MW01284512

The Hour of Fatality

A Jane Rochester Mystery

LeAnne McKinley

Published by LeAnne Mckinley, 2019.

THE HOUR OF FATALITY

First edition. October 22, 2019.

Copyright © 2019 LeAnne McKinley.

ISBN: 978-1077285743

Written by LeAnne McKinley.

To my husband, with grateful thanks for his loving heart.

CHAPTER I

"At dead of night!" I muttered. Yes, that was ever the hour of fatality at Thornfield.
— Charlotte Brontë, *Jane Eyre*

Ferndean Manor lies in a secluded spot. The house sits deep in sylvan splendour, among woodland streams whose musical laughter sounds perpetually in one's ear. It was six weeks to the day that I had first arrived here and I had been wed to Mr. Rochester for nearly as long.

"Jane, where are you?"

I turned away from the parlour window at the sound of my husband's voice. "I am here, sir."

A smile effaced the grim lines of sadness he habitually wore. "Your voice is a banquet to a famished soul. Come, sit with me awhile." Mr. Rochester was seated in his habitual place near the empty grate, his head cushioned by the massive, wingback chair. He spoke cheerfully, but an expression of melancholy marked his granite-hewn features. It was thus he had appeared when I first found him again, in this very parlour.

I approached his chair and dared to drop a kiss on his ebon brow, then I took my preferred seat: a little stool at his feet. He kept his mutilated hand tucked in his coat but the other sought my own. I noted the edge of an envelope protruding from his pocket and guessed the source of his harrowed expression; something had occurred to remind him of his infirmities.

"I need you to be my eyes," said he, "as you shall ever be in our married life. Prompted by your generous pity and magnanimous heart, you have pledged your life to a blind man, helpless and depen-

dent on you even for such sorted and sundry tasks as letters of business. John has brought the mail this morning. Are you prepared to
enter on your new duties?"

"Yes, sir."

"Here is the first then."

He passed me a letter sealed with plain wax. I read aloud.

Dear Mr. Rochester,

For many years I have had the management of your estate,
and I hope I have given satisfaction. But now, sir, I must
give you notice of my departure. I've done my best to take
over every concern since your mishap, but my brother's
farm has prospered, and he asks me to assist him. The
truth be told, I am not sorry to leave Thornfield Hall.
There is not much of the hall left, of course, but there is
something uncanny about the old place. I go to my brother's farm on the fifth.

Malcolm Granby

I looked at Mr. Rochester to see how he would take the news of
the sudden departure of his land agent. He rubbed his chin for a long
moment. "Curious letter, isn't it?"

"What could he mean? What could be uncanny about Thornfield?"

"Ex-act-ly. Pre-cise-ly. That's what I would like to know, but we
won't get it out of him. Gone on the fifth, eh? That was yesterday.
He didn't want to be interrogated and made good his retreat beforehand. Peculiar."

My husband meditated in silence, his visage darkened as he contemplated his agent's behaviour. Thornfield was now a wreck; a hol-
lowed-out shell. It was of no use to anybody, save as resting place for

the crows. I had no doubt it could be uncanny at times, but enough to drive a man from his duty?

"Well, here is another. Do you recognise the seal?"

I studied the elaborate imprint in the red wax but it was unfamiliar to me.

My Dear Rochester,

I have just heard the news of your marriage from the minister himself. My best congratulations to you and Mrs. Rochester. I have long had it in mind to invite you to stay with us at Ingram Park, only I feared to obtrude any importunate invitation. Should you be disposed, however, you and your bride are welcome to pay us a visit. My mother and my sister are in London, to prepare for Blanche's wedding, so it will only be myself to keep you company. Of course, the whole party will join us in a few weeks' time, including Mr. Hardwick, Blanche's fiance. Should you choose to come, you may pick the day of your arrival.

Lord Ingram

"Well, how about it, Jane?"

My husband's face had changed to a curious blend of sarcasm and severity. I knew him in this mood, but I could not tell just what was in his mind. "It seems a well-intentioned letter. He shows more delicacy than I would have expected of him."

"Oh yes, Ingram is the very type of gentleman. I've had several of these sorts of invitations. The whole county has felt sorry for me at one time or other. I refused them all. I have been in no mood to be plagued and coddled by the pity of my neighbours. And now that I have you, my fairy, what need do we have for anyone else?"

The circumstances, such as they were, did not make Ingram Park a place that I would wish to reside in. I had no taste for the scornful disdain of Miss Ingram, which I was sure would not be absolved by my position as her former suitor's wife.

I would have said as much, but pain, acute and sharp, made my headache. I closed my eyes and waited in silence for it to fade. When my attention returned to my husband, I could see that he had once more become absorbed in his own curious thoughts.

"But I ought not to speak for you, Janet. Perhaps you grow weary of our isolation. You might prefer to be a guest in a noble house. How would you like to be a fine lady waited on by a host of servants, surfeited with elaborate dinners, honoured as the new bride by those who once dismissed you as a nonentity? It is no less than you deserve." He gripped my hand tightly, as if I were going to hurry away to pack my trunk. "Would you be pleased by the turn of Blanche Ingram's countenance when you are announced on the arm of the man she sought to marry?" He chuckled to himself. A sardonic smile flashed across his face.

"You are sneering, sir. It is not her fault that you flattered her so."

"The mortification of her pride would certainly change her hauteur, would it not? She might meditate on her own deficiencies when she is presented with what a woman ought to be; when she sees what a good, guileless, clever, wise and noble woman actually is. When she acknowledges your superiority— "

"Now you are flattering *me*. It is foolish to speak so. There is no call for comparison between Blanche Ingram and myself."

"No, thank God. Now I have secured you, I care for no other woman's opinion, but what might you feel in such a circumstance?" He sank back into his chair. All his levity was gone, but a deep furrow across his forehead remained. "To enter the home of such fine beings on the arm of a blind and crippled man, ruined and blighted, who cannot walk but where you lead him? Would it not be mortifying to enter company on such terms? I'm sure you would find it repulsive."

I looked with concern at the grim melancholy settled once more on his face. "I am always glad to be by your side; to lead you anywhere I can. Fine company can whisper whatever it pleases. I care for no one's good opinion but yours."

"They would shake their heads in sorrow when they saw me. I would be 'poor Rochester', a miserable worm among them. How they would grieve for my misfortunes in my presence; and rejoice in spite when my back was turned!"

He was fretting himself into unhappiness. Immediate measures were called for. "It is a kind invitation," I said, rising to my feet.

"Yes, yes, a bit of salve for a pricked conscience. Now he has done his duty and can think no more of me. Where are you going, Jane? Why do you leave my side?"

"I intend to call John, to ready the horses and carriage."

"What the deuce for?"

"We are going to pay a visit to Thornfield Hall. If there is anything uncanny among the ruins, I, for one, would like to know what it is."

I stood outside on the steps of the house with Mr. Rochester's arm through mine. The sun was dropping golden beams through the many boughs and branches of the wood, and all about me was bathed in rich verdure. I described the beauty of the wood to my husband while we waited for the carriage to come round. In spite of the glorious morning, a strange malaise afflicted me; I leaned more than I intended on my husband's arm.

"Jane, are you well?"

My head still ached, it was true, but I would not own that. I was sure a morning in the open air was all the cure I needed. "It is nothing. I've never been sickly."

"But you are not strong. Ferndean is an insalubrious spot, too damp for good health."

"Never fear for me. I am perfectly well." I belied this assertion by turning my head away to cough. Mr. Rochester frowned, but the subject was put off by the arrival of the carriage. Seated in its comfortable interior, I succeeded in resting my temple against the cushions. I was sure my strength would return soon.

As we began our ascent through the woods, I composed my voice to sound as hale and well as I could. "It is a lovely morning. The fields are a vivid green, and there will be tassels in the hay fields soon."

"And the sky?"

"Nearly cloudless, except for a few pale wreaths on the horizon."

"A lovely morning, Janet. Do you know, I have not been to Thornfield since its destruction. I left the management of the estate and its tenants to Granby. He was an able manager, by-the-bye, and very trustworthy. It will be no easy task to replace him." With a sly smile, he added, "Perhaps we should advertise. After all, it brought me an excellent wife."

I chastised my husband for the impertinence of this statement, but before long, the ruin of Thornfield was visible, a blackened gash upon the pastoral landscape. I grew silent as the white roads led us thither.

I knew of no spot in England so compelling as Thornfield Hall. The dawn of love, the weariness of despair, the promise of blissful union were all encompassed in the life I had passed there. My thoughts turned and turned upon Thornfield, as if some tether bound me to the place, and kept me flying always within its orbit.

The carriage ran sedately up the road and clattered over the pavement. John called out to the horses, and we came to a stop. After he opened the door and helped us each of us down the step, he said, "I'll let the horses graze a bit."

"Not for long, though," said Mr. Rochester. "We'll just have a look around and go on to the Rochester Arms for dinner."

"Yes, sir." John pulled his forelock and stepped aside. John and his wife Mary were the only servants of the hall left. The three of us turned as one to face the solitary wall, its windows stark and empty. On the far side of the tumbled remains, the long garden wall still stood, though one stretch of it had been knocked down by falling wreckage.

I observed John, who looked on the desolation of the great house with an expression of deep dismay. John had been with the family since Mr. Rochester was a boy. It was likely, I thought, that he had spent more of his life in this house than either of us.

He turned his head and saw my eye upon him. "It's a sorry sight, ain't it?"

I could not but agree with this pronouncement. The old servant turned slowly away, his head bowed, and attended to the horses.

Mr. Rochester took my arm. "Tell me what you see."

With a heavy heart, I reported to my husband what had become of his ancestral home. "There is still a wall of stone standing. And several beams remain, pointing out of the ground like factory chimneys. Blackened rubble lies at their feet. There are charred remains of wood, but the reek of smoke is gone. The stones are heaped about in eerie shapes. Nothing lives here but the birds."

"An uncanny place?"

"Even on a lovely summer day."

He slipped his arm round my waist, a customary position when we walked together. "Might we reach the orchard?"

"We might."

"Lead the way then, Jane but step carefully."

Beyond the pavement stretched an awe-inspiring sight. Rose bushes rambled in undimmed splendour and gazing up through the vigorous weeds, primroses offered their petals to the bright sky. While farther down the path, I could make out the broken chestnut tree wearing a veil of ivy over its dead limbs. It was a wild, lonely place; a startling reminder of the transience of man. I attempted to do justice to such a scene in my husband's ear.

"Bring me a flower," he said when I had finished. I fetched a half-blown rose to place in his hand. He breathed in its incense, then pressed it into my fingers.

"This was always the best part of the house, I think." His face was sombre, but not doleful. My hand lay on his arm, and now he seized my fingers in a tight grasp. "The destruction of this house was perpe-trated by my folly. It has stood on a foundation of greed, avarice, self-ishness; the devastation before you is the natural result. We are for-tunate to have escaped without greater harm."

"You are being morbid again, sir. It is only a house."

"Only a house, she says. Yet I hear the trembling in her voice as she speaks of it. It troubles you, Janet."

"I loved Thornfield. I never thought to see it undone."

I turned my head at the sound of a rook in the distant thorn trees. As I did so, the broken chestnut caught my gaze once more.

"May I leave you here for a moment? There is something I wish to see."

"Very well, but take care where you step."

I followed the garden path, keeping my feet on the gravel. A wide swath of grassy turf lay on either side of it, and even a stretch of mud-died sand. At the edge of a dried puddle were the minute footmarks of birds, and overlaying them, a deep half-circle mark, as of some-thing heavy pressed into the mud. I moved further and found anoth-er.

"There are the marks of horseshoes here, in the mud. A horse has been here."

"A stray farm horse, perhaps."

"Could it have been Granby, do you think? Would he have ridden here?"

"He told me nothing new when he stated his dislike of Thornfield. I believe he avoided the house since the fire. There was no call for him to wander back here."

"But suppose he saw something strange? Something unusual? His letter made it sound as if he were frightened."

"Well, whatever was here has gone on its way, and so shall we."

"Are you not curious, sir, who is visiting your house without your knowledge?" I asked.

"It is not my house. There is no hospitable chair, no glowing hearth, no serene couch here, is there? Do you see anything of the kind? This is a decaying wreck. Time only is wanted to bury it in the ground. Let it remain so. Come, take me back." I put my arm around him, but my feet did not move. "Jane, why are we not moving?"

"It does not seem altogether right to me that Thornfield should be abandoned."

"Oh, never mind about Thornfield! I have been cursed with it for long enough. Divine justice has blotted it from the earth—let it so remain."

"Edward, I may as well tell you at once that I am not leaving until I have taken a closer look at that path."

"I see you have not given up your witchery yet. Very well, get on with your prognostications." He folded his arms across his chest and leaned heavily on one foot. He did not look pleased, reader, for he hated to be reminded that his blindness rendered him feebler than I, but I would not detain him long. Thornfield had become an unsettling place, an eerie vision that bore little resemblance to the refuge I had once found it to be. I felt there was still something strange here, however, some tale that was left untold.

I walked on the grass, treading lightly, watching out for more marks of passing man or beast, but I could make out nothing definitive. I came to the old horse-chestnut tree, blasted and broken by the lightning that had struck it over a year ago. The trunk had broken high up, so that the stump still stood well above my head, while at its feet lay the wreckage of its once noble crown. My foot came down on something hard; I bent low to examine it; I found a heavy coin: a guinea, with a glossy sheen upon it. This was no long-forgotten gold piece, fallen from Mr. Rochester's pocket in better times. This was a recent arrival at this forsaken spot. Perhaps there was something uncanny about Thornfield after all.

"What the devil are you at, Jane?"

I slipped the gold into my pocket and rejoined my husband. We retraced our steps to the waiting carriage. I was relieved to be carried away from the remains of the shattered house. It seemed a mere dream to return to this place as a settled home, yet I doubted my fate could ever be divided from Thornfield Hall.

CHAPTER II

We were wholly unexpected when we entered the Rochester Arms. I stopped near the door to remove my gloves and wait for the innkeeper to appear. My husband stood by me, his arm hooked in mine.

A loud crash arrested our attention. The innkeeper occupied the doorway, an apron tied round his waist and a glass smashed at his feet. He still grasped a towel, but its occupation was no more.

"It's you, miss!"

"Does he know you, Jane?"

I could not repress a smile at this turn of events. "I came here weeks ago, fresh from the scene we just left, seeking information that Thornfield could not give. This man told me all your story, and somewhat of my own besides."

"Is it really you, then, miss? Were *you* the governess?"

"Governess no more!" Mr. Rochester declared in thundering tones. The wine glasses might have shaken in their racks. "She is Mrs. Jane Fairfax Rochester, and she is the mistress of everything in your sight!"

My husband has an expressive face, fully capable of displaying his ire and even inspiring dread. The man visibly cowered before this display of wrath.

"I beg your pardon, sir, and yours too, miss—ma'am. I meant no offence. Only being taken by surprise—quite off my guard—beg pardon."

Mr. Rochester's expression altered instantly and the room filled with a jovial laugh.

"You can make it up to us with the best dinner your kitchen can contrive in half an hour. In the meantime, a glass of wine for us both. This is James Hart, is it not?"

"Yes, sir." A timid smile showed on his face and gathered strength as he went on. "It's good to see you out and about." I remembered that the innkeeper had once worked in Mr. Rochester's household, although it was long before my residence at Thornfield. "My very best congratulations to you and your missus."

"Thank you, Hart, thank you very much. Come and sit with us a moment if you have the time."

"Oh yes, sir. I'll just be a minute."

The man hurried away, and I led my master to a table in a pleasant corner; the dining-room was empty. There was no fire in the massive fireplace on this summer day, but the brass trimmings and burnished wood radiated a pleasing mental warmth. The innkeeper returned, his apron left behind, and wine glasses in his hand. He sat down at the table and smiled hospitably at us both. His expression showed plainly that he was delighted to see Mr. Rochester in a happy estate. My heart warmed to him.

"I am come to make a request of you, Hart."

"I'd be glad to do you a service, sir."

"It's an easy duty for one placed as you are. I'm looking for a bit of gossip, and I'm hoping you've got some news for me."

"There isn't much news to speak of in this part of the world, but folks need to talk about something. We make what we can of it."

"I've received a letter from Malcolm Granby. You are acquainted with him?"

"Of course, sir. I know him well."

"He's told me there's been some strange report concerning Thornfield; something uncanny going on. Have you heard of anyone visiting the ruins?"

"Not in the ordinary sense, no. As a matter of fact, I think folks around here are determined to leave them alone. They'd rather visit any spot but that."

"Why? What do they say about it?"

"Well, of course, they've been told to keep away from the house itself, lest there's some falling brick or the like. And then, you know, people say your misfortunes were all some wicked curse. They think the ruins themselves are bad luck."

"Has Granby ever mentioned it?"

Hart laughed and leaned back in his chair. "Granby? No. He's a solid, trustworthy, unimaginative man. He'd be the first to discredit that kind of talk. Besides, he's a good churchman, and not much given to flights of fancy."

"So you've heard nothing unusual about Thornfield?"

"Well now, I did just happen to hear something. I dare say there's nothing in it."

"Let's have it; speak out."

"One of my stable boys told me a story the other day—I don't rightly know how much of it is true. His family lives right close to the hall, over on the near side of Hay. He was out late at night looking after a horse that had got the colic. While he was walking him round the stable yard in the middle of the night, he noticed something strange up yonder at the hall."

"Well, go on, what did he see?"

"Lights, sir. As if someone were walking about with a lantern."

"Ah! Anything else?"

"I don't think so."

"And what do you think?"

"What do I think?" Hart leaned in, his hands folded on the table before him. "It's plain as plain to me, sir, although I haven't got any proof for it. There are gipsies camped out on Hay Common. They come round every year just about, and get into unaccountable mischief."

"What have they done?"

"Only petty thievery, here and there. Although half of its mere talk, as like as not; but if anybody was making himself inconspicuous at the old hall, I expect it was them. *They* wouldn't mind a curse, you know. They'd be just as likely to cast a curse themselves."

"Did you tell Granby about it?"

"I'm planning to when I see him next."

"Did you know he's left my employment?"

"Left? Granby?" The man's benevolent look was abruptly replaced by wonder.

"Says he's gone out of this part of England altogether."

The man opened his mouth; then closed it. "I'm sorry to hear it, very much so. I never would have expected him to go off in such a sudden way."

"That was my idea. You haven't heard anything about it then?"

"Not a word."

"He says he's gone to help with his brother's farm in the South. Have you ever heard him mention the scheme?"

"He did just speak of it once in passing, but he never was much of a talker. I suppose he thought it warning enough."

We contemplated Mr. Granby's taciturn nature in silence and finished our meal. When it was time to depart, Mr. Rochester reverted to the subject once more. To the innkeeper, he said, "What day did Martha's brother see all this?"

"It would have been the night of the fourth, I believe."

"Jane."

"Yes, sir?"

"Do you note the date?"

"Mr. Granby's letter was dated the following day."

"Is it a coincidence, do you think?"

"But what could lights at the hall have to do with Mr. Granby leaving?"

Mr. Rochester gave me an enigmatic grimace, but his only words were, "What indeed?"

We left the tavern to find the afternoon pleasant and warm, almost balmy beneath thin clouds moving high and distant. A farmer and his ox made their slow way in the direction of Hay, the nearest market town, but the yard of the inn was calm. I helped Mr. Rochester to mount the carriage, and John, in his turn, aided me.

Such scenes as fire and darkness seemed remote; I gladly forgot them. I was more tired than I expected, and I was grateful to be resting in the carriage, with my master's hand twined in my own. Ferndean was already deep in shadow when we arrived. The manor looked all the more striking against the black outline of leaf and bough.

"I would like to paint that sky," I said, after describing it to Mr. Rochester.

"Do you have your paints with you still?"

"I keep my drawing pencils with me. They are in my room at this moment, ready when they are needed."

"It would be a pleasure to sit by you while you draw, though I cannot enjoy the fruits of your labour. Mary," this he said to the servant at the door. "We would like some tea." We repaired to the parlour, and soon I was seated once more on the stool at my master's side. I felt fatigued still, but thought only of the delight of resting my aching head against my husband's shoulder. I had ample opportunity to examine my Mr. Rochester's face; I searched its lines for a return of melancholy and regret. I could trace neither, but observed instead the deep composure of reflection. Ere long he spoke.

"There, Jane. You have your explanation about Thornfield Hall."

"Gipsies? It does not seem likely to me. It would be an eerie place to abide in by night. Surrounded by tales of ghosts and woe, I think a gipsy would prefer to remain at a distance."

"Well, what else could it be then? It's unlikely enough that the peaceful tenants of Hay, or the farmers busy with their harvest, are lurking about the blackened desolation; and it hardly seems fitting for a fairy ring. The little people prefer the fresh fields and quiet bowers." He seemed to stare fixedly at a distant wall but this I knew was coincidence. Although he could perceive bright lights, tonight in the darkened parlour, his eye beheld no forms. Mary arrived with the tea tray, candles, and Pilot, who burst into the room with a clamorous bark.

"Down, Pilot!" Mr. Rochester commanded. The dog sheepishly put his muzzle near my fingers, entreated for a caress, which I gave, and retired to the cold fireplace. The tea poured, the candles lit, Mr. Rochester placed his hand on my knee.

"Very well. I will not let Thornfield remain unwatched. We will find a new agent to oversee what remains of my house and put a stop to midnight visitants. He must be a man of the right sort, however, immune to idle vapours or suspicions. A man capable of battling the powers of the air. Jane, was that a cough?"

"No, sir."

"Are you certain?"

I would gladly have disavowed this, but I was forced to acquiesce by coughing once more. I decided to rise, but when I tried the experiment, my knees failed me.

He put his fingers to my cheek and forehead; he held my wrist and counted my pulse. "You are not well, Jane. Your head is hot, your pulse is laboured, your fingers ice cold! You are to go to bed at once. I'll send for Doctor Carter."

It was a shame to disturb the doctor so late in the evening; Ferndean Manor would be a long journey for him at this hour. I resolved to show my strength and right myself, but my efforts were futile. I reached for the back of the chair only to behold the room whirling round me. When I attempted to steady myself, my limbs would not obey. I fell, and even now I can remember no end to that falling.

I came to Thornfield Hall at the hour of twilight. My path wended among hayfield and hawthorn, and when a bend in the road blocked my view of the house, I even ran in my haste. The battlements on the roof loomed darkly against the glimmering west. If I could touch them, the blackness would rub off on my skin like soot, and cling to me; such is the strange presentiment of dreams.

I reached the pavement near the door. It, too, was black, and I stepped cautiously, fearing the sound of my own tread in spite of the silence that lay on the dead air. I mounted the steps, their stone faces worn smooth in well-remembered grooves. The vaulted hall within was deep in shadow, but a blaze of light shone from the dining-room, majestic and warm. Was I welcome there? Mr. Rochester entertained fine company in that room, gentlemen and ladies endowed with wealth and grace. No, I had no place in the dining-room. I would see where else he might be found. I went to the library, but the grate was cold, the chair tenantless. I searched the long gallery; every door yielded to my hand, but the rooms were vacant shells.

I stretched out my hand for the dining-room door. Here, I was sure, I would find him at last. There was smoke curling across the ceiling, and the handle was hot to the touch. I tried to fling open the door, but it would not yield. I could hear a sound within, a laugh, lugubrious and low, that grew louder and more mocking, that penetrated the darkness like a living thing—

I suppressed the shaking in my limbs and threw open the door—a wreath of fire embroiled the room and heated my face. Brocaded curtains, purple cloth, rich damask, all writhed together in flame. A motionless form reclined in the chair, senseless and still, his head sagging to his breast. I called out Mr. Rochester's name, but he did not stir. Before I could come to his aid, a different being approached, hauntingly familiar in its ghastly shape. The flame did not touch her, yet her dark hair moved and lifted in the heat. Bertha Mason, black and menacing against the crimson light, barred the way. Her eyes burned, too, with a blue flame in their depths. It was *her*, Mr. Rochester's first wife, whom he had hid from my knowledge. In her madness, she raved and flung herself upon me, keeping me from my master.

Mr. Rochester!"

I woke at once to a darkened bedroom; I struggled to place my whereabouts in the dim firelight.

"Jane, I am here. I am here, Jane."

I felt such weakness in my frame that I could scarcely move. Someone brought water to my feverish lips and bathed my brow in cool water. Mr. Rochester chafed my hand in his. I longed to speak and reassure him, but the effort of words proved elusive; it was beyond my ability. My husband lay down beside me on the bed; his hand gripped mine.

"Dear God in heaven, spare her. Be merciful—I have only just found her again—my darling Jane— "

The moonlit room vanished from my sight. Perhaps, it too had been a dream. I would fain have retained it, but I had no control of my restless, roving mind. I arrived at yet another present, yet another Thornfield. The cold moonlight left stark shadows beneath the leaves; the primroses opened wan faces to the growing starlight. I was in the garden, walking the well-remembered path to the orchard, but this garden was not as I had left it. The once neat hedges of box were overgrown into fantastical shapes. The roses spilt from their beds in untidy heaps and rank weeds towered among the fragile blooms. Dark vines of ivy overreached everything in sight, gathering wild and domestic alike in their gnarled creepers.

I knew the sweet fragrance of this garden, but when I breathed deep, I was reminded instead of Lowood, the school that had been my childhood home for eight long years. With sudden clarity, I recognised that scent; it was the dank, heavy air of the dell, dismal and disease-ridden. I remembered again the camphor in my nostrils, and the fever ward lined with forms huddled beneath the bedclothes. All around me, the pale flower blooms along the path melted into the pallid faces of children, wasted by their suffering. They lifted from their beds and slipped away with lanterns burning in their hands.

A heavy mist came creeping over the ground, obscuring sky and earth alike; it even drowned the moon. I no longer followed the path but was rooted in place as the fog engulfed me. All directions were equally bewildering. I watched in helpless immobility as the first light appeared. It moved in the smoking darkness like a beacon, but it gave me no comfort. The lights waxed and waned around me. They brought no warmth to me; rather, an icy fear stole over me, inhabiting my very bones. Alone in that formless and desolate world, I could not take my eyes from their luminescent gleam.

A light shone near me. With trepidation in every step, I followed; it was further off than I thought. I followed first one, then another, down winding, unfamiliar ways. Some of them began to fade; I would not be left alone in this gloomy, sightless world; I followed as well as I could.

The *ignis-fatuus* led me on; I knew not where. I too was ill; perhaps I was also dying. I dared not guess what shadowy paths the strange lights would lead me to, but I could only stumble on into the gloom, abandoned to the fate that lay ahead of me—

A woman's voice, it's accent gentle, familiar, and firm, assailed my ear. It was soothing to hear. I tried to listen.

"It is morning. Come, dear, wake up."

I opened my eyes. It was a summer morning; sunshine fell on the sash of the window, and on the coverlet stretched over me. A smiling face bent over the bed.

"Diana!"

My cousin, Diana Rivers, sat in the chair by my bed. "How are you feeling?"

I considered before answering. "I am glad to be awake."

"You have been very ill, but the crisis is passed, I think. Does the light distress you? Shall I draw the curtain?"

"No." I stared greedily at the morning brightness that I might impress it on my mind. "No, I would rather see the sun, but I have had such strange dreams."

"I do not doubt it."

She took my fingers where they lay on the pillow. In my sojourn from Thornfield, by the mysterious hand of providence, I had found Diana, Mary and their brother St. John, and had learned that they were my family, the children of my mother's brother. I had had no knowledge of my relations as a child and had been united with them only months ago.

Diana's presence was truly comforting. Her ardent, cheerful nature was a real support to me. It was still an effort to draw breath or to speak, but my questions must have shown on my face.

"In my last letter I promised to pay you a visit after your marriage and thought I would give you a pleasant surprise, but it seems the power of suspense was in your hands instead of mine. I arrived to find you bedridden with typhoid. It is not an illness I have been acquainted with before, and I admit I would not like to become more familiar with it."

She squeezed my fingers, and with a faint smile touching her features, she added, "As soon as I could persuade him, I convinced your Mr. Rochester to go to bed. He was up late last night waiting for Doctor Carter. They gave you a sleeping-draught at midnight. You were so very restless." Diana held her hand to my forehead. "This house is a dreadful place for a lamb like you. The doctor agrees with me."

"Mr. Rochester spoke of it once as an insalubrious spot."

"It is an absolute breeding ground for fever, but there is strength in you yet, Jane. Will you have anything to eat? The servant has made a lovely broth for you."

I could not sit up for long, but I was nourished by the soup and lay back on my pillow with content. "You will not leave, Diana, will you?"

"I will be here. And as soon as Mr. Rochester is awake, he will be here as well. He may be angry that I didn't wake him to see you, but he is worn to a shadow from trying to look after you himself. He is truly devoted to you, Jane."

I smiled; it took effort, but I could hardly help it.

"Rest now. I know you are tired."

The weeks that followed are dim in my memory. Sometimes Diana would read to me, or Mr. Rochester sit by me with my hand grasped in his. I could do nothing else. Diana's words were a true prophecy however, and my body mended, albeit slowly.

"Are you awake, Jane?" Mr. Rochester asked. Mary had led him to my bedside so that he might sit beside me.

I declared that I was and smiled with what energy I possessed. Both tenderness and sadness showed in the expressive lines of his face.

"Your breathing is not so laboured as it was." He felt about on the covers until he found my hand. He pressed my fingers to his cheek and held them there. My heart wrung with pity for the sorrow he had endured.

"I am recovering, Edward. I am truly sorry to cause you so much trouble."

"Sorry! Sorry!" He clutched my hand close to him. "Jane, I owe you a thousand apologies for keeping you in this house. It was utterly reprehensible of me to allow you to reside in such an unhealthful place as Ferndean, even for a few weeks."

"You could not have known I would become ill. It is not your fault."

"I shall take no more risks with my most treasured possession. As soon as you are well enough to be moved, we leave for Ingram Park."

The name called forth the image of Blanche Ingram, dressed in spotless white, her haughty eye turned on me in contempt while her lip curled in a sneer. I remembered, too, sundry speeches and looks from her mother, the Dowager Ingram; I recalled with clarity her denigrating words; her scornful expression when she happened to glance my way.

"Ingram Park? Must we?"

"I won't have you in this atmosphere any longer than necessary. I have already written to Lord Ingram and made all the arrangements. It is not your idea of a pleasant situation, nor mine either, but I want you someplace safe where you can be well looked after. There is no location in the country in a more healthy situation. There will be servants to attend you, a doctor just at hand, and we have already been invited."

I much preferred the quiet isolation of our sylvan bower, but I could hardly argue for such an alternative. "If you think it best."

"I do. You are my wife now and must do as I bid. Your health is in my care and will not be far from my mind. Janet, my love, you raved in your fever. Do you remember your dreams?"

"They are fading now, but I remember them. They are not worth speaking of."

He rubbed my hand with a restless thumb. "You are haunted by the past? Burdened by that wretched house? That tent of Achan? It has plagued me enough, by God. I pray it does not prove a burden to you."

"I shall think no more of them, for it is of no importance. I am thinking now of the future, and of the present. I am with *you*, Edward, whom I love."

This inspired a tender kiss, but a look of humour soon followed. "If puzzles about Thornfield are not enough to occupy you, we can be sure of diversion at Ingram Park. There ought to be plenty of curious faces and figures to distract you. Of course, the house is worth seeing, even if the inhabitants are not exactly to our taste, but at least we will not be dull."

"You will not be alone, either." My cousin Diana had come into the room. She approached the opposite side of the bed and felt my pulse. A firm nod showed her satisfaction with my progress. "I intend to go with you."

"It is not necessary— " Mr. Rochester began, but Diana forestalled him.

"I know her constitution. And I know that she is far too likely to abandon her sickbed before she ought to. I will nurse her until she is without need of nursing. I trust that some little nook may be found for me at Ingram Park."

"I should not keep you from home," I said.

She laughed. "You are keeping me pleasantly occupied. My sister Mary has gone to London with dear old Hannah to have her teeth drawn. And there never was a more fractious patient than Hannah. They are gone to stay with friends and will be in no hurry to rush home. I was to join them there, but I am just as pleased to remain with you."

Diana turned to the window while she spoke. "I find it strange to be a woman of means, with no required labour to perform. While I was still a governess, I longed for more time for my studies, but I think my energies are superfluous to the task. I require something more active to do." When she turned back, she wore a sly smile. "I would far prefer to keep you company until you are well. Provided Mr. Rochester does not mind *too* terribly."

"I owe you a great debt, Miss Rivers, for ministering to us in our hour of need. I only wish I could offer you my own hospitality instead of another's. For all you have done for my Jane, I owe you far more."

"We are family, are we not?" Diana replied. "Besides, even if I did not love her so well, I owe Jane a far greater debt than any I have discharged."

On the day of our departure, I reflected with amusement on Mr. Rochester's promise long ago to adorn his young bride with jewels and finery. Here I stood, preparing for our first bridal journey wrapped in two dressing gowns and a great beaver bonnet more suited for January than June. I was propped up between the servant Mary and my cousin Diana as I descended the stairs, and bodily lifted into the carriage by John, who placed me on the bench as tenderly as he would a sleeping child. Diana sat by to support me, but where was Mr. Rochester?

He emerged from the house on the doctor's arm; the doctor assisted him into the carriage. "You'll come and see us soon, Carter, won't you?"

"I'll be there tomorrow afternoon, but don't worry over-much. She'll be right as rain before long."

Mr. Rochester called to the coachman on the box outside, and the carriage sped along the drive. He relieved Diana of all need to support me. His strong arms cushioned me against the quaking vibration. "We are finally on our way. We are wanderers, Jane, born to travel the earth like a roaming jinn."

I could just see out the window, and I recognised the road to Hay and then to Millcote. I was pleased to find myself so cognizant; no longer in the grip of delusion. I felt I might safely trust my own powers of reasoning once more.

"Edward, have you sought a new land agent yet?"

"No Jane, I have not. Between weeping tears of blood and holding your burning fingers in my own, I have not had the opportunity. Why do you ask?"

"I do not wish to neglect the matter while we are away."

"Forget Thornfield. Forget all this unhappy time. It is too grim to bear remembering."

"I can not help remembering."

"The mental effort will make you ill."

"The satisfaction of curiosity will make me well."

Mr. Rochester laughed, his chest shaking beneath me. "You are an impudent, irrepressible elf, Janet. Be quiet now and do not talk. You must rest. The journey is already more than you ought to undergo at present, but I promise you Thornfield will not be forgotten."

CHAPTER III

"Jane, what is in that tree?"

Our carriage ran swift and sure beneath the lofty oaks; their noble branches arched above the road to Ingram Park and stretched their arms wide over the landscape, like partners in an elaborate dance. The house was still hidden from view by a rise in the land, but on the crown of the hill stood an enormous tree, the monarch of an ancient wood. A little more than halfway up, clinging to the branches, was an upright figure in a blue coat.

"I believe it is a man."

"A man?" Asked Mr. Rochester, starting from his reverie. "Up in the tree? Does he appear distressed?"

"Not at all," Diana said, with amusement in her voice. "I think he is on the lookout."

"Tell the coachman to stop up ahead," Mr. Rochester said. Accordingly, we came to a halt at the foot of the mighty oak.

"Hello up there!" Diana called gaily. "How do you find the view?"

With swift confidence, the man descended from the tree.

"My apologies if I startled you," he said as he approached the carriage. He still held a telescope tucked under his arm. "It's such an old habit from my time at sea. The day isn't quite in order if I don't get a good look at the horizon."

"And do you see signs of fair weather?" Diana asked.

"I do indeed. Not a squall in sight. You are coming to Ingram Park? You must be the Rochesters?"

His eyes were fixed on Diana but travelled now to myself and my husband. I bowed my head, smiling faintly. I am sure I looked quite pale and plain. I was never a beauty even when in good health. Mr. Rochester bowed also, but he seemed at a loss, turning this way and that as if he might 'see' who was speaking.

26

"I am Mrs. Rochester. And this is my cousin, Miss Diana Rivers, who accompanies us."

"A pleasure to make your acquaintance. My name is Captain Fitzjames. I'm staying at the house as well. With your permission, I will join the coachman. I may be of service to you when we arrive in the yard."

He mounted the box, and the carriage started off. "It must be quite a view from the treetops," Diana said merrily in my ear. It gratified me to think of the captain's polite and cheerful demeanour. I hoped it presaged future benevolence from Ingram Park.

Our carriage rolled once more through the woods preceding the house, and I fell to contemplating our arrival. I had little experience of fine society: elegance, airs, and polished manners were all foreign to me. I would have felt hesitant to approach any domicile so noble as this, but in Ingram Park, there was even more to intimidate. On my last introduction to this family, I was still a governess, a lonely subservient without claim to rank or fortune. It was simple enough to conduct myself then; I had only to keep my own counsel. I was not altogether certain how to act the part of the wife of a wealthy, landed gentleman. I have always been desirous to please, and I wished to betray no awkwardness, but my most earnest attempts at pleasing others had often met with failure.

Diana, however, did not seem at all put out on learning that she would be introduced to a peer of the realm. Seated on the other side of me, dressed in soft blue muslin with her curls neatly arranged under her bonnet, she looked far better suited for introduction at Ingram Park than her companions, and much more cheerful besides. Even now, she was leaning forward, almost craning out the window to get a clear view of the road ahead. I soon found that the view was worthy of attention.

Our equipage descended the slight incline, and we beheld the house for the first time. It was a majestic edifice, built of yellow stone, and fitted with a multitude of windows that glinted in the westering sun. Towering spires adorned the roof and elegant carvings thronged among the masonry.

A pool of water, silvery and calm, lay just below the house, where it reflected a mirror image of that stone visage. We crossed the bridge that spanned it and then passed through the shrubbery of an expansive garden. The hedges were trimmed in orderly rows, but occasional gaps in the greenery revealed tall statues; it was not unlike travelling through a giant chessboard. A tidy, respectable knight waited, perhaps, beyond that garden gate, ready to approach the next square. The grounds were innocent of wild, rebellious growth; only the blooming hollyhocks betrayed the impropriety of nature's will.

Our team of horses slowed to a stop, the captain leapt from the box, and we dismounted the carriage. The captain hesitated, turned as if he would take Diana's arm, then glanced curiously at Mr. Rochester. I answered his unspoken question.

"Captain, would you be so kind as to look after our horses for the present? John is accustomed to leading Mr. Rochester." John would soon be returning to the region of Ferndean with the horses, but for now, I wished him to help my husband through this strange new setting.

"I would be happy to," said the captain with a bow.

Our party thus arranged, we ascended the stone steps. They were both wide and steep, as if moulded for some giant's tread. We passed beneath a great portico in front of the house, and I felt dwarfed indeed by the ionic columns soaring above my head. The wooden door was massive and dark, but our knock quickly yielded an attentive butler.

He led us through the great entrance hall where our footsteps rang on the black and white squares of marble. I inadvertently prevented the party from advancing when I first glimpsed the painted ceiling. I stopped to gaze above me, despite the pain in my head, at a rosy heaven of gilded splendour inhabited by a host of angels, and painted with clouds that blushed with vermilion tints. No artist, however amateur, could be unmoved by such a masterpiece.

"I thought it would please you," was Mr. Rochester's comment.

We were led to a drawing-room, a noble apartment bedecked with spotless white couches and gilt-framed mirrors and waited in patient silence. I, for one, was relieved to be out of the quaking and rattling carriage. My temples throbbed, while my joints, so recently wrought upon by fever, ached uncomfortably. The novelty of my setting, however, was sufficient distraction, and my position at the end of the room allowed for further inspection of the beauties therein.

Mr. Rochester was seated on a divan supported by spindly wooden legs. He, in course, had nothing to look at. The waiting grew long and my attention returned to my husband. He sat with his head slightly bowed and tipped to one side. He was listening for the owner of Ingram Park.

Directly behind him stood a polished grandfather clock. Its sombre face, nested in a dark square frame, echoed the square countenance of my husband. As the minutes ticked slowly by, I watched Mr. Rochester's face furrow with deep lines, his expression suffused with choler. I looked at Diana, who raised her eyebrows at me; the waiting was protracted indeed. Would my husband take it as a slight? An insult accorded to his changed position, to be thus ignored so long? I tried to read his thoughts but with little success. Mr. Rochester retained a stony immobility, his lips sealed. Diana and I followed suit and continued in silence.

At last, a small distant door opened and the butler reappeared.

"I beg your pardon," he said. "It seems that Lord Ingram is—ah—has not returned to the house."

"Where the devil is he? It's not like Ingram to ignore his guests."

"I'm very sorry," the man said, his voice echoing strangely in the spacious room. "We are not sure yet where he is."

"You might at least bring us tea then."

"Yes, sir, of course." The man slipped away, no doubt relieved to escape our further notice. Another dreary wait seemed about to follow when the opposite door was flung open with violence. The long stride and tall form that paced quickly into the room immediately suggested the arrival of our host.

"Nichols!" He called out, yanking a glove from one hand. "Nichols, where are—Oh!" He glanced round him for the first time and noticed his guests. "By God! Rochester! I do beg your pardon! I'd forgotten you were arriving today. You of all people too. Have you been looked after?"

Before waiting for an answer, Lord Ingram gripped Mr. Rochester's shoulder in friendly greeting. "Please, don't get up." He turned to me and bowed. "My apologies to you, Mrs. Rochester, for leaving you unattended on your arrival. How did you find your journey?"

"Well enough, I thank you." I looked up at Lord Ingram. My acquaintance with him was very slight, but I retained a clear recollection of him. I remembered the languid posture and pallid face, lacking in both fire and vibrancy. Now, however, a faint flush showed on his cheek and he moved with more energy than I expected. "Allow me to introduce my cousin, Miss Diana Rivers."

Diana stood and bowed, while Lord Ingram settled into a wingback chair just nearby while laying aside his gloves. "I hope you will find your stay at Ingram Park meets your expectations. It is rather dull here at present. Mary has gone to visit our cousins in Bath. There's only the captain here. You must meet him."

"We already have," Mr. Rochester said. "We found him in a tree." The far door opened, and a stout maid entered with the tea tray. The butler followed in her wake.

The bustle of tea being served kept us occupied momentarily, and the clock struck the hour: six solemn tones echoed sonorously throughout the chamber. Lord Ingram, I noticed, peered at the clock's face with a mild anxiety, but it was so quickly dismissed that I wondered if perhaps I had misread him.

He accepted a cup of tea from the servant and began to question Mr. Rochester on the state of his health, the roads, and other such easy and familiar topics. He spoke with an elegant languor I remembered from his stay at Thornfield. I made use of the opportunity to examine my host further. His skin was not so dark as his sister's, but his hair, like hers, was raven black. His face was handsome, his form tall and well-proportioned, but his eyes shifted from one object to another a little more than necessary. His posture communicated ease, yet his eyes betrayed a look of impatience, although it was politely repressed. His coat was flung open and I noted a scrap of matter clinging to the pocket of his coat. A fragment of bracken, moss, grass, or something of that kind lingered there undetected.

At that moment he turned his attention to me. "The house and its staff are at your disposal. Things are rather empty, you might say, without my mother and Blanche here to keep us all on our toes. Of course, we're all old friends here, are we not? Practically speaking?" He favoured us with a smile, but the expression was just a trifle too earnest and I only bowed my head, as did Diana.

"You won't find us very demanding guests," Mr. Rochester said. "At the moment, my chief concern is getting my wife to bed. The journey has quite done her up after being so ill."

"Oh yes, yes. Of course. Nichols? Get Mrs. Smith and—"

"I beg your pardon, my lord," Nichols responded, in a well-modulated tone. "Mrs. Smith is not here."

"Of course. I was forgetting again. Head housekeeper has gone off. Some family crisis or other. The old place is at sixes and sevens without her. Fetch one of the girls from the kitchen—I hope you'll be comfortable, Mrs. Rochester. If there's anything you need, just ring the bell, do." He turned to my husband. "You'll come to dinner,

won't you? I'll send my own valet to look after you. Thoroughly reliable man. He remembers you, you know." Mr. Rochester thanked
him but without much cordiality. Even the most tactful mention of
his infirmity could cast a gloom upon him.

I rose to my feet and Diana stood also; she was distracted, however, in the search for one of her gloves that had fallen under the
table. I happened to glance at Lord Ingram at the same moment in
which my companions gave their attention to the floor. At that moment, a nearby door opened up and Nichols appeared, along with a
young woman in the garb of a house-maid.

"Here's Sally, sir."

"Sally! What for?" Ingram cried. He righted himself in a hurried
movement that brought his head into violent contact with a neighbouring lamp, and he came to his feet with a flushed face. He held
one hand to his head.

"You asked me to bring a maid— "

"Oh yes—just so, yes. Thank you, Nichols. Yes." His cheek was
mottled white and pink as the sudden stimulus faded. He gestured to
me. "Mrs. Rochester, here is Sally to assist you. Nichols, have a look
for this lady's glove. You've got it? Very good. All taken care of then?
We'll meet again at dinner."

John was dismissed to return to his wife now domiciled in the
village of Hay. Whereas I was destined to become better acquainted
with the vast regions of Ingram Park. I was grateful for Diana's arm as
we passed out of the room and into the broad gallery. The house was
as an enchanted palace to my inexperienced eyes, and yet it struck me
as overburdened with ornament. The accumulated wealth of many
generations made a display that was overwhelming in its extrava-
gance.

We obediently followed the young house-maid. When she had
first entered the drawing-room, the house-maid had given no more
than the impression of a trim young woman, but as I paced slowly

up and down the stairs and halls of Ingram Park, with Sally as my guide, it was impossible not to analyse her more closely. It was obvious she was gifted with more than the ordinary share of beauty. Her eyes were blue and her hair golden yellow where it escaped her plain bonnet. She was well-formed and walked with grace, in spite of the black stuff dress and dull apron. The maid would be a fine and glittering adornment to the richest ballroom in the land were she attired in satin and pearls.

We mounted the stairs and approached a long row of bedrooms, but before I could be installed therein, a red-cheeked maid bustled out of one of the doors.

"Sally! What are you doing here?"

"Bringing guests to their bedroom. They've been travelling all day." She added the last with a sort of defensiveness.

"Well! I'm sorry, madam," this with a nod to Diana, "but you can't stay here. All these rooms are being aired. Didn't they tell you, Sally? With the ladies of the house gone, we're having everything done over."

"Where am I to take them then?"

"Well, let me see. His lordship didn't say anything about guests. I don't suppose he thought of it." She sighed; then she pondered as if we were not present. "The west wing will have to do I suppose."

"Isn't there somewhere else?" Sally inquired.

"Not that I can think of. It isn't so modern, but it's dry and clean, which is more than I can say for where you're taking them now. Why? What's amiss in the west wing?"

Sally made an indistinct mumble and led us away. As she turned, the other maid said, "Put her in the blue room. She'll be comfortable there."

Another labyrinth of passageways followed as Sally led us back to the gallery and into another wing of the house. Although spotlessly clean as the rest, there was a feel in the air that suggested this region was unfrequented. On the second floor, Sally held open the door for us and said, "There's no one else sleeping in this part of the house now. It'll be main quiet for you."

This was no grief to me, as quiet repose was all that I desired. We entered a spacious room with pale blue walls and walnut furniture of an intricate, delicate style. I had expected something more formal and grand, less doll-like, but I was not displeased. It was a pretty room, more lovely than any I had ever slept in before.

"Do you need anything, ma'am?" Sally asked. "A bite to eat, perhaps?"

Diana spoke up. "You've had nothing since breakfast except tea. You must be hungry, Jane."

"No, I am not." I had already sunk down onto the bed. My faculties were fading quickly and my stamina was at an end. "I only want to sleep. You need not stay, Diana. I will not stir."

"A bit of soup, maybe?" Sally doggedly pursued her theme. "Cook always has a pot of soup on, for any who need it. I'll fetch you some. You do look poorly, ma'am."

Diana pressed her hand to my forehead. "There's a slight increase in temperature, but that's hardly surprising after the long day we've had. Go to sleep now, if you can, but Sally, you'll stay on hand, won't you, if she needs anything? I must change for dinner." Sally made her bob, and I paid no more attention to them. I stretched out beneath the covers without bothering to get undressed; my trunk was no doubt in transit between the carriage and the house; and closed my eyes, relieved at last to sleep.

Sleep came, with its hearty, wholesome restoration, but not without the sharp condiment of dreams. I had thought my journey well over, but even when confined to bed, I continued my weary travels, wandering dim hallways and strange passages, until my search seemed futile. It would be hard to say what it was I wished to find, for my dream offered scant information on that head, but I searched nonetheless earnestly. A door opened at last, but the room I entered was enormous in its proportions. I was as a tiny linnet among giants; I wondered how I might escape into the garden. I sought for some glimpse of daylight, a portal to lead me to some fresh, living thing, but the lifeless house ran on and on, deep in shadow.

The following day I lay in a torpor. While I retained my couch, nutriment scarcely passed my lips. My body demanded sleep, that it might husband its own resources. Mr. Rochester and Diana both stayed near to me, rarely leaving my side. Doctor Carter did not neglect to visit, but his services were not needed. Rest was the only palliative called for.

I found a profound sense of peace in that bed; the powdered blue chamber became a pool of Bethesda to heal my poor and sickly frame. Another day of quiet rest followed, but the third day dawned bright, and I woke early, as the sun first touched the eastern horizon.

My room was dark, but the coals of a fire still smouldered in the grate. My chief thought was of something to eat. I noted the wire in the room; I could summon a servant to bring me some breakfast; I could wake the staff from their comfortable repose and send them hurrying at my beck and call. I was a guest of importance, after all, replete with lands and a great many thousands of pounds. I smiled, reader, at this representation of myself, and knew well that I would not touch that bell until the sun was up and the servants were already awake.

I tidied myself at the basin and sought my shawl against the chill in the air. Then, I arranged for the entertainment of my morning vigil. I went to the window and watched as the first tint of cinnabar red painted the eastern sky; sunrise was not far off.

There was something peculiar about this early morning vista. I saw now that Ingram Park lay in a sort of dell; low, rolling banks hemmed in the expansive grounds, and the noble wood of oaks ringed round it. In the full light of day, it had been majestic. Now it looked solemn, old and mysterious.

The lake that stretched before the house no longer reflected the sky. Instead, a great bank of cloud smothered it. The fog hung also in the branches of a dense patch of trees. I could see there the dark leaves of holly and the massive boughs of yew trees. It reminded me of the garden at Moor House in the North.

I wished to be outside, to explore the gardens, and particularly that dark yew walk, to feel the cool and solemn aspect of that shaded avenue, but this, I thought, would not be the first order of the day. I was a guest in a strange house, and furthermore, a married guest. I must see to my husband and find out what he needed. I left the window seat, now overlooking the anticlimax of ordinary day, and stretched out my hand to ring the bell.

The summons was promptly answered. It was not Sally, whom I expected, but the stout personage with startling red hair that we had met in the east wing the day before.

She made her bob, introduced herself as Mrs. Harper, and added, "You're up early, ma'am! I thought you'd still be a-bed."

She went at once to the wardrobe, only to find nothing hanging in it. "Didn't Sally air out your dresses, ma'am? Why, that silly girl. I don't know when she'll learn her business."

"I have had no need for them as of yet."

"Well! Are your things here? Where is your trunk?"

"I believe it's by the door."

"What, this little thing? Surely you brought more?"

I smiled. "I am accustomed to travelling light."

Mrs. Harper opened her mouth, and promptly shut it again, no doubt perceiving the rudeness of any more questions.

"Would you like help getting dressed, then, ma'am?"

"I would, but I called you on a different errand. I had almost nothing to eat yesterday. I would like some breakfast."

"Certainly, certainly. I'll have something sent up directly, but we'll have breakfast served in the dining-room before long."

"Tea and bread and butter are all I require for the present." She was soon on her way to the door, but I called her back. "Can you tell me where Mr. Rochester's room is?"

"That's an easy one to answer, ma'am. You see that door in the wall?"

I had already noted it. Not only was there a door leading into the hall passage, but a second door was placed on the neighbouring wall.

"This was the master and mistress suite at one time, and the chambers are connected. Your husband is just through there."

She bustled her way out again, and I stepped to the side door. I perceived no sound from within. I tested the doorknob; it turned noiselessly in my hand. I passed through. The room was different from my own, although formed of the same generous proportions. Here the walls were papered in grey, the furniture massive and dark. A particularly imposing wardrobe stood not far from the bed, quite dwarfing me. I was reminded of my dream. Yet the room was still tasteful, the furnishings majestic rather than gigantic.

I approached the bed and found Mr. Rochester asleep beneath the covers, his good eye sealed in slumber. Pleased with the prospect of approaching my husband, I was seized by a playful mood, a lightness of heart unusual with me.

I crept across the room with a silent step, then took a seat on the bed beside him. He did not stir. I leaned close, prepared to surprise him. I put my lips near his ear. I was about to speak his name when his eye flashed open.

"Jane."

I remained bent over him, frozen in my awkward position. "Good morning, Edward."

"I am gifted with singularly acute hearing, Jane. Perhaps you were not aware."

"You shall be my hearing for me, then. And I will be sight for you."

His lips curved in pleasure, a saturnine smile of singular satisfaction. His strong arms found my waist and held me fast. I settled into place beside him. He inquired after my health, and I was pleased to give him satisfactory answers.

"Are you indeed well, my fairy? Are you restored to well-being at last?"

"I am a little weak from hunger, but that is soon repaired."

"I am sure you are not as well as you think you are. We must not overdo things for a great while yet. But if you are hungry, ring the bell."

"Breakfast is already on the way. It may well be on the stairs at this moment. I will just leave you for a brief time to eat."

"Leave me? Just now?"

"I am very hungry, sir."

"Jane, why do you still call me sir? Am I some tyrannical overlord, that you salute me thus?"

"No, of course not. I rather like the word. It suits you."

"Does it?"

"I like to think of you as my master still."

"Not just your master."

"And my dearest friend."

"Yes?"

"And my kindred. My closest family."

"And?"

"And my lover, dear Edward."

He drew me even closer to him, for the sake of a kiss, a caress, a murmur in my ear, but he released me soon after.

"You must eat your breakfast. You shall not want among so much plenty. Only come to me when you are finished."

I returned to my room to find Mrs. Harper waiting for me. The welcome sight of the tea tray was placed by the fire, and while the maid was busy with my trunk, airing my dresses and hanging them in the empty wardrobe, I devoured my morning meal. I watched as she arranged my things, her mouth pursed up as she examined them.

"I hope you slept well in this part of the house, ma'am. There's a draught that comes sometimes when the wind is in the North, but as this wing isn't used much, they've never done anything about it."

"If all the rooms in Ingram Park are as pretty as this one, surely the house must be much admired."

"Oh yes! People often come to see it, but there isn't much to compare to this room, even in Ingram Park."

"I suppose Baroness Ingram's chamber is very grand."

"Very fine, to be sure, although not quite in the same style. I admit I always liked this one myself, but her ladyship never favoured it. Now then, shall I help you on with a new dress, ma'am?"

"If you please."

"Sally's the one who'll be doing for you regularly, but she's not well this morning. Although she'll be right as rain in a few hours, like as not. She's a scatterbrained creature, but not so bad at heart."

"I won't be too hard on her."

"No, I don't suppose you would."

She selected a gown of soft grey and helped me into it. The robing process completed, I examined myself in the glass. I was trim and neat and as presentable as I was likely to be. The lovely, fairylike chamber reflected behind me made my usual costume appear particularly drab and dull, but there was little enough I could do about it at present. I did not think the tenants of Ingram Park would accord me greater affection if I attempted to dazzle them.

"We met a Captain Fitzjames yesterday on the way into the house," I said. "Is he still staying here?"

"Oh yes, he's been here a great while. Doesn't show any signs of moving off."

A curtness had come into her voice, which prompted me to ask, "Do you like him?"

"Seems a gentlemanly sort. He's easy enough to look after, but I don't know what her ladyship will say when she comes home to a house full of guests. It's not like Lord Ingram to fill the house with people. He's usually off on his own holiday whenever he gets a chance."

I wondered what to conjecture about our invitation to the park, but Mrs. Harper added quickly, "I need to be getting back to the kitchen, now, ma'am. Unless there's anything else you're needing?"

"I will do very well, thank you."

I approached the window, to view the gleams of early morning burnishing the gossamer waters of the lake, and contemplated the answer to Mrs. Harper's question. What would Lady Ingram say when she arrived and found us here? She would not be very keen on a former governess occupying a position of honour in her household, of that I was sure.

CHAPTER IV

The morning that followed was kind, the sky clement and calm. Mr. Rochester and I passed it with a walk in the gardens nearest to the house, he providing strength and I vision. My cousin Diana went arm in arm with Captain Fitzjames, who accompanied us on our excursion and condescended to walk at our rather slow and tedious pace. A carpet of grass set down in a stand of flourishing roses provided a dry and commodious resting place.

"Ingram Park is famous for its roses, I think," said the captain. A profusion of blooms surrounded us, their pale pink hues rendered vivid by the strong light. He indicated a half-open blossom reigning in solitary glory against a background of greenery. "What do you think of them, Miss Rivers? Are you fond of roses?"

"It would be a poor mind that could not delight in a rose, but I confess they sometimes have melancholy associations. That one reminds me forcibly of Goethe's little boy. Do you remember the poem, Jane? 'Far, far off it pleased his sight; near he viewed it with delight: soft it seemed and glowing.' " Diana quoted from memory.

"I remember you attempted to teach me to translate it, but I did not make much progress."

After a quiet pause, the captain chimed in, "Spake the rose, "I'll wound thy hand, thus the scheme thy wit hath planned deftly overthrowing."

A faint line of astonishment crossed Diana's forehead. She glanced at me with a conspiratorial glow, to see if I also noted this accomplishment in our new acquaintance.

"Do you read very much poetry, Captain?"

"Oh, I am no great scholar, I'm afraid. I have only read Goethe's poems in translation, but crossing oceans leaves one with many empty hours, and I have tried to use the time as profitably as I can. The music of poetry has been a great consolation to me, but I envy you your ability to read it in the German." He stood and approached the rose for further study. " 'In the dingle glowing'. Yes, this would just do for Goethe's heedless youth. Nor are the thorns wanting, I see." He turned his back on the flower and stood with his hands folded behind them.

"There is something about a rose," Diana proceeded. "Something almost of Eden, of a garden once lost, in its radiant depths and heady scent. As if they beckon us to another existence we can never quite attain. What do you say, Jane?"

"I admire the greatness both of the rose, and the poet, but I find the one uninspiring, and the other rather cold. As lovely as they are, I am more drawn by that stand of trees on the banks of the stream."

"What, that gloomy grove?" The captain asked. "Does it appeal to you? In contrast to this?"

"Very much. It reminds me of the garden at Moor House—Diana's home in the North. It has a wild remoteness that charms me more than this neatly cultivated spot. I long to walk there."

"Yes, I understand you," the captain said. "The wild rose we labour among thorns to gather may be more treasured than the flower plucked without love or tears."

Diana looked up at him with her eyes shining. "You speak my mind exactly, Captain."

In return, he bent and offered her a rose that he had concealed behind his back, a fresh, full bloom he had secreted into his hand without our seeing. A more lovely tableau I had rarely seen. Diana looking up, her skin flushed, lips parted, face brilliant in the glowing sunshine; the captain, bowing low in one elegant movement, his eyes alive with interest; it was a scene that I did not soon forget.

Before she had time to thank him, he straightened and busied himself with something in the pocket of his coat. A moment later, he had produced the segments of a flute and proceeded to assemble it. Diana looked at me as if to say, what other wonders are we to expect?

"Shall I play for you? Rochester, do you care for a little music?"

"With all my heart," my husband replied. The captain played a haunting, charming melody, imbued with strange aeolian intervals that spoke eloquently of the sea. It was an amateur's performance, but it was played with a sensitivity that belied the captain's bluff, weathered appearance. The soulful tune came to an end; he took a seat beside us. Diana, meanwhile, had offered me the rose for closer inspection.

"It is very like the kind in the hedgerows of Thornfield. It will not be long before they are blooming there."

"Thornfield," said the captain. "That was your house? The one destroyed in the fire? I have heard of it. But surely the roses are still there. Is it far?"

"Only ten miles or so, but it is not very hospitable at present."

"No, I suppose not."

"We are exiles," Mr. Rochester said. "Indefinite exiles by all reports, but not entirely without hope of restoration. If the roses do not despair of Thornfield, we shall not give it up just yet. A rose may be more than the loss of paradise; it might be also the bearer of future promise."

"So it may," said the captain. I saw his eye on Diana as he spoke. His next words, however, were to me. "You read German, did you say?"

"Only a little, but Diana can read it well. She taught me the rudiments last winter."

"And how do you find her mode of instruction? Would you recommend her as a teacher?"

"I would, heartily. We spent many happy hours in study together."

He bowed to me, but his eye returned to Diana. "Perhaps, you might be willing to teach me a little, Miss Rivers. I doubt I will ever make a master at it, but it would be gratifying to better understand the language."

Her eyes lifted once more in surprise, but it was a pleasing expression. I could see she was gratified by the request.

"I would be happy to, Captain."

The baroness and her daughter Blanche remained in London for more than a week while we continued in residence at Ingram Park. At first, our amusements were little, for I was still fatigued and wearied easily. My husband attended me, as did Diana. Lord Ingram attempted to keep us company, but as the days remained dry, sunny and innocent of inclement weather, he visibly chafed at being confined to the house. I assured him that it would be no injustice to his guests if he pursued his own diversions. Consequently, he resumed riding out.

Mary Ingram, Lord Ingram's second, and youngest sister, soon returned to the house. I had seen her before and had not forgotten her tall and willowy form, nor her rather dull and lifeless eye. Compared to her sister Blanche, she had seemed a wilted thing, lacking in vivacity and wit. I was curious to see how she would be among us.

I found her hospitable enough before entering the dining-room. We first met in a small salmon-pink salon, used especially for assembling before dinner. She was standing by the window, looking out onto the portico.

She turned when we entered. "Oh!" she cried, in a faint voice.

"Good evening, Miss Mary. Perhaps you don't remember me? I'm— "

"Yes, of course. I remember you, I was only—Mrs. Rochester, is it not? And Mr. Rochester, of course, I remember *you*."

This was all spoken in a high, light, breathless voice, and with the last statement, her eyes fixed on my husband with that sort of unpleasant fascination one knows when looking at a maimed and crippled thing that one must nonetheless be kind to. Her eyes quickly flitted away. I felt a mild pang of pity for her.

Edward bowed and said, "So you are returned from your travels, Miss Mary. I hope you took great benefit from Bath."

"Yes, thank you. I have cousins there."

"The weather was very fine for your journey."

The conversation continued in such trivialities between the two of them. Mr. Rochester had known her since she was a girl and spoke in a comfortable tone that put as nearly at ease as possible. At length, however, a dull pause filled the room, and I felt I ought to make a remark.

"It was good of you to leave your enjoyments behind to be host to us here, although we have been well looked after by your brother."

"Have you? He can be a little thoughtless about everyday matters, but he wrote to me and said it would be better, if I came, to— " She did not finish this statement, but only gave me a curious glance. "You *have* been well looked after?"

I answered in the affirmative, and soon after the bell rang, summoning us to our repast.

The dining-room at Ingram Park was a long, gaunt room, high-ceilinged and hung with rich tapestries that glittered in the firelight. The black walnut table shone as a mirror and candle light glowed in its depths. I wrapped my arm round Mr. Rochester to steady his step when he crossed the threshold. As I was most accustomed to lead him, I was allowed to escort my own husband to dinner.

Lord Ingram went ahead of us with Diana on his arm. Diana is taller than I, yet Lord Ingram towered above her. We were followed by Captain Fitzjames, who escorted Mary Ingram. She was nearly as tall as the captain and offered sedate answers to his kindly inquiry about her journey.

When the dishes had passed to and fro and the wine was re-freshed, Captain Fitzjames raised his glass and said, "Mr. Rochester, I have sadly neglected my duty by you. I have not yet congratulated you on your choice of state. I have long believed marriage to be the apotheosis of a man." He drank off his toast and addressed himself to me. "I trust you shall soon cure him of all his vicious ways. No more smoking in bed or dining in his oldest clothes. You shall have him in decent order. It takes a wife to properly form a husband."

"The habits may be altered I think, but the true nature of a man is not always so malleable."

"And what cannot be expected from a change of habit? Is not the mind, the spirit, the very nature formed through the long exercise of habit? If you were witness to daily life aboard ship, Mrs. Rochester, you would be amazed at the remarkable changes that take place in men. Some come aboard timid or lazy, or even guilty of crimes, for our government does not scruple to man our navy with criminals from the gaols, but they are transformed, madam, by the steady rou-tine and discipline. In a long commission, especially, the change can be remarkable. You would hardly credit how a person's nature may change if enough pressure is applied in the right points."

Captain Fitzjames fixed me with an expectant eye, but I was at a loss. I myself had ascended from the role of a governess, a posi-tion scorned and ridiculed by the very people of this household, to a woman of fortune and now wife of a landed gentleman. I did not regard my nature to be much changed by these transpositions, but I also did not feel that I could offer myself as proof of my conviction.

I looked at Mr. Rochester, but he merely took a drink of wine; he remained immobile and impassive. I could not tell if he were even listening. Fortunately, Diana came to my rescue.

"I disagree with you, Captain," she said in her frank way. "I do not believe a man's nature is changeable. Men may become more brave or thoughtful or noble under the right education, but the bravery or nobility must be there beneath the surface, ready to draw out."

"So human nature is fixed then? You are no arbitress for democracy, I see." He smiled at Diana. I think he was pleased with the acuteness of her argument.

"On the contrary, I believe men and women of every station in life are inclined to nobility, or the opposite, depending on the nature God has given them. It is a very democratic view."

"I see, I see." He laid down his fork and turned in his chair to address her. "And supposing your sailor or parlour-maid is made of the same fine stuff that you yourself are? What is to become of them? Shall their finely tuned nature not be allowed elevation? It is hardly allowable. Ingram, you'll take my side of the issue, won't you? Surely a lord must maintain the superiority of the aristocracy." He shifted with a smile to face his host.

"Well, there is something in what you say. Just look at France. Or all these Chartists about, upsetting the natural order of things. It doesn't do them a bit of good, you know, all these notions. The established order has done more for England than all the revolutionaries combined."

"What say you, Miss Rivers? Would you have us embrace a revolution?"

"I shall not attempt to defend the French, Captain, or anyone else who enlists violence in their cause. But if I may be allowed, I would suggest an addition to his lordship's views. Where God has endowed a man or a woman with greater powers, it is no just act of society to prohibit him from the use of them."

"There's something in *that*, to be sure," his lordship replied. "But we can't fix the world for everybody's convenience. You can't change what you were born to, so it stands to reason you had better accept your lot."

"I don't suppose a lord would have much difficulty accepting his lot in life," Diana said, with a smile. "To be born to such an inheritance must not be an undue burden on contentment."

"Well, I see what you mean, but there it is. You can't change your station in life, and it's only a stick in the wheels to go about trying to do it. People ought to stay to their own level, for the sake of society. Stay to their own level," he repeated. His voice had gathered warmth as he went on until he finished this speech with a certain energy. I looked at him curiously; he noticed my glance and looked away, his face flushing. I wondered if he had been drinking a great deal before dinner.

"Bit hot in here, isn't it?" To the butler, he said, "Nichols, open that window, please."

The servant stepped forward to do as he was bid, and a cool draught blew through the room that flickered the candles. I tightened my shawl over my shoulders, although more in anticipation than from any actual sensation of cold.

Captain Fitzjames, in the meantime, had turned to my husband. "What say you, Rochester? Can I tempt you with my philosophical conundrum? Might one find elevated natures among the rough-handed farmer or the coarse and slavish governess?"

"What right have you to speak ill of a governess?" Mr. Rochester demanded. His fist slammed against the table, rattling the glasses. I put my hand on his arm, but he paid me no notice. An instant chill fell upon the conversation and Captain Fitzjames looked around the table with a bewildered look.

The silence was broken by Diana's merry laugh. "You have quite successfully proven my point better than I ever could, Captain. For both myself and Mrs. Rochester have worked as governesses, and I do not believe our natures have suffered degradation because we earned our bread with a bit of hard work."

"You—ah—I do beg your pardon. Miss Rivers, Mrs. Rochester, I was not aware."

"Of course you were not," Diana said. "You would never have said as much if you had. I am not at all offended and I am sure Jane is not either."

"No, of course not."

An awkward quietness continued at the table, however, until Mary Ingram made a pronouncement, her weak voice a sign that she was attempting to gain confidence rather than being in possession of it. "I always liked my governess."

This, I think, was meant to be a kindness to me, for she glanced uneasily in my direction, as did the rest of my dining companions. I felt it incumbent upon me to speak. "We are all made in the likeness of God. If we possess any virtue greater than what all men are capable of, it should be as a fine ornament to an already beautiful image."

"Well said, Jane," Mr. Rochester said. "Ingram, tell me how that new mare has got on. The one with the injured leg. Did she ever heal?" The conversation benefited from a different direction. Lord Ingram visibly relaxed his features. Captain Fitzjames addressed his food more assiduously until Diana began to question him about the various ports he had visited. He proceeded with a lively description of Minorca. Her questions were many and seemed to gratify his able tongue.

When it was time for the ladies to retire, I was astonished to see Lord Ingram hurry from his chair and pull mine out for me. "Allow me," he said. And as he did so, he leaned forward a little, and I heard his voice close to my ear. "I didn't mean *you*, Mrs. Rochester."

I would have turned to look at him, surprised as I was by this confession, but he had already traversed the room to help himself to wine at the sideboard while telling his companions about its vintage. I left the dining-room wondering, if it wasn't me, who did he expect to stay on their level?

Following Mary and supported by Diana's arm, we repaired to the parlour. The gentlemen would come in time for the tea, while the three of us must rely on one another for our entertainment. It was a grandiose apartment, bedecked in ornaments of cut glass and silver. We were soon ensconced in a comfortable corner where we had a clear view of the evening sky giving up the last of the sun's rays; only a pale tint of amethyst glowed beneath the bright orb of Venus. The trees beyond the house were all a dense mass of shadow.

I stole a glance at Mary and saw that she was a trifle pale. I did not think she was much in the habit of playing hostess with a mother and older sister normally on hand to fill the role. I could not imagine Diana and myself to be very intimidating, but I wondered if her reserve were not merely the effect of shyness. At any rate, it seemed a welcome opportunity to put a question or two.

"Miss Ingram, I understand your mother and sister have been in London for some time. When do you expect them to return?"

"Soon, I believe. Blanche is fond of London and unlikely to leave unless required, particularly while Mr. Hardwick is there. My mother, however, desires to depart before the summer heat encroaches, and they are returning home for her sake."

"Mr. Hardwick is your sister's fiancé?" Diana asked. Mary nodded. "Has she known him long?"

"I believe she met him once or twice in society and thought him handsome, but as far as I know, there was no interest on his side until recently." For the first time, I saw a glimmer of animation in her face. She leaned forward from the couch where she was seated. "It's been hinted he admired her before, but was only able to say anything after he came into his money. He now possesses nearly ten thousand pounds, while my sister and I will receive comparatively little. The estate was entailed on my brother, you see."

"Yes, but that's almost romantic, isn't it?" Diana said. "They are able to marry at last."

"Yes, I suppose it is. Romantic." Mary repeated the word, as if weighing it in relation to her own thoughts. "Blanche is very much looking forward to having her own establishment."

I struggled to suppress a smile. I was quite sure Blanche Ingram would be delighted to have her own household to order about.

Mary went to the window and opened it wide to the clement night breeze. "What a lovely evening," she said, with a sigh in her voice. "It's almost a shame to be in the house."

Diana and I rose and joined her at the window. "Oh look!" said my cousin. "There are moths about."

"They love the copse down there. I often see them."

"I thought as much. Surely those yew trees must be very old."

"They're quite ancient."

"I suppose they encourage ghost stories," I said.

Mary turned quickly from the window and spoke in a sharp voice, "What do you mean?"

"Nothing in particular. It was only a passing fancy."

Her face continued to betray an abstracted air.

"There is something rather mysterious about a yew walk. I always find an alluring quality about an old wood, as if their hoary old branches might spin a tale of all the history they have seen." Diana spoke calmly, and I thought, reassuringly, but Mary seemed not to be listening.

"There is a sort of ghost story, actually, but it's not one I care for much. It's a bit of a family secret, you see." Her voice lowered a little, and I saw in her face something of the child who may at last unburden herself of some guilty knowledge. "At least, Mama thinks it should be, but I'm sure it's no worse than half of what one hears about one's neighbours, but no one would talk about it when we were children. Except for Old Bill who works in the stables. He loved to make our flesh creep. He's quite good at telling a scary tale. At least he seemed that way when I was a girl."

She paused to draw breath. I had never heard Mary make such a long speech. Certainly there was a pleasant feeling of liberty without the gentlemen in the room.

"They say that my father's first wife had a garden there. She was very fond of it, though I can't imagine why. She was killed in an accident. I think she was thrown from her horse. She had only been married to my father for a year or so. They never had any children, and of course, he married Mama a few years later. The garden has never been tended, and the yew walk has been neglected since then. It's positively overgrown. My mother often complained of it, but father insisted it be left alone. It has grown quite wild in that spot." A husky whisper lowered her voice further. "Some said the marriage wasn't happy, and perhaps, well, perhaps the first wife was jealous and—but that's all nonsense, isn't it? One can't be jealous after one is dead, do you think?"

"I think it is a subject we can hardly conjecture on," Diana said. "The grave does not give up its secrets."

A brisk wind blew into the room, swinging the open window shutter so that it cracked smartly against the outside wall. Almost simultaneously, an enormous bang shattered the silence. It went on ringing in the dead air. Poor Mary jumped and cried out.

"How dramatic!" Diana cried, and she reached forward herself to close the window. "It's as good as a play, isn't it? What will be next?"

Several minutes passed, in which we drank our coffee with nervous composure and waited for some sign from the gentlemen in the next room. Finally, I heard the voice of my husband just outside the door.

"What was that racket, Ingram?" he demanded. At last he came, entering the parlour on the captain's arm.

"It was the window slamming shut," Mary said.

"Nonsense," Mr. Rochester said.

"It sounded almost like a horse pistol," Captain Fitzjames said. He darted to the window to open it once more and take a long look around. "God knows I've heard enough pistol shots. I hear them in my sleep sometimes and leap out of bed in search of the enemy boarding in the night. That is, until I remember where I am."

Lord Ingram followed the gentlemen into the room, but he called to the butler over his shoulder as he entered. "Send them outside to have a look around! Find out what that was." He crossed the parlour to examine the grounds through the opposite windows. "It may have been a gunshot," he said thoughtfully. "But you ladies need not take alarm. More likely than not, it's only Old Bill. Irascible fellow, but he's been with us for ages, and cares for the horses like they're his own children. He keeps a pistol by him to scare off foxes and things."

"That's an unsettling entertainment to have on hand, but I suppose old Bill must get his pleasures somehow." Mr. Rochester said. "Jane, did the noise upset you?" He stood alone, not far from the door, where the captain had left him. I went to his side.

"No, sir. We are all well. It was only a noise."

The butler returned ten minutes later, with the welcome intelligence that Old Bill confessed himself responsible. The rest of the evening passed off without incident. Lord Ingram persuaded Mr. Rochester to sing, and the captain favoured us with a rather good performance on his flute. Diana accompanied them on the piano. She was a good performer, and the captain in particular was attentive to the business of arranging her music for her.

The piano was silent for a time when coffee and dessert made their appearance. I had removed to a seat a little apart from the company, as the evening breeze from the window had begun to chill me. Diana had taken refuge with Miss Mary, while his lordship was engaged with my husband, to discuss some estate matters having to do with Thornfield. I was interested in their discussion, but soon found my attention drawn off to another quarter. Captain Fitzjames approached and took a seat by me.

"Shall you join us in making music, Mrs. Rochester?"

"I play a little, but not so well as Diana. I prefer to listen. Do you find many opportunities to play music at sea?"

"It is one of our only entertainments. You would hardly believe the boredom of sea travel, madam, although sometimes disrupted by hasty and even violent action, much of a sea journey is spent in long, slow, monotonous hours with the same company, and very little diversion. Music has saved my sanity during many a cruise." He smiled pleasantly, and I was once more struck by his lively cheerfulness. I could not but acknowledge a sympathy of nature between him and my cousin. Her spirits were good, her temper equable, her manners unaffected. I did not know much of the captain, but in temperament, there certainly seemed a similarity.

"Do you expect to return to the sea in the near future?"

"Alas! No," he sank back in his chair, his merry smile dimming. "No, I'm afraid my sea time is about over. We have no enemy to sail against, and I have little interest at the Admiralty, while they have a great many men to offer commands to."

"It must be an enchanting life, to sail the world."

"It has many advantages, I must admit, but it is also frequently cold, wet, strenuous, and somewhat lacking in the comforts of a settled home. It is indeed."

"You anticipate settling down then?"

"If I can contrive it, yes. I'm afraid I have not yet figured out how to go about it." His eyes and mine were both turned towards the rest of the company, although our words were heard only by ourselves. He leaned towards me, and although his voice remained cheerful, he spoke in a more confidential tone. "I am to inherit a small estate someday. A fine old place, nothing grand or noble, you understand, but good farmland. I'm in no hurry for it, however, and now that I'm not at sea, I'm not sure what else to do. My father manages the land very assiduously, but I'm afraid I've never been able to take much interest in it. It's a shame, really, I ought to learn, but my father dislikes teaching me as much as I like learning, so perhaps we're better off as we are."

"Is your father very difficult to get along with?"

"No, he isn't. That is to say, with other people, he is not. The trouble is, Mrs. Rochester, that when I have a matter in hand that requires immediate action, I have no difficulties. Be it a privateer under my lee or a mainsail blown out of its bolt rope, I am ready and willing to act, but give me a mere intellectual matter, a long, drawn-out, deliberate assessment, I grow impatient, and will simply act on the first suggestion made to me in order to be doing something. My father prefers to mull over every decision as if the state of the nation hangs upon it. I can hardly stand it, and I'm afraid I affect him in much the same way. So, to preserve the peace between my father and myself, I have taken up a wandering life."

"So that is why you stay so long with our host?"

"Why yes, there's that. I suggested leaving some time ago—I abhor the thought of being a hanger-on, but Ingram insists I stay."

"He must enjoy your company."

"Yes," he said, but he looked doubtfully at his lordship. "Yes, I suppose he must. Very much to my credit, too, isn't it?" He leaned back in his chair. "Is your cousin to stay with you for very long?"

"I don't know her plans. She accompanies me of her own volition, and may take herself off at any time."

"She's a very engaging young person. I don't recall ever meeting a young woman who spoke so well on so many different subjects. I suppose she is content in her studies and her independent life. Seeks no change for herself?"

I had been watching the others in the room, like himself, but now I turned to get a good look at the captain's face. His eye was carefully examining me.

"That's a difficult question to answer. I wonder if any of us can truly say that we seek no change for ourselves. Have you ever found yourself wholly content with your lot in life?"

"I see you bear the family resemblance to your cousin. You are a close questioner also."

"Where has the captain got to?" Mr. Rochester exclaimed.

"I'm right here, sir," the captain called out. He nodded to me and rose to his feet. "I was just being grilled out of countenance by your wife."

Mr. Rochester laughed. "You may delude yourself into thinking that you will get the best of her, but you will find it no easy matter to outwit Mrs. Rochester."

Neither my husband nor my cousin suffered me to remain long in company. I was still easily fatigued, and Mr.Rochester insisted on retiring with me. I entered his chamber with relief. He took a seat by the fire.

"What are you doing?" He asked me.

"Brushing out my hair."

"You might have a servant do that for you."

"I'm accustomed to doing it myself."

"Well, come here, then." I seated myself on his knee. He took command of the brush and attended to my locks.

"I was not aware you were so qualified to be a lady's maid."

"I can only hope to make amends for all the good that you do me, my angel."

He brushed with faithful consideration for a few moments, but the task was soon neglected for a close embrace. I felt, however, that his attention was not entirely given over to me, so that when a log dropped down into the flame, I was not surprised to hear him say, "Fetch me a drink, Jane. I am not ready to sleep yet."

I went to the bottle of brandy on the dresser and promptly followed these instructions. When I returned to his side, he began, "You have a trusting nature, Jane. You are willing to believe the representation others make of themselves."

"I must admit my faith in appearances is not what it once was." I didn't like to speak what was in my mind, but he supplied the words for me.

"You owe that to me, do you not? Very likely no one has deceived you so much as myself, to my own shame and regret. When I think of my past treatment of you, I am overcome by repugnance at my own conduct."

"Never mind that now, sir."

"Never mind it! I do well to remember it. And so do you. Not so that you can remind me of my misdeeds and hold them against me, much as I deserve it. I know your heart is too generous for that. But you ought to take a lesson. Fine gentlemen and ladies are not always what they seem. Captain Fitzjames, for instance, cherishes some particular views toward your cousin."

"I've noticed it."

"*Tré bien, madame.* And perhaps you have perceived a certain unease in our aristocratic hosts?"

"I have."

"And how do you account for it?"

"I believe it's your infirmity that embarrasses them, and the recollection of my previously humble position. They do not wish to offend, but cannot make out how else to behave."

"No doubt, no doubt, but there is something else not altogether right about our company. Can you put a name to the enigma?"

"No, sir."

"Neither can I." He couched his chin against his fist, emptied his glass and offered it to me to replace on the waiting tray.

"Like you, I was rather burned by deceit in my youth. By dint of hard knocks and broken promises, I learned to read the hearts and minds of my companions, that I might ferret out their motives. This faculty you cannot be expected to possess." He considered this a while. Then he took my hand. "I liked your innocence in the early days of our acquaintance, Jane. It suited my purpose to find you so trusting, so dependent on the judgment of your master. And I have suffered for trespassing on your naïveté. I suffer still."

"How do you suffer, sir? Where is the pain?"

"Not in the body, but in the spirit. I flattered myself once that I should be your protector and guardian. I trusted in my strength and sagacity to defend you from the wolves of this world."

"And do you find an abundance of wolves at Ingram Park?"

"My little simpleton! You are in need of more protection than you know! If you are to be a woman of the world—to navigate all the wily notions of the creatures around you, you must call scepticism, suspicion, doubt to your aid. They are your surest friends—your truest counsellors."

I studied my husband's face, impassioned and earnest. I laughed. I could not help it. "It is small wonder, Edward, that you have spent so many years in wandering, friendless pursuits. Is there anything more sure of disrupting home and happiness than the comforters you suggest?"

"Oh, you need not doubt all voices, you need only test them—trust only in what is sure. Be wise as a serpent, Jane, and do not rely on any source of knowledge that has not been thoroughly tried."

"Is there any particular bit of knowledge I ought to be doubting? Anyone of our acquaintance I should suspect of double motives?"

"At present, I don't know that there is. Perhaps you are blessed with a sure instinct to guide you to those who mean you good and not harm. Maybe it is that very instinct that led you to me, hindered and hampered as I was by lies and misdeeds, but even when wrapped in my darkest deceptions I wished nothing but good for you. From the moment I first laid eyes on you, I wished you well."

"Even when I felled your horse? In Hay Lane?"

"Even then, my mischievous sprite, even then."

CHAPTER V

I confess I thought little of my husband's dire warnings. As I prepared for my bed, I lingered instead on the deep assurance of his affection. I was no longer a lonely wanderer on the earth, no restless Israelite sundered from her promised land; I went to my pillow gratified and content.

But a few hours of passing sleep may sometimes alter our notions, change our idle fancies into lingering nightmares; the calm security of day might make way for morbid thoughts in the coldest hours of the night.

I woke up near midnight, for I heard the chiming of a clock somewhere in the house. I was by my husband's side, secure and safe still. Except for a pall of moon glow, the room was dark. Memory presented plainly before me my husband's face, as he spoke of my innocence, of my naive, trusting nature. Perhaps I *had* been too trusting, I thought, too reliant on the opinion of others. I reflected on my former days as an inmate of Thornfield, when all around me knew well the deep secrets of the Hall, yet I continued month after month oblivious of the true nature of those secrets. I had trusted the interpretation presented to me and never inquired for more explanation.

In retrospect, I thought myself little to blame. On what grounds ought I to have suspected the motives of those around me? But now it seemed to me that I had allowed my faculty of curiosity to grow too complacent, too docile beneath the cloak of a humble schoolgirl, regarding myself as too insignificant to question my betters. Was it not well that I throw off such restraint? Allow myself to question, wonder, puzzle over the society I was now thrust into? If in the past, I had been too easily lulled into trusting appearances, it might now be wise for me to be more circumspect. No doubt an alteration in my position demanded an amendment to my habits of mind.

I little expected such sentiments to be put to the test. Yet while engaged in these meditations, I was startled by a noise – curious enough at such an hour. It was the sound of footsteps outside the door. I listened and perceived the stranger's footfalls pacing with heavy solemnity down the hall. I rose from the bed. Mr. Rochester continued in deep slumber. I went to the door, which I knew to turn noiselessly on its hinges. I looked out into the hallway. All was empty and quiet. And yet, I perceived a certain glow, a faint light, as of a candle, moving away from me.

On my left was a stair we had never used. I did not know where it led but presumed it carried one deeper into the west wing. Down this narrow and seemingly unused stair, the last strains of light mingled with darkness.

Well, it is no business of mine. Besides my feet are cold against the floor. My bed I know is close and warm. The distant light grows dim, fades and vanishes to nothing. My hand lingers yet on the clasp of the door. I had not thought to exercise my curiosity so soon, but when in life are we given the choice of how and when we are to employ our faculties?

I went back for my shawl, wrapped it hurriedly around my shoulders, and slipped out the door. My feet passed silently down the hallway. I saw very little, but the way was straight and smooth, and when I reached the top of the stair, I could yet perceive a faint glimmer of light. Unexpectedly, I heard a new sound—no footfalls this. It was a laugh; a gay, careless laugh of a low timbre. I thought it likely that it was the laugh of a man.

With catlike tread, I descended the stairs and arrived in a narrow way that opened onto a room I had not yet visited. The portal was made visible by a slender blade of light on all sides of the door. I tried the handle—I pushed open the door—the room was a deep den of shadow, with only a circle of candlelight at the centre, so bright to my night-adjusted eyes that at first, I could make out nothing. When the glare of the candle no longer blinded me, I just made out the slight form of a woman. She whipped around to face me. There was no sign of laughter in her visage. Rather, she wore a look of unmistakable menace, as of a small animal cornered at last.

"Sally?"

Her face changed at once, and the wild defensiveness was gone, but she looked wary still. "What are *you* doing here?"

I felt no need to defend myself to such an interlocutrice, but a little explanation seemed fitting. "I heard footsteps pass my room and came to find out what it was."

"Is that all?"

"What else would it be? I had no idea what might be transpiring. What are *you* doing here at such an hour?"

The symmetry of her features appeared even more perfect in the fitful light of the candle. She wore no bonnet, no nightcap, and her blonde hair was loose round her shoulders. A fierce defensiveness still lingered in her eyes; I felt as if I were accosting Boadicea. Then the expression changed, literally changed as I watched. Her blue eyes softened, her stiff brow melted, her whole frame altered, the upright, defiant posture seemed to shrink before me. She sighed.

"Oh! Mrs. Rochester. You'll think me so silly." She took a small step forward. I saw for the first time that there was something about this room I had not seen. The walls were cast in darkness, but there was a faint glittering sheen from beyond the shade. This was no ordinary chamber. "You don't know what it's like to be a servant in a house like this. We're so short-handed and I'm run off my feet all day, and then at night—we're all packed into the servants' quarters', with Mrs. Harper watching our every move—some nights I just long for a little time to myself."

"You came here for privacy?"

"Yes, ma'am. Just to be alone. That's all I wanted."

"Is there no other hour when you can slip away? It must be dreary in the dark."

"Not tonight there wasn't. And I particularly wanted to get away tonight. I sound foolish, I'm sure, but it's all I have." She spoke in a low voice. "I feel like a caged-in creature sometimes. Nothing ever happens to break up the sameness of the days. I have to invent something, you see, just to keep myself from growing miserable."

How plainly I understood the deep monotony, the abiding loneliness, of serving in a great house where one was bereft of hope, and without sympathy from any living creature.

"I do not think you are foolish. Indeed, I believe I understand you perfectly well."

"Do you really, ma'am?"

"But you must try not to give way to melancholy."

"Oh, I do try, ma'am. I try to think of happy things, so long as I can get a little time alone, just to think my own thoughts."

I nodded, but a new thought struck me. "And is this why you are so often ill in the mornings? Because you are up half the night wandering about in the darkness?"

"It's not so often as all that, ma'am. Only a time or two." A new light came into her eyes, a shadow of worry. She folded her arms over her stomach. "And I've really been sick some days."

"Well, it's all right. You need fear nothing from me. I suppose this is a secret of yours?"

"Oh yes, ma'am. Mrs. Harper wouldn't be pleased to find out I was here. I'm not harming anything, but she wouldn't understand. You won't tell, will you?"

"No, I will not."

"Thank you, Mrs. Rochester, ma'am. Do you need the candle? I know the way very well. You may have it."

"No, it's all right. I haven't got very far to go."

"Do take it, please. You'll need it on the stairs."

"You'll come with me, won't you? Why don't you lead the way?"

"Oh, yes, of course."

Our curious procession ascended the stairs, lit by Sally's candle. I don't know if I would have found the right chamber in the darkness. Restored once more to my room and to my husband still asleep in the bed, I smiled at myself and my attempt to unravel any mysteries at hand. My intrepid adventure had turned up nothing more than a bored house-maid. No doubt a bit of fruitless knowledge was the usual reward for undue curiosity.

As I laid down, I heard the wind rattle the window panes. Soon after, it hurried down among the oaks and shook them vigorously; a great, rushing sound filled the night as the gale of wind blasted both house and wood. I was not surprised some minutes later to hear rain commence. It pattered against the glass and the walls outside, hushing me gently to sleep.

When I woke, the sun was already far advanced, but its progress was hard to measure; a dense curtain of rain cloud closed the view of Heaven's fields. I left my couch and discovered that I was alone. I thought Mr. Rochester would be there and quelled a momentary disappointment. Yet I was relieved, too, for I now had a chance to explore the scene of the previous evening's encounter. I dressed with my usual simplicity and left the room, descending the spiral staircase with care.

I recognised the door at once; it stood open; I entered the room. I had come to Ingram Park anticipating a beautiful mansion, furnished with unexpected beauties, but I had not been prepared for this. It was a small room, of octagonal shape, with tall, mullioned windows looking over the gardens. The walls were adorned with murals, shimmering cherubs and angelic forms that glowed with an unexpected brightness against the sombre cloud beyond the glass. The paintings bore a similar hand to the one that wrought the elegant masterpiece of the gallery. This, however, was executed with a flawless detail that astonished me. The only furniture of the room was a weighty object covered by a dust cloth. A peek beneath its folds revealed a harpsichord of the last age. Sally's secret retreat was a music room, apparently unused. I went to the window and found once more that I was viewing the yew walk. She had chosen her hiding pace with care; residents of the house would be unlikely to notice a midnight visitant here.

I left the room and travelled the hall towards the gallery, pausing to examine the portraits on the wall. A great many old frames enclosed the likenesses of previous generations. I studied the faces, some grim and stern, others handsome and expressive. One young lady in a close bonnet glowered from her gilt frame with an expression so familiar that I paused and stared. Here were the majestic features of Blanche Ingram, or nearly so. The portrait's lips even bent in a subtle line of scorn; yes, it was her forebear without a doubt. I passed on through the hall, meditating on what sort of reception I was likely to receive from Miss Ingram. In the little I had experienced of her, she had treated me with condescension and disapproval. The governess of Thornfield Hall was of a caste beneath her notice, worthy only of contempt.

Perhaps I should have triumphed, to be thus installed as an honoured guest in her house, but I confess I would rather have done without my glory and so evade the dragon. Cold disdain from my fellow creatures has never been much to my taste. I reached the gallery and thought I heard strains of conversation somewhere. No morsel had yet passed my lips, and I hoped for some sign of breakfast progressing.

The long gallery laid a hushing spell on me, however. I walked carefully, feeling the hollow echo of my footsteps to be an intrusion on such pregnant emptiness. I paused to look up at the magnificent figures emblazoned on the vaulted ceiling; to feel once more the stirring rapture inspired by those brilliant images. I was startled out of my reverie by a voice.

"Do you like it, Miss Eyre?"

I turned in haste. Before me stood the living likeness of the portrait I had so lately examined. I curtsied to Miss Blanche Ingram; then hesitated. Was that right? What was formal etiquette for a guest and equal? Where was Mr. Rochester? I had depended on him to keep me in countenance for this interview.

For her part, she did not bow. She stood at her full height, her arms folded across her chest, and looked down on me with a faint smile. "I beg your pardon. I ought to say Mrs. *Rochester*. Forgive me."

She approached me, and to my complete surprise, she put a gloved hand on my shoulder and bent to study my face. She leaned forward and kissed my cheek. It was a formal act, but even the pretence of affection from her carried with it a sort of electric shock that stunned me.

"I wish you my congratulations." She stepped back from me.

"Thank you, Miss Ingram. I did not know you had returned to the house."

"We spent last night with the Eshtons. You must call me Blanche. I shall not accept formality from *you*." Again, she revealed a tight-lipped smile. "You have married into one of the first families in the county, and furthermore, are wed to one of my oldest friends. You take precedence over me, as a newly married woman. I hope you find Ingram Park to your taste."

"It is certainly a beautiful house."

"It does not have its equal in this part of the country." She spoke in a plain, matter-of-fact voice, as if proclaiming a universal truth. She began to pace around me, with a slow measured step, her gaze directed not at the room and its magnificence, but at myself. "They told me you were ill. I am surprised to see you about the house alone."

"I am considerably better than I was. I understand Ingram Park has a reputation for its healthy location. It has certainly acted thus upon me."

"I am glad to hear it, but this draughty gallery is no place for you. Take my arm, if you please. I will bring you in to breakfast."

Was this the cold and haughty Miss Ingram I had known at Thornfield Hall? Still, there was that smile, neither affectionate nor kind, only watchful, such as one might expect a cat to inspect a goldfish in its bowl. I took her arm and followed her.

I soon found a more formidable introduction was yet to come. If I had been surprised by the semblance of affection from her daughter, I had no repetition of it with the mother. The dowager baroness of Ingram Park stood by the window of the breakfast parlour. She was clearly in confidential conference with her daughter Mary. They both looked at me when I entered the room upon Blanche's arm. Mary glanced at me, her cheek tinged with pink, but she quickly dropped her eyes. She was silent as long as I remained in the room.

Her mother's black eyes fixed on me a penetrating gaze, while her mouth compressed into a hard and haughty line. I have long accepted the necessity to remain calm when presented with natures at variance with my own. Nonetheless, a quick rush of temper welled up within me. I looked away momentarily, to master the impulse and compose my features.

"Mrs. Rochester," began that august lady. "I did not expect to meet you here." Her voice expressed no pleasure. After a prolonged pause, she added, "I hope you have benefited from the hospitality of my son."

"Lord Ingram has been very kind."

"He is not here. I have not seen him yet; do *you* know where I might find him?"

"I do not, ma'am. I imagine he has gone out shooting with Captain Fitzjames. If I meet him, I will be sure to direct him to you."

She responded with a sniff, ran a condescending eye over my gown and took no more notice of me. A quick movement of her head communicated with her daughter Blanche, who dropped my arm and left my side. She did not do so without a final glance back at me. Her look evinced neither regret nor apology; on the contrary, she looked more self-satisfied than ever. I no longer had any appetite for breakfast.

A fitful period of rain kept us within for the morning, but the rain departed in the afternoon, leaving a promise of deliverance in the calm and balmy air. I ventured to request a walk out of doors, for I found the grandeur of the house mildly oppressive, as if I could not draw a good breath.

"Nonsense, Jane," Diana reprimanded. "The ground is still far too damp for you." As if to emphasise the point, a low murmur of thunder from some distant region sounded in our ears.

I stifled a sigh at my enforced inactivity. "We might study then. I am by no means so sure of my German verbs as I could wish."

"There will be time enough for studying when you are fully recovered."

"Then I must see to Mr. Rochester. Perhaps he has need of me."

"Mr. Rochester has an army of servants to attend him."

We had retired to my room for the afternoon, where a fire burned in the grate against the damp atmosphere. I did not wish for a fire and looked down at it with faint disapproval.

"You are a terrible invalid, Jane," Di remarked as she watched me moving fitfully in my chair.

"I cannot help it. Besides, I feel well enough."

"That is because you are being quiet and keeping still. Typhoid is not an illness to trifle with. Your lungs are still weak."

I drew a deep breath in resignation. I could not argue with my cousin. I must consign myself to dogged inactivity, but it was wearisome to my spirit. I was tired of my knitting needles, so I examined the contents of my pockets, and brought forth the guinea that I found under the shattered tree at Thornfield. I contemplated its golden sheen, but could make nothing of it, and returned it to my pocket. Then I took up my knitting and endeavoured to be tranquil.

A knock at the door summoned me to attention. Di opened it to reveal a maid bearing a vase of hot-house flowers, bountiful lilies and orange blossoms that scented the air. In her wake appeared Blanche Ingram, dressed in snow white with a sky-blue sash round her.

"I've brought you flowers from the conservatory." Blanche dismissed the maid and took a seat beside me.

Diana took a chair opposite her. "That's very kind of you."

"We have so many," she said carelessly. She looked at me with a searching gaze and asked after my health. I made a few inquiries after our common acquaintance, the Eshtons and the Dents, and our conversation lapsed into silence. Blanche stood and took a turn around the room.

"I suppose you have not been to Thornfield Hall?"

"Before I was ill, we visited. It is quite a wreck now."

"I know it is."

"You've been?"

She stopped her pacing. "Once, yes." She hesitated, then resumed her walk. "On the way back from London. I had the coachman drive up, just to see what had become of it. I did not stay long. I wonder what you must have felt, arriving there. Did you see anything—unusual?"

"Unusual? What do you mean?"

She stopped at the vase of flowers and rearranged them somewhat more aggressively than the blooms required. "One hears things—stories. Tales for the servants' hall I make no doubt."

"What sorts of things?" I asked, genuinely curious now what she alluded to.

"Oh, I'll not repeat any of it. A hundred years hence there will be legends about it all, and children will fall asleep thrilled with tales of the ghost of Thornfield Hall."

"I was not aware that Thornfield possessed a ghost," Diana said.

"Who said that it does? I did not." She stood before a vanity mounted with a mirror. I could see her face in its reflection, and presumably, she saw me. She flashed a rather coined smile in the glass and turned around.

"Jane, have you ever thought of wearing flowers in your hair?" My bonnet was off, laid to one side, and my hair braided neatly against my head, as was my wont. She plucked a cluster of lilies from the vase and took up a position behind me, that she might place the flowers in my hair with a deft hand. "What do you think, Miss Rivers? Is not that an improvement?"

"It does bring more bloom to her cheek," Diana said. "You have an eye for natural beauty, Miss Ingram."

"I consider it heedless to ignore an opportunity to be beautiful. One never knows when it might prove advantageous. I must leave you now and you must get your rest."

She departed at once. I went to the mirror and examined my face in its frame, to first remove the flowers from my hair, and then replace them. It was true, my pale skin gathered colour against the pure white petals.

"I believe she expects me to dress as a peacock now that I have wealth to spend."

"She is certainly very showy. I should feel ridiculous dressed up as she is. Still, it is natural to have a taste for finery. It would not hurt you to indulge in it a little."

She stood beside me at the mirror and placed a flower in her own hair. "There, we are a matched pair."

"We are perfect opposites, Diana."

"You were pretty before she brought you anything." She reached behind my head and tucked a bloom more firmly into my braids. "But the flowers are not a-miss, either."

I smiled at Diana's words, but my mind quickly dismissed them. I was far more curious about the nature of Blanche's inquiry. What had provoked her questions about Thornfield? And what of these ghost stories? It was almost as if she wished *me* to tell *her* something, but what knowledge she hoped to elicit from me I could not guess.

I did not find dinner to bring much improvement. Faint echoes of thunder continued throughout the evening, but no rain ever came. Conversation at the table was subdued, and as usual, divided. The dowager remained firmly in possession of her children's remarks, while Captain Fitzjames paid particular attention to Diana's description of the moor country and its inhabitants. Mr. Rochester held my hand beneath the tablecloth but said little.

"I shall be glad to remove to our own home," I remarked quietly to Diana after we departed with the other ladies.

"But what home will you go to? You cannot return to Ferndean."

"That is all the more reason to lay plans. We must depart somewhere."

"You must not think of leaving us," Miss Ingram interposed.

I had not known her to be so near to me. I turned in my seat and looked up at her. "I am deeply grateful for your hospitality, but we cannot trespass on your kindness forever."

"I depended on you remaining with us for two months at least."

I glanced at Baroness Ingram, that I might assess her opinion of a prolonged stay. Her eye was on Blanche, her lips compressed in a hard, impatient line.

"It rests upon her recovery," Diana said. "Until I have the doctor's blessing, I would not wish for a removal."

"You speak wisely, Miss Rivers. We must abide by such sage advice." Blanche brought her ample garments to the window, before saying, "What a strange light we have this evening. If the air were not so close I would seal all the windows to block out the sight of it."

The final rays of the sun slid over the edge of a dark and shifting cloud, while an eerie and sombre glow lit the shadowy lawn. She turned from the window; and stopped, startled, and gasped. So did we all. For a shot sounded in the night air.

"Oh, not again," Mary said. With a sigh and a prosaic shake of the head, she stood and went to the dining-room door. "Nichols, pray go to the stable and take Bill's pistol away from him. We want no more gunshots."

"Very good, madam." Nichols departed.

The dowager looked about her in frightened consternation. "If he had not served your father so well, I would have him sent away at once. I could never bear such noises. It is unsafe for my constitution."

"It shall not be repeated, mama," Blanche said. She closed the window shutters after all, blotting out the unearthly light, and went to the piano, to play a calm and restrained melody.

Mr. Rochester and the other gentlemen joined us soon after, speaking confidently of Old Bill's possible punishment for frightening foxes in so unorthodox a manner. I went at once to my husband's side.

"Are you tired? You ought to rest." He spoke quietly in my ear.

"I am a little. I think I will go soon."

"I'll go with you."

"Do stay," I urged him. "You have not had company for so long, and I am going to do nothing more than lie down. It would be no peace to me if I knew you were confined unnecessarily."

"Very well, Jane, but I'll not stay long. And you must promise to rest."

I bid goodnight to our hosts and departed for my own room, and my candle soon illuminated the spacious chamber of my bedroom. I ought to rest; I knew it, reader; but it has long been my habit to walk when my mind is occupied. The invalid's impatience for free movement clung to me too. Tender and devoted as the care of my husband and cousin had been, I was eager to be free of it, to exert the power of independent movement. Though my frame was not so robust as it had been, yet my mind demanded refreshment that could not be attained within these walls.

The window was open, and the darkling sky had changed once more. The setting sun left no more than a violet shadow, whilst the evening breeze blended the pleasing scent of lily and jasmine. A marble basin erected at the base of the hill gave a soft, Arcadian mood to the scene. I half-expected a slender nymph to appear behind those laden willows. The lawn was smooth and dry, the air clement and gentle. A short walk, I felt, would be the best aid to rest.

I secured my shawl and left my room, moving quietly down the stairs to a little door beyond the music room, and exited the house. Beautiful and majestic as the mansion was, I felt a pleasant delight in being free of it. I made my way over the lawn towards a path that followed the garden hedge. As I rounded a corner, I saw at once that the path approached the distant copse. I had not intended to get quite so far from the house. Now that I was down low, however, I could see more clearly into the dense shadow beneath the trees and there, winking like a tiny eye, was a light.

There was nothing ghostlike about this light; nothing eerie or incorporeal, but to see a light burning at so late an hour in so strange a place—I looked back at the house. The west wing which I had left was dark and still. The east wing was brilliant with candlelight, but it was quite distant from me. I doubted I had the strength of lung to hail so far. I took stock of my own limbs and bodily frame. Torpid, yes, but not weak. My strength would hold.

Perhaps, I thought, this was mere illusion, an *ignis fatuus* in the dusk. I hesitated as the path dipped lower, taking me into the dell occupied by the copse. Well, it was not so far. I looked at the sky and saw a pale crescent moon, yellow and dim at its rising, but gaining in brightness as it ascended. There was light enough now for this dim path. I went on.

A stream flowed along its pebble bed from my left. I approached it. The banks were muddy and soft, and I could no longer see the light. I walked round the trees, listening to crickets grow silent at my feet, and chime once more behind my back. The light was on the ground. The thick branches cast eerie shadows in the moonlight, and the air smelled damp and stale within. Hard to conceive a more fitting dwelling for a spectral inhabitant.

I ducked low to avoid the overhanging branches and lifted my skirts to avoid fallen bracken and stones. I was told that this had once been a garden, but there were no signs of cultivation here. Green moss clustered thick around the rocks; I felt the dense softness beneath my feet as I passed. The stream was in sight once more; so was the light, a dark lantern that had fallen to the ground. It lay on its side with the slide open. And there, in a crux in the rocks beside me, was a face.

Stricken white, deathly pale, I recoiled at the sight of its ghastly visage. It was the face of a man, his head bent back and his dark curls dragged in the mud. I cried out, but only one eye rolled beneath a half-open lid. I willed my feet forward and beheld the rest of the apparition. The man lay in the stream, his face, neck, chest glowed with unnatural pallor in the gloom. And across his white shirt was a thick band of red. The man was bleeding, wounded. Was he dead?

I dropped on my knees in the mud and turned the waxen face toward mine. The lips parted; a moan issued forth. There was life still in this spent frame. I took hold of his arms and tried to move him, but it was useless. My already taxed strength failed me. I called out for help, but I knew there could be none here. The house! I must get to the house.

I was struggling to my feet when the grip of an icy hand seized my wrist. His eyes opened; they were lidless in frightened panic. His black irids looked direct into mine. With a grasp more powerful than I had expected, he drew me back to his side.

"You've come! I've longed to see you." His voice shook with terrible energy. "I could not find her." An anguished grimace distorted his features.

"Please, be still. I must get help." I attempted to pull my arm away, but his grip grew strong, surprisingly strong for one so afflicted.

"I have looked so long for her." His eyes closed; deep lines of grief crowded his face. He pulled my fingers close and pressed them to his cold lips. An awful fear bore into my soul. "I did my best. Do you believe me? I did my best." His palm rose to my cheek. It trembled against my skin. "I missed you so, my dear, my love. You have come to take me with you— "

He sank back into the stream, his exertion telling on his weakened body. "I only wish I could have found her. I wish— " I pulled away, his fingers slid away from my face, and yielded to my efforts of escape.

I fled the copse, stumbling over root and under branch. My sinews wavered as I ascended the path; my knees shook; they threatened to give way, but I willed them to obey. The gentle slope now felt steep in my need for haste. I cut across the lawn and up the path to the house. Here was the massive front door. Was there a butler there waiting to answer? Music sounded from the light-filled window not far away. I dashed as best I could towards it, praying my legs would carry me so far. Already my chest burned; I was suffocating.

"Help! Help! Oh, come quickly!" I beat on the window casing to arrest their attention. The music stopped.

"Jane!" My husband's voice answered swiftly. "Is it you?"

"What is the matter?" cried Ingram.

"There is a man on the ground. In the grove. He is injured, bleeding. Oh!" My lungs demanded air that they could not get. I gasped and coughed; my frame shuddered; I sank to my knees.

"Good God!" Ingram cried. "Fitzjames. Hurry." To the butler. "Get the lady."

They were off, running full force across the grass. A man's arms encircled me. A moment later, Diana was with me, supporting me. My husband's voice was speaking, but I yielded to utter exhaustion; I listened to nothing more.

CHAPTER VI

"Jane."

In the firelight, I gradually pieced together my surroundings. I felt a sense of urgency that I could not place at once. Vivid images of blood and darkness rushed upon my inner vision, and I shuddered beneath my blanket. I did not recognize at once these golden bed curtains or this cavernous ceiling, but I knew that voice, beloved and well-remembered. My eye searched for his familiar form, and at last, discerned him, a stark silhouette against the firelight. I was in Mr. Rochester's bedroom.

"You are shaken, Jane?"

"Only for a moment."

"You are weary?"

"I have slept. I am not so weak as before."

"Tonight has called for great labour on your part."

I tried to search his face but I could make nothing of it in the gloom. His tone of voice was curious; passionless and cynical.

"Is something the matter, sir?"

"Pre-cise-ly! With your usual acumen, Jane, you have hit the nail on the head." He sat down on the bed beside me. "Something is very much the matter."

"The man—is he going to be all right?"

"I don't know. Without the gift of second sight, or indeed of any sight at all, I can hardly say what the morrow will bring. Tonight has already been more adventure than I might have foreseen. Certainly, he is badly wounded. Does it grieve you to hear that?"

"I am grieved that any man should be injured. Are you not?"

"In Christian duty, I ought to say yes, but compliance from my feelings depends upon circumstances."

A light began to dawn as to what the matter was. I tried to raise myself but struggled vainly against soft sheets and overstuffed pillows.

"What are you doing?"

"I want to sit up."

Mr. Rochester leaned forward, moving his hand over my legs in order to discern my position. He slid his arms under mine and helped me up with a gentleness that belied the caustic tone of his voice.

"Jane, what were you doing down there in the middle of the night, when I had expressly told you to go to bed?"

"I am truly sorry to have disobeyed you."

"Are you? Are you? A curious time and place for a secret tryst! Unless it was your desire to be secretive; your aim to be undetected. An ideal location for meeting a secret lover, Jane."

Now the trouble in my master's mind was laid bare. Jealousy, an old phantom of his, had come to haunt him. I rallied my thoughts, trying to piece together an argument in my favour.

"Mr. Rochester, before tonight, I never set eyes on the gentleman. And even if I had, I would no more betray you than betray my own self. Do you not know me? Do you not trust me?"

His dark brows narrowed with anxious penetration, as if his blind eyes willed to see into my secret mind.

"Trust you! Why should I?" He rose to his feet in haste and paced the narrow lane before the fire. "I tell you to go to bed and find instead that you are wandering in the woods! This is a devilish business, Jane!"

"Perhaps it is, for that poor man found in the stream, but my part is easily explained. Will you sit down and hear it?"

"Three months ago you stood at God's altar with me. You promised to love, cherish, even to obey me. Is this your notion of obedience, Janet? To rush around in the dark of night when I have told you to rest?"

He stopped where his stride had brought him and grabbed the back of the chair to help him find his way to the bed. With an expression of pained resignation, he took a seat on the bed beside me.

"Give me your hand, Edward."

"If you promise me that you are not wishing for the hand of another. I'm a wretched enough husband, blind and maimed and ugly as I am, but I believed in your fidelity, your constancy, your character— "

"They are unchanged, I assure you. Absolutely unchanged."

I was not pleased to find my devotion questioned. What dark doubts had taken root in my husband's mind? What suspicions lay there that he would second guess me so easily? It hurt me to be so accused. I wished to defend myself, but I longed far more to be believed honest and true.

"I forget sometimes that you are so inexperienced. So much sagacity and temperance are rarely to be found in so young a girl, but young you are, and I must have patience with you."

"I am sorry to try your patience."

"Let us hear your story then, and we'll make what we can of it." He looked away a moment. He did not seem to wish me to speak. Almost in a quiet soliloquy to himself, he went on, "God knows I *want* my Jane to be cleared of all suspicion. There is no deceiver so persuasive as a loving heart."

"Edward, you can trust me, truly you can."

The bold lip trembled a moment. Then his hand arrested mine. "Well, what of it then! What omniscient spirit informed you that fate had abandoned a stranger in need? Perhaps an angel visitor called you forth to discover him."

"I don't know what it was exactly. My sickness left me impatient of lying still. I felt I would find little rest in the mood that had seized me."

"Humph," was my husband's only response.

"I went to the window; the air was warm and enticing. I thought only of walking around the edge of the house. Then I began following a little path. You know how a little path always draws one on. And then I saw the light."

"A light?"

"The glow of a lantern beneath the trees."

"You didn't see it from the house?"

"No. A rise in the ground concealed it. Once I was lower down, it was just visible."

"So you went to investigate?"

"Yes."

"What was it?"

"A dark lantern fallen to the ground."

"Anything else? A weapon?"

"I did not think to look."

"Footmarks?"

"There might have been. The ground was muddy by the water. Where is he? Do you know how he does?"

"He has lost a great deal of blood, but the doctor was sanguine in his hopes."

"What was the cause of his injuries?"

"Can you wonder? A gunshot."

I meditated on this information. "The same gunshot we heard at the house?"

"It's probable."

"Has anyone offered an explanation?"

"None that I know of. The man said nothing. Did he say anything to you?"

I was silent a long moment, trying to decide if I ought to disclose all. To a jealous, passionate nature like Mr. Rochester's, the tale might cause consternation, but having already inspired his distrust, I felt that concealing the truth would only add insult to injury.

"He spoke to me."

"To ask for help?"

"He seemed to know me. He spoke to me as if—as if he recognised me and loved me. He clearly took me for someone else, someone who had already left this life behind. He seemed to think I had already passed over to heaven."

Mr. Rochester released my hand to rub his chin, a not unusual trick when he was thinking hard.

"He must have been delusional with pain," I added.

"Humph! What did he say to his delusion?"

"He said, 'I looked for her, but I could not find her.' He did not have the strength for anymore. I ran as soon as he released my arm."

"You ran yourself ill again. You shall spend the day in your bed tomorrow, as much as you may abhor it. And I expect full obedience, mind you. No slipping away without permission!"

He rose from the bed to take off his clothes, tossing them carelessly in the direction of the chair. Half of them landed on the floor, but he could not see that. His weakness smote my heart with pity. With an awkward and clumsy effort, he tugged his dressing gown over his head by himself. A servant might have helped him, but in this distressed mood, he scorned any outsider.

"This is a curious business, Jane. There is more to this than we can, as yet, discover." He flipped the covers down and slid into bed and wrapped his arms protectively around me. His warm cheek pressed close to mine.

"Jane, my love. You must never disobey me like that again."

I woke late in the morning to the sound of voices outside my door. One of them, I was sure, was my husband, although he spoke so low that at first, I could not understand his words. The other was a woman's voice rising in shrill tones.

"I'm to look after her, sir. Master's orders."

"I will not have her disturbed."

"I only want to see what she needs."

"I shall attend to her. Your services are not needed."

"You, sir! But you can't see anythin'! Beggin' your pardon, sir."

"Go on! Off with you! You're not wanted I tell you, now go away!"

The bedroom door opened and closed with a slam. Mr. Rochester stumped across the room to me.

"Impertinent girl!"

"That sounded like Sally."

"Do you know her?"

"She helped me dress yesterday."

"Presumptuous thing! No doubt she taxed you with her ignorance."

"I am more patient with ignorance than you are, being little more than an ignorant girl myself, but I suppose I should be thankful she inspired your ire, or I might be tempted to jealousy myself. I have rarely seen such a beautiful young woman as she is."

"Oh, I am sure of it," he subjoined sullenly. "I have known a great many beautiful young women, and none of them could hold a candle to you for native pith and intelligence."

"Where is Diana?"

"She was here all morning to attend you, but you slept the perfect rest of the righteous. I persuaded her to go out for a drive with the Captain and Miss Mary. Lord Ingram is gone to meet with the Magistrate and Blanche is attending to her mother. Jane, I have changed my mind."

"Changed your mind about what?"

"You sound hardy enough today. How do you feel?"

"I am hungry, sir."

"There is porridge, seed cake, soft-boiled egg, and who knows what else they've sent up for you. You will forgive me for asking you to pour your own tea." He groped for the tray on the dresser and brought it to the bed with a slow and tentative step, feeling his way with his bad arm. I sat up eagerly to consume a very welcome breakfast.

"How is the wounded man?"

"He is as well as can be expected I believe."

I refreshed my cup of tea, pouring slowly, retracing my thoughts of last night, but I was not ready for any revelations yet. "You have not told me what you've changed your mind about."

"I want you to leave your bed, as soon as possible. I would like a good look at that devil's den under the trees. Will it disturb you to return there?"

"I don't think so."

"Do you feel well enough? We will not be above half an hour, and we'll take our time."

"Edward." I laid down my spoon.

"What is it, Jane?"

I would communicate what vexed my mind, I decided; surely justice demanded it. "I am not going anywhere until I speak to you about last night."

"What about last night?"

"You plainly suggested that I am not to be trusted to keep my marriage vows."

"Oh! Now for it! Give me the full volley, Jane. Doubtless, I deserve it." His dark eye flashed as he spoke. He folded his arms over his chest. Was I teasing a repentant sinner or reprimanding a haughty doubter? I could not tell.

"Do you think I would deceive you? Betray you? You, whom I love with my whole soul? Do you believe me capable of such a thing?"

"I admit I was roused, perplexed, nay, overwhelmed, last night; my anger was directed primarily at myself. To see the signs of your illness manifest once more, while I was idling! My self-reproach was keen indeed. The confidence in your voice this morning is enough to dissolve all memory of trouble."

"Well—and will you doubt me again in future? Will you harbour constant fear of my betrayal? Surely you can have confidence in me?"

"That's just it! That is the very spot! I have had the misfortune to see my confidence trodden upon like so much dirt. I'm afraid it is a worn out, wasted thing. That is the wretched ugliness of jealousy, my darling, that I can seldom keep myself from doubts, for they have been proven true time and time again. Do not let it grieve you. It is not your fault."

"Do you mean I must put up with your lack of trust as if it were a bad habit?"

"Yes, I suppose you must."

"It's hardly fair. I cannot bear to be thought a liar."

"And I suppose I am to overlook this little matter of your disobedience? I hope you can understand that an untrustworthy spouse is my greatest abhorrence."

"It was only a thoughtless lapse. I am not accustomed to anyone taking much interest in my movements. I scarcely thought of you."

"No, I don't imagine you did."

I realised what a poor palliative my words were. "I am sorry, Edward."

"We will learn the ways of this marriage business yet, Jane, given a little time and opportunity. Have you finished your breakfast? I'm sorry to make you dress without the benefit of your maid, but I would prefer to pass unnoticed just now."

I put on a simple gown and fastened the hooks successfully.

"Do you have a shawl about you? You must not catch cold."

"Yes, I am ready."

"Then lead the way."

We descended the little path, walking slow enough for my husband to take each step with care. Judging his steps was difficult enough without the power of sight; on an uneven descent, the challenge was even greater, but he showed little reluctance, only his movements were necessarily small.

"By-the-bye, Jane, I heard a strange thing from Ingram yesterday, about Thornfield Hall."

"Thornfield!"

"Rumour has improved upon her story, adding embellishments as the distance grows from the source. They say a ghost resides there. You may guess which one."

Mr. Rochester's brows contracted in a shadow of his old melancholy. It was not hard to imagine the spectral tenant of Thornfield. It must be that of the mad hand who brought about its demise. "Your first wife."

"Yes." He paused to feel his way around a depression in the ground by tapping it with his toe. "Such a malicious witch would hardly rest easy in her grave."

"Do you still hate her so much?"

He stopped in the midst of the path and turned in my direction. "Unhappiness made me vindictive. Contentment in my lot has eased the rancour in my soul. She did me great injury in her profligacy, but I have endeavoured to forgive her for it."

"So she has made the ruins of Thornfield her abode?"

"Ingram says the servants tell him so."

"You do not accept such a story, do you, sir?"

"I verily believe there are stranger things roaming the face of the earth, but to own the truth, I think Bertha spent her wrath so fully in life that there is little left to excise after death."

Sombre memories of my dreams in illness shadowed my thoughts, in spite of the warm sunshine. I diverted my reflections by discussing the question further. "I wonder if your old agent had any notion of this rumour." We resumed our walk down the hill, his arm snug around my shoulders.

"I have no doubt that he did. I wonder—how far do we have to go now?"

"We have just come to the spot where I could make out the light."

"Good. The stream, you said, flows into the grove. Take me to the bank first. But don't step on the soft ground."

I paused well away from the stream, a little distance from where it entered the trees. A thick carpet of mud bordered the water, but I could see nothing except a few bird tracks in the soft soil.

"I wonder which direction Ingram and Fitzjames came from."

I turned and looked at the house, and noticed something I had not seen before. It had been hidden by the hill. "There is a little foot-bridge closer to the house. Ingram would have gone that way. The path runs further down the hill, and then turns toward us here."

"So he would have come up from below, rather than from above, as we are doing. Very well. Take me closer."

At length, we arrived at the spot where the path entered the trees. "I could not see the light from here and did not care to enter the dark woods without being sure of my destination. I walked around last night."

"Was it difficult going?"

"It was. Rocks, sticks, thick moss— "

"I suppose you followed the path on your way out?"

"Yes."

"Do you see any traces of your flight?"

I searched the path. "I see the marks of many feet, but I cannot tell one from another."

"Janet, my love, I have told you before that you must be my eyes for me. Today, you must be more. I can neither see the evidence nor interpret it. I believe you possess faculties for intelligent observation. Look closer."

I let go of my husband to move up the path, my head bowed low, that I might see anything that would gratify him.

"Take care not to step on anything important yourself!"

To the left of the path was a grassy plot, dry and unsullied. I perched there and looked at all I could.

"I see the mark of more than one boot on the path. Some of the tracks are quite heavy. Here is the heel of a boot pressed deep."

"Which way is it going?"

"Towards the house."

"When they carried the man up. Anything else?"

"No." I led Mr. Rochester deeper into the trees. There were shadows here, but the noonday sun cast plenty of light.

"Where are we now?"

"We are very near the place where I found him."

"Have a good look around, Jane. Tell me everything you see."

"There is a trough at the edge of the stream where the body lay. If he fell back—he must have hit his head on the stones."

"Yes. True. There are scratch marks in the mud."

"Scratch marks?"

"I think—he grabbed onto this tree branch, and the branches dragged across the ground."

"Ah."

"There are several marks here, on the other side of the stream, but they're rather mixed up."

"A struggle?"

"Yes, I think so. And here, on the path. A puddle has dried recently—a man stood here, feet spread apart."

"Looking which way?"

"He faced away from the stream."

"Where is the lantern?"

"Gone. But here is where it fell. I think it must have been placed
on this rock."

"He stops," Mr. Rochester said. "And puts down his lantern.
Where is his interlocutor now?"

"I see his tracks! A man stood facing him I think. There is the
imprint of a boot, close to this boulder."

"His assailant stood with one foot on the ground, the other on
the rock?"

"The moss is disturbed here. Yes, I think so."

"They face each other for a few minutes at least. No hurried attack in the dark. Suppose a strange robber delivered a threat before
resorting to force. Was there anyone else? Any branches broken?"

"There are some snapped twigs, but I don't know if it's anything
or not. I see another set of marks leading away from the house, but
the ground is quite dry further from the water and then it turns
mostly to grass. I can make out nothing." I turned back, looking left
and right. The trees seemed filled with signs that I could not read.
Was that broken cobweb the sign of a passing hand? That crumpled
leaf the effect of a stranger's passage?

Mr. Rochester had his fist over his chin, his mind busily engaged.
I stopped close to the rock and searched the ground.

"Ah!" I cried.

"What is it?"

"There is something here!"

A noise, like that of a branch breaking, sounded behind me. I
turned to look. Someone unseen flailed about, and the violent mo-

tion caused the branches to crack and tremble. An impenetrable holly bush partially blocked our view.

"Hi! Who's there!" Mr. Rochester called out. "What is it?" I had already taken a few steps away when he called me back. "Jane, stay put!"

"There's something in the tree back there. I can't see it."

"What is that?"

Something was moving quickly behind us, on the far side of the holly. I thought I saw a flash of grey, as of fabric, but there was nothing more. I hurried to my husband's side.

"Someone has just run away, down the bank."

"Man or woman?"

"I don't know."

"I'll not have you running round the hillside. We'll let him go. Are you sure it was not a bird? An animal?"

"I don't think so."

"You've been out long enough. Come, Jane."

"Just a moment."

I stepped down to the stream's bank, to the flash of silver that had arrested my eye before. A small rectangular case lay in the tall grass, quite near to the path. I scooped it up and slipped it in my pocket. The rattle of carriage wheels and stomp of horses' hooves carried over the lawn.

"It's time to be getting back. And you'll mention none of this to anyone."

CHAPTER VII

"Jane, I could have sworn I made sure your things had been cleaned." Diana stood by the dresser, running my shawl through her fingers. I sat in the chair of my own chamber, a book open and face down in my lap. I was in no mood for reading, as my mind was fully occupied with the mysteries of the morning. My cousin picked a dead leaf from the fringe of my shawl.

"Tell me about your ride with the captain," I asked. "Did you speak much?"

She laughed. "We talked the whole way. He seemed a bit starved for conversation."

"Perhaps he likes your conversation especially."

She smiled pleasantly, without shyness. "He has very affable manners. I enjoyed our outing. But I'm worried about you." She came to the chair and put her hand on my shoulder. "I am afraid your efforts last night will hinder your health. You are supposed to be resting, not finding half-dead men in the bushes."

"I am glad I happened to find him."

"So am I! But I do not feel you are fully recovered."

"I am tired, I suppose, but I do not think I am injured by the exertion."

A light knock sounded on the door and Sally came in.

"Is there anything you need, ma'am?"

"Thank you, no."

"Or you, miss?" She turned to Diana.

"No, thank you."

"Oh. Well." She faced me and inquired, "Will you be coming to dinner?"

"Not today. I'll have my dinner here, please."

"Oh."

I waited for the girl to go, but she did not. She looked at me, at Diana, at the window. She wrung her hands.

"Do you know how the injured man is doing?" I asked. "Are there any reports about him yet?"

"The doctor says he's in a fair way to recovery. As well as can be expected. That's what Mr. Nichols told me." She paused. "He's the one who actually spoke to the doctor. Not me."

"I'm glad to hear of his good progress," I replied dismissively. Still, the servant lingered. "You may go now."

"Oh. Thank you, ma'am." She bobbed and went away.

Diana laughed at her absurdity.

"She's new to her work," I said. "I suppose she doesn't know exactly what to do with me."

"Well, she will find you a model patient, at least for one more day."

I sighed. Then a thought struck me. "Diana, do you know if Captain Fitzjames takes snuff?"

"I don't know for sure. He said nothing about it. Why do you ask?"

"Oh, just—idle curiosity. Edward does, sometimes. Or he used to."

Diana narrowed her slender brows at me. "What are you thinking about? Something is going on inside your head."

"I'm just puzzled, that's all."

"You ought to lie down. And try not to puzzle too much."

Diana helped me into bed. "I'd like to speak to him. The injured man."

"I understand he has said nothing coherent yet. The captain sat with him all through the latter part of the night. He said he was accustomed to taking his watch at odd times of the day. I believe he is with him now as well."

"That is very good of him."

"Goodness seems quite characteristic of him, from what little I can tell."

I slept throughout the early evening and woke to a darkened room. There was no fire in the grate tonight, nor was there a need for any. A candle by the window had burnt down to a mushroom wick.

Diana sat in a chair nearby with a book in her hand, but the volume had settled in her lap and her head listed to one side. The curtain had been drawn back, no doubt to let in the cast of moonlight, but heaven's cold sickle was no longer visible. The night must be far advanced. I rose from my bed and was pleased to find myself regaining strength. I went to Diana's side and touched her shoulder; I spoke her name, but she did not wake. She was quite sound asleep.

I went to the door of Mr. Rochester's bedroom and entered. The bed was still made; the room empty. A clock somewhere below boomed the hour; it was midnight. They must be holding high revelry in the drawing-room tonight.

I went to Mr. Rochester's window to study the vista before me. All looked serene and calm. No curious lights or shadows moved about, and if they did, I felt no temptation to follow. I would not risk my husband's displeasure again. I was about to turn away when something caught my notice. No, surely it couldn't be—small and pale in the trees, I could see a light.

At any other time, I might have envisioned a fairy holding a tryst under the yews, but no such pleasant fancy could arrest my imagination this dark evening. I viewed it with an agitation in my spirit that could hardly be suppressed. What tragedy was *now* passing within that dense thicket?

I hurried to my own room and went to Diana's side. I shook her shoulder.

"Oh!" She yawned and looked about her, trying to get her bearings. "What time is it, Jane?"

"Midnight. Wake up, Di, and come with me, quickly. There is another light in the trees."

She rose from her chair, the book still caught between her finger and thumb, and followed me to Mr. Rochester's room without question. I half-hoped the illumination had been the turmoil of my own mind, unsettling as such a conclusion might be, for a real light was haunting in its reminder of last night's horrors.

No such consolation was afforded me, however, for Diana said, "Yes, I see it! Has it been there long?"

"I just noticed it. I only woke a few minutes ago myself. Diana, suppose there is something else going on there, something— " I did not like to specify my fear.

"Someone hurt, or in need of aid, like last night?"

"Yes."

"We ought to call the servants. Alert the household."

Ready to act on this suggestion, I turned from the window, only to feel Diana's hand close upon my arm. "The light is moving!"

I looked for myself; yes, a lantern was gliding up the path, bobbing gently as its owner carried it. It disappeared a moment later, hidden behind a rise of the bank.

"The footbridge."

Then it reappeared and steadily climbed the path towards the house.

"This way."

I hurried to the hallway while Diana followed close behind. We ran as quickly as we could, but without speaking a word. I believe we already understood one another perfectly. If the apparition passed close to the house, we might see something to unlock this mystery. Tall windows by the front door faced the path and would give us a clear view. Was it the prone man's attacker, returning to the scene of his wicked machinations? Was there something else attractive to midnight visitants among those dense branches?

We turned down the maze-like passages and into the open gallery. My weakened chest hindered me and my step slowed, while Diana ran ahead. The front hall was empty and shadowed, except for the starlight cast through the windows on either side of the door. Her pace was halted in the middle of the room. The great oaken door was opening. Quick as thought, Diana slid against the wall where stood the imposing grandfather clock, and pressed herself into its shadow. I slipped quickly back into the arch I had issued from, hoping its gloom disguised me.

The front door opened and disclosed the hand that had moved it aside. A tall gentleman stood there, his shirt pale in the dim light and his coat hung over his arm. He set the lantern on the side table and leaned over to blow it out. In the faint glow, I could see plainly the mild features of Lord Ingram. He strode quickly through the gallery, his footfalls echoing on the marble tile, and approached the hall that led to the drawing-room, from whence the strains of music could still be heard. He paused, however, at the hall opposite to where I stood. Perhaps he could feel the weight of watching eyes, for he turned and looked around him. I stepped back, hunching into the shadow and lowering my eyes so that he might not see them gleaming in the darkness.

"Who's there?"

There was nothing for it now; I had been seen. I raised my head and righted myself.

"Who is that?" He said again. He was already thrusting his arm through one of his coat sleeves. I told myself firmly to avoid any glance in Diana's direction and left the shelter of the doorway.

"It is Mrs. Rochester." My voice threatened to shake unaccountably. I clenched my fingers in an attempt to steady my thrilling nerves.

"What are you doing here?" His speech sounded raw and rose uncomfortably at the last word. As I approached, I could see that his eyes were wide and strained.

"I woke in the night and decided to look for my husband."

"He is in the drawing-room." Lord Ingram stared hard at me a moment. "You saw me come in, I suppose." His coat was neatly in place now, and he waved his hand in the direction of the door, with a nonchalant movement that was more nearly like his usual manner. "I was having a look around. Just to be safe, you know."

"And in the grove?"

"What? There is nothing in the grove. Why? Why do you ask?"

"Only nervous fears. After last night— "

"Yes, yes, of course. When you find something dreadful once you expect to find it again. I only went as far as the front step, but every-thing is quiet and dark. No lights abroad tonight."

"I'm glad to hear so good a report. I'll return to my room now. If you would just tell Mr. Rochester that I only wanted to check on his whereabouts." I turned to go. "Good-night."

"Good-night, Mrs. Rochester."

Diana met me in the hallway after Lord Ingram had safely quit the field. She put her hand over mine and looked into my face. A pale shadow of worry coloured all her features. No doubt I looked the same. She let go, and we paced in silence to my room. We went to the window, our eyes on the copse; all was dark and still. We looked from Mr. Rochester's room, fearing to see some other strange glim-mer in the darkness, but there was nothing. We sat down before the cold fireplace in my room, with the long-suffering candle on the table between us.

"Jane," Diana said at last. "Do you have any inkling of what busi-ness Lord Ingram could have down there in the middle of the night?"

"I can think of no obvious purpose."

"Neither could he, seemingly. He clearly lied. Does it not seem strange that a gentleman should wander his grounds at midnight and lie about it?"

"Yes, it does."

"Was he looking for something?"

"Or for someone," I suggested.

"Do you suppose he's in league with Mr. Barnett's assailant?"

"Or— "

"Or what?"

"Did he do the shooting himself?"

Diana made a grimace. "He was in the drawing-room still, was he not?"

"As far as we know."

A gentle knock sounded at the door, and then my husband's voice: "Jane, are you up?"

I opened the door for him. "I am, and Diana is with me."

A servant was holding his arm. "You may go," he said to the man. I led him into the room and towards a chair, but he would not sit down. He leaned his arms on the high back of it.

"Ingram told me you were wandering the hallways. You must learn to be more helpless, Jane. To lie a-bed and do nothing for yourself and order servants about."

"I was trained early to independence."

"Nonsense! You were born that way. Independence is in the marrow of your bones. What were you doing roaming the house alone at midnight?"

"I was not alone. Diana was with me. Did Lord Ingram tell you that?"

"He said nothing about her. Well? I am waiting for an explanation."

Diana and I exchanged an uneasy look. How much was right and fitting to tell? Knowing Mr. Rochester's keen inquisitiveness, I felt it would be fruitless to suppress the truth.

"I woke a little before midnight and went into your room to see if you were there. I looked out the window and saw a light, in the trees."

"Another one? Janet, you seem to have a gift for these things. There must be some sympathy between you and that druidical grove."

"I think the angle of the window has more to do with it."

"Well, get on with it then."

"I woke Diana, and we went to the window together and saw someone was carrying a lantern up the path to the house. We ran to the front hallway and saw the light bearer enter the house."

"It was Ingram?"

"Yes."

Mr. Rochester frowned deeply. He began pacing the room, his good hand hooked around the elbow of his bad arm behind his back.

"After he saw me, he explained himself by saying that he was looking around the front step, to be sure all was safe."

"He did not mention the grove?"

"When I asked if all was quiet there, he said specifically that he had not left the steps."

"He lied?"

"I believe so."

Silence fell as we considered this.

"Have you always found Lord Ingram to be an honest, reliable man?" I asked.

Mr. Rochester did not answer this question. Instead, he said, "Jane, what was it you found in the trees this afternoon? There was no opportunity to discuss it when we returned to the house."

"Got back to the house?" Diana asked. "I never knew you were out of it."

"You are well into our confederacy, now, Miss Rivers." Mr. Rochester said. He reached out his hand to find the mantelpiece, that he might lean against it. "Come, let us see your evidence, Janet."

"I took it from my pocket and left it in my dresser."

I went to the dresser by the bed. I had slipped it beneath my stockings; I remembered well where it was placed even in the dark, but my reaching hand discovered nothing. I lit a fresh candle to aid my search, but it was a search in vain.

"It's gone."

"What was it?"

"A snuff-box. A silver one, not unlike the sort I used to see you with."

"Well, it wasn't mine. I stopped taking snuff months ago after I dumped a whole boxful trying to help myself to some. Silver, you say? You didn't happen to open it, did you?"

"I did."

"What was in it?"

"Snuff."

"Nothing else?"

"Not that I am aware of."

"Who has been in your room today?"

"Myself and Diana only. And Sally."

"The house-maid? Was she near the dresser?"

"She hardly left the doorway while we were there. I couldn't speak for while we were at dinner, however."

"Well, another piece left without a place in the puzzle. Who knew you had it?"

"No one but you."

"And whoever was hiding behind the holly bush this afternoon. Someone knew you found something, Jane. Someone who was so surprised that he lost his footing in a tree."

"His name is Barnett."

It was the first time since the incident in the grove that I had appeared at the breakfast table at Ingram Park. However, I was more famished for news than for tea or toast. In fact, the captain could hardly ask for a more captive audience than he had at present.

"Donovan Barnett. He is not from this neighbourhood at all."

"But what was he doing there?" asked Mary. The cup in her hand was halted on the way to her lip.

"He has recently entered the service of Mr. Hardwick."

"Blanche's Mr. Hardwick?"

"Yes indeed. Mr. Hardwick asked him to come to the house on business of some kind," and here he nodded to Lord Ingram.

"But why come up the little path and not by the main road?"

He smiled at her eager curiosity. "Even that mystery is cleared up, Miss Mary. His horse threw a shoe at Millcote and he was forced to leave his animal at a blacksmith there. He was directed how to get here on foot, but the directions must have been poor ones, for he wound up at the Three Brothers, and they sent him up the path as the quickest way."

"An unprofitable shortcut," Mr. Rochester said.

"Indeed."

"And how does he account for his injuries?" Diana asked.

"He says a bandit attacked him to steal his money."

"Right on our property?" Mary cried, with a small gasp.

Lord Ingram leaned forward and took up the story. "He says he thought he recognised the man when he was in the tavern. In his consternation at being lost, he was not very guarded about inquiring the way. A tramp was on hand and listening to every word. He believes the fellow followed him on purpose to attack him at the darkest place."

"How dreadful!"

"It *is* distressing," Ingram said, consoling his sister with a hand on her shoulder. "I went early this morning to the Magistrate, and I believe they are already searching the countryside for the thief."

"I would be surprised if they find one," Mr. Rochester said. As usual, his eye was fixed on a sort of middle distance, being unable to focus on any particular object in the room.

His voice was low, but I was sure Lord Ingram heard him speak, for his lordship turned to him with a most particular look. "I suppose if Mr. Barnett had much money on him, the thief may have had means to take himself far away."

"Let us hope he had the wits to do so," the captain said. "Although it would be gratifying to catch the villain who did this, I would rather know we are safe from such creatures. For the time being, however, I think it best if the ladies keep indoors during the evenings." I was not surprised to see the captain glance significantly in my direction.

"A wise precaution," I admitted.

It was an injunction all the easier to follow, as the morning began with a cold swath of cloud blotting out the sun and threatening rain before the day was far advanced. Breakfast over, our party dispersed for various employments. While my husband discussed hunting with Lord Ingram, Captain Fitzjames approached me, and with a tip of his head, suggested I move to the corner of the room. I was surprised at the familiarity in his manner; I soon found out his purpose, however.

"Mr. Barnett has asked me to convey a message to you."

"To me?"

"Not a message exactly. A request. I have explained to him how he was found and by whom. He says he was not himself that night—which is not to be wondered at—but he does recollect you, and wishes to thank you as soon as may be. He is still very weak, but he is presentable and able to speak. Will you come?"

"Yes, gladly, but— "

I paused and glanced at Mr. Rochester. "Perhaps my husband might come with me. He has not asked to see me alone, has he?"

"No, ma'am. I'm sure Mr. Rochester would be welcome as well, provided he speaks softly. An invalid's ears can be strangely sensitive."

At that moment, my husband called to me. "Jane, we're going outside to the barn, to meet this new spaniel of Ingram's. Would you care to come?"

I looked at the captain, who merely shrugged his shoulders. "I'll remain inside, sir, if you don't mind," was my reply.

"Very well. You'll stay out of trouble, won't you, Jane?"

"We'll take turns keeping watch over her," the captain replied, in a good-natured voice. Mr. Rochester's face contorted into one of his enigmatic expressions, but he only took Ingram's arm.

"Rochester, what do you think about— " Lord Ingram's question, and Mr. Rochester's reply to it, were blotted out by the closing door.

"Perhaps I will come alone. Will the present do, Captain?"

"It will do very well, madam. Come with me."

CHAPTER VIII

I hesitated in the hall, just outside the bedroom door. Mr. Barnett's words came vividly back to me—his great woe and desperate grief; the pathetic sadness of his soliloquy echoed once more in my mind. Mr. Barnett, I felt, had suffered many pangs before he ever entered the mysterious grove of Ingram Park.

"All ready?" The captain asked.

"Yes. Thank you."

I followed him into the room. A small fire burned in the grate and a vase of chrysanthemums nodded at the bedside. The blankets were taut over the figure in the bed. He wore a dressing gown drawn awkwardly over his shoulder, and I could just see the edge of the bandage wrapped close to his neck.

"Here she is, Barnett," the captain said. His voice was quiet but cheerful. "I have brought Mrs. Rochester to see you."

I had no distinct impression of the man in the bed. Not until I reached the bedside, and was seated in a wooden chair alongside him, did I have leisure to study his face. He was pale, very pale; the skin beneath his eyes showed blue, but I imagined he was normally a high-coloured man. There was a fullness about his lips and chin that suggested a romantic ancestry far from England's chilly shores, but there was such a lassitude about his face and limbs that it was difficult to judge his temperament, except as melancholic. His eyes were quite black, more like a mirror to reflect one's thoughts than a window into the soul behind them.

He immediately sought my hand with his, and I felt an awful dread that a strange confession would break out upon me again. I nearly snatched my fingers away, but his first words showed his intention.

"Mrs. Rochester, please allow me to thank you, from the depths of my heart, for coming to my rescue. I owe you my life. I can only offer my gratitude, a small repayment for such a debt."

His voice was hushed, but nonetheless had a curious power to hold the listener's ear. "There is no question of obligation, sir. I did only what I thought was right. I believe a divine hand led me to find you."

"I sometimes doubt whether the Lord was at his wisest then. Except for an unresolved matter of conscience, I am quite resigned to death— "

"Come, come, Barnett," the captain put in. He was tending the meagre fire—no more was needed on a day like this, even for an invalid. "You remember what the doctor says. We must not be too morbid."

"Morbidity is an easy temptation under the circumstances. Out of courtesy to the captain, however, we will speak of something else. Mrs. Rochester, since you decline to accept my thanks— "

"I do not. Although the service rendered was small enough. Other hands have contributed more to your healing."

"Well then. Since you decline any honour for your actions and make yourself out to be the mere instrument of God, I will confess that I would like to know something more of His instrument. The captain has no information about you but that you are newly married and have been ill. I hope your work of saving me was not the cause of your illness."

"It was my illness that brought me to Ingram Park." I related a brief account of my sufferings from typhoid.

"You are made of stern stuff, I find."

I smiled. "So my husband tells me."

He released my hand. "And you have been married only a short time?"

"Nearly three months now."

"Were you long acquainted?"

"In a way, I suppose we were. It was a rather—peculiar courtship. I will not attempt all the details now." No doubt he would hear it all from someone. I preferred that it not be me.

"I understand your husband is blind?"

"He was injured in a house fire, many months ago. We are somewhat homeless at present."

"Ah. I know that plight. I am a little homeless myself. And what of your family?"

"I have none. That is, I have my cousins now. When you are well, I hope you will meet my cousin Diana Rivers—she is staying in the house with us—but I was cast off by my known relations as a child and grew up as an orphan."

"Were you?" A new interest came into his eyes. "An orphan! Were you happy, Mrs. Rochester, in spite of that misfortune?"

"There were many causes for sorrow in my early years, but it was not all grief. And, I grew strong enough at need."

He examined my face, as if attempting to trace some likeness in it, but his eyes wandered off, fixing on nothing. "I have thought much on the plight of the orphan. It seems such a burden to entail on a child."

I thought of the anguished confession he had made beneath the trees. *I tried to find her,* he had said. A light of understanding seemed imminent, and a question trembled on my lips, but he forestalled me with a question of his own.

"Mrs. Rochester, would you be so kind as to come a little nearer?" His voice was already so low that I had to lean forward to hear his words. He glanced quickly at Captain Fitzjames, but the captain was humming a sea chanty to himself, while his attention was engrossed by his telescope. My confusion must have shown in my expression, for Mr. Barnett added, "Come closer, please. Bring the glass."

A glass of water occupied the stand by the bed. I took it and brought it near his lips. He did not drink. Instead he looked at me, his dark eyes an inky well of some emotion I could not fathom. His voice was just audible when he spoke.

"I am under an obligation to you, for more than just my life. I must also ask you to keep a trust with me. Do you think you can?"

"If there is nothing wicked in your request, I am sure I can comply with it."

"There's no wickedness in this. Only, it's imperative that nobody know what I said to you, under the trees, about—when you first found me. You will not tell?"

I withdrew the drinking glass; I leaned back in my chair. Barnett's haggard face glowed with a curious energy.

"I will speak to no one of it. But— "

"But what?"

"I have already told my husband."

He closed his eyes briefly, then he returned my gaze. He looked resolute, I thought, a curious expression for a tired invalid. There was unusual power in this man; a controlling force was acting on him. Was it a force from within, or from without? What stroke of doom threatened to fall on him?

"Mrs. Rochester, please tell me the truth. Can your husband be trusted with a secret?"

When I considered all of my past experience with Edward Fairfax Rochester, I could not repress my surprise at this question being put to me. If the occasion were not so solemn, I would have laughed. Barnett himself looked at me curiously, the stern set of his features melting a little.

"You just passed through the strangest turn of countenance. What is it?"

"Mr. Barnett, if you knew all the past history between my husband and myself—it would take so long to explain, but I assure you, if anyone can keep a secret, Mr. Rochester can."

I left the invalid's room greatly confused. I found my way into the long hall but made little progress. As the captain had remained with the patient, I was free to wander unobserved, and I walked idly, without direction, following one passage after another without observing where I would arrive. I felt certain I had got somewhat near the truth. There must be a child, a girl, who had been entrusted to his care, and was now lost to him, but who was she? Where was she? And who was the woman he had wanted to find her for? The matter was incomprehensible to me. There was such sorrow in his mien; he wore the very look of despair; it was not an easy look to forget. What comfort or help could be brought to such a man? The deep anguish in his eyes seemed a kind of request, that I might find some tonic to soothe his agitated mind, but I was sure there would be no pill or bolus to heal such a wound of the spirit.

I looked up at last; without thinking of where I was going, I had arrived at the library. Perhaps Mr. Rochester was within. He might wait for me here if he had returned to the house.

I entered the library—and beheld a stranger instead. It was a man in gentleman's dress, much stained from travel. His back was to me at first, but he glanced swiftly over his shoulder. There was something in his hands that I could not see. He was a tall man, broad-shouldered, with tawny hair and penetrating blue eyes in a tanned face. A mud-spattered riding coat hung from his shoulders.

"Go to the kitchen and fetch Sally," he demanded, turning his eyes once more to the object in his hands. "Tell her I want a cup of tea in the library."

"I beg your pardon?"

He looked up at me again. "You're a new servant, aren't you?"

"I am not."

He turned far enough to look me over. My dress was not especially costly or pretty, just plain black satin, with few of the flounces that were in style at that time. It was a serviceable rather than a fashionable dress.

"Well, I'll not trouble you then. Unless you are in a benevolent mood, young lady, and would like to find me someone who is."

"Perhaps you would be so good as to do so yourself. I am otherwise occupied."

"Are you indeed?" I could see now what was in his hands. It was a pipe that he was vigorously cleaning. "Who are you, anyway?"

Rude fellow! I wished for something clever to say, but cutting repartee has always failed me when it might be of service. The simple truth would have to suffice. "I am looking for my husband, Mr. Rochester. Have you seen him?"

The pipe slipped from his fingers and fell to the floor. He muttered an oath under his breath, but instead of picking it up, he turned to look at me, his gimlet eye taking in divers points of my dress, hands, and face.

"*You* are Mrs. Rochester?"

"Yes."

"Mr. Rochester is your husband?"

"Yes, sir."

With a sudden movement, he bent and recovered the pipe from the floor.

"I've heard of you." What was one to say to this? "You're not exactly what I was expecting. Thought you were some sort of phoenix, to charm a man with Rochester's money." He gave the bowl of the pipe one final twist with the brush and extracted a handkerchief from his pocket. "No accounting for other people's taste I suppose." He polished the outside of the pipe, then proceeded to blow his nose with energy.

"You will excuse me," I said, and I departed from the library. To my surprise, I found that my hand was unsteady. I had not realised the casual judgment of an ill-mannered man could have such an effect on me. Until now, the inmates of Ingram Park had accorded me the esteem belonging to my station. I had valued the respect I had received, but now I saw plainly that it was the work of hearts well inclined to me and my husband. There was plenty of scorn reserved for me if anyone chose to show it.

I confess I brushed away a miserable tear. I had been caught unawares by the capricious venom of a stranger. I thought I had long since developed a shell hard enough to withstand the bitterness of others, but it appeared there were weaknesses in my armour susceptible to sneering contempt. I began to walk away when the door opened behind me, and the man spoke to me once more.

"Barnett is here somewhere, isn't he? Is he up and about?" There was a little less of contempt in his voice.

"He is in bed, sir," I answered, though I could barely meet his eyes, knowing as I did that a flush of shame likely coloured my cheek still. "He was wounded not many days ago."

"Yes, yes, I know all about that. He's still here, though? He hasn't gone off anywhere?"

"I don't see how he could. What business is it of yours?"

The man smiled, a broad grin that turned his right eye to a narrow slit. "He is my *man* of business, young lady. Any other questions?"

"No, no— "

So this, I thought, must be Mr. Hardwick, Blanche Ingram's fiancé! When had *he* arrived at the house? I turned my back as quick as I could and hurried down the hall. There was no heart in me to contend with such a man as that; a fleet retreat was the only alternative open to me.

I stopped at the dining-room, where a manservant was occupied. I steeled my voice against any quavering weakness. "Do you know if Mr. Rochester has returned to the house?"

"He's gone up to his own room," the man answered. His voice was low and even, his face composed into a blank. Had I committed some blunder that had brought me in for general disapproval? I hurried away through the halls, counting the turnings still to find my way, and went to Mr. Rochester's room. As I approached the door, I realised I must explain to him all that had transpired between myself and Mr. Barnett, that I might persuade Mr. Rochester of the need for keeping the other's secret. I had no doubt my husband was capable of great secrecy and discretion, rather, he was all too adept at concealment, but would he feel bound by a promise I had made on his behalf? Would his jealous nature be renewed by such confidences? Well, the experiment must be tried, no matter the outcome, but I resolved not to open the situation yet. My nerves were still shaken by the tumult of emotion the morning had brought on. Mr. Hardwick's sneering contempt remained traced on my brain. I felt, above all, a need for comfort.

I knocked and entered, announcing my presence. My husband sat in his chair by the empty fireplace—his boots, knees, arms, and chest liberally plastered with mud.

"Oh! Edward, what happened to you?"

He did not move, but replied, "Ingram forgot to tell me about the step in the stable yard. I am never leaving the house without you again."

"Did no one help you out of your wet clothes?"

"I sent the servant away. Prating old fool! The man would be telling me what I should have done!" He added a few more choice curses to his opinion of the servant—small wonder that I had received a blank look from one of his fellow workers, or perhaps the man himself.

"*I* am here now. You cannot sit in wet clothes."

I took him by the hand to guide him to his feet and divest him of his muddy ensemble. This was a familiar process that we underwent every day, albeit with less earth involved. It was not a ceremony without its charm. Only after he was nearly dressed in fresh garments, did I notice the tiny specks of mud scattered over his face. I went to the basin in the corner and dipped my handkerchief in it. Then I proceeded to wipe away each tiny spot of dirt. One from his cheek. I followed it with a kiss there. Another from his forehead; I planted a kiss there too; he claimed a kiss of his own, his strong arm circled my waist, his hand sought my neck.

"Your pulse is skipping like a hare. What have you been at this morning?"

"I went to see Mr. Barnett."

My husband instantly released his hold on my waist. I had underestimated the discord that name would occasion between us.

"What! Barnett! Already? The moment I step outside the house you rush to see him? And is that why your face burns— " he raised his palm to my cheek. "And your pulse rattles!"

"No, it is not because of *him*. There was another man, in the library."

"An*other* man? The deuce take me, for marrying a young woman! Too young by half!"

"Mr. Rochester, you must lay these doubts to rest. I have no wish for any man but you."

"This is an unpropitious beginning, Jane, that you would tease me with these devious plans, sneaking behind my back to visit with other men. Where is your steadfastness, Jane? Where is your faithfulness?"

"These accusations are baseless. I passed a few minutes in conversation with a man who wished to thank me for saving his life. Then I happened to meet Mr. Hardwick in the library."

"Hardwick? Is he here?"

"I believe he only just arrived."

"And what was his manner to you?" Mr. Rochester's voice had changed. Suspicion was not far off, but a new note of curiosity was mingled with it.

"Brusque. And rude. I did not like him."

The flicker of a sardonic grin appeared on my husband's face. "And Mr. Barnett. Did you like him?"

"I pity him for his sufferings. He inspires compassion, nothing more."

"Then your heart remains with me, does it? Grim and cross as I am?"

"It always has been with you. I would rather you than a dozen young men."

"A curious taste for a young woman, is it not?"

"I couldn't say. I only know that it is my own."

An empty pause followed this remark. With hurried movements, he attempted to fasten the rest of the buttons on his shirt. He met with little success and I was struck anew with pain. I longed to return to his arms, yet my pride held me aloof. I could not allow his unreasonable doubts to taint our union. I wished for some perfect speech to reconcile us.

"I ask nothing more than to be your wife, and I conceive it my solemn duty, as well as my joy, to honour our marriage. What more can I do? If your heart cannot confirm my faithfulness to you— "

"Oh, never mind my heart, Jane. It's no more than a bruised and battered organ, ground down by the faithlessness of your sex, leaving only a rough and ragged thing to beat my blood with. What heart do I have left?"

"How cynical you are, Edward! You never used to speak thus." I spoke gently and took his hand, grieved for the harrowing heartache in his voice.

He bowed his head. His craggy features assumed an aspect of stony acquiescence. I deftly undid the buttons and slipped them into their proper places, then I held his face in my hands and left a kiss on his troubled brow.

"Never mind it, Jane. Never mind. Do up my collar, will you?"

When he was dressed, he stumped to the bedroom window, feeling his way. I left him alone, deeming it best for him to recover his self-possession without me. "I will go to my own room a moment. I won't be long."

All was trim and neat in my chamber, just as I had left it. I glanced out the window; a watery gleam of sunlight slipped momentarily through the veil of cloud and then vanished. I had left my shawl in my dresser and decided to keep it with me. I opened the drawer, drew out the garment, and saw, tucked haphazardly among the stockings, a flash of silver. I laid the other articles aside. There was the snuff-box, the very same.

"I have something to show you," I said, when I returned to Mr. Rochester's room. I explained what I had found and put it into his hands. His fingers knowingly groped the outside. "Yes, an ordinary snuff-box. You must have overlooked it."

"No. It was not there before and now it is back."

"By what hand?"

"I don't know."

"Someone staying in the house, judging from appearances."

"Yes, yes. It must be." I found this to be a disturbing thought.

"Now then, bring me my boots. The tall ones, in the back of the closet."

"You are not going *riding*?"

"Heavens, no! We're going outside before the rain begins. I believe I know where to find one of the missing pieces of our puzzle. We're going to the barn."

On the way to the back door, Mr. Rochester inquired about the man in the library. I passed over what I could of Hardwick's insolent badinage. He then required every word that passed between Mr. Barnett and myself.

"He asked you enough questions. Did you think to ask him any?"

"What else should I have said?"

"You could have asked why he lied."

"Lied? About what?"

"About the tramp in the grove."

"But how do you know he was lying?"

"We found a gentleman's snuff-box in the trees, close to where his interlocutor stopped to question him. A common vagrant would not have an object like that with him."

"Suppose it was a thief who had stolen it beforehand."

"A thief takes care to secure his property. He knows well enough the dangers of neglect."

"Maybe the box belongs to Barnett."

"We could ask. Still, there are other mysteries about that little box of yours. Don't speak to anyone about it at present. I am forming a plan that requires a little more time to be thought out, but I will not enter into that now. Are we at the door?"

"Yes."

"Does it rain?"

"Not that I can see." I opened the door for us and we stood on the step.

"There are some buildings about somewhere, off to the right, I believe."

"Yes, I see them. What are we looking for?"

"Not what. Who."

A long expanse of stable graced the back regions of the house. The buildings were freshly painted, and the white trim glowed against the sombre grey clouds. Except for the deep groove in the mud, freshly impressed by Mr. Rochester's fall, the yard was neat and clean. I led my husband carefully over the step and found the open door. A smart groom inquired if he could help us, but Mr. Rochester dismissed him and we went round the outside of the building.

A long field of green, newly sprung alfalfa stretched away behind the stable, and bees made themselves busy among the wildflowers. An ancient cane-bottomed chair, with one leg missing, leaned against the outer wall of the stable. A sullen hound lay underneath, his eyes watching our every move.

"Bill!" Mr. Rochester shouted. "Where the devil have you got to?"

"Coming, com—ing," grumbled an old man's voice.

While we waited, I stepped through the open door of the stable. The loose hay was swept and the stalls quiet. By the door, there stood a rough-hewn bench made of split logs, and on the wall above, an old and dusty key hung from a peg. I returned to my husband's side when I saw a grey-haired figure with a bent back approaching.

"Ah, it's you, sir, is it? Back so soon?" The old man's hand touched his battered hat. "I'm glad to see they've cleaned you up a bit, sir. That was a nasty fall, that was."

"I've no time for idle chat," was Mr. Rochester's peremptory reply. "I've got a question for you and I expect honest answers."

"Aye, you'll get naught but the truth from Old Bill. You can be sure a' that." The man eyed his weathered chair eagerly, then glanced at my husband. "Would you like to have a seat, sir?" The dog looked grimly at us from under the chair and uttered a low growl.

"No," I said. "I don't think so, but you may sit if you prefer it." The old man hunkered into the seat and the dog lay down beneath his master. Mr. Rochester began his inquiry.

"Do you remember the night when the injured gentleman was found?"

Bill nodded sagely. "Mr. Barnett, that was."

"Did you notice anything unusual about the house during the day?"

"Not that I recollect."

"Ingram said you sometimes shoot foxes in the evenings."

"I only did that a time or two—and so would you if your horses were scared of 'em."

Did you hear the gunshot? On Tuesday night?"

"No, sir."

"No? Why not? Do you sleep with pillows over your ears?"

"Why, it was Tuesday, sir."

"What then?"

"Tuesday's my night off. I always go to the Three Brothers."

"Do you?" Mr. Rochester considered the matter a few moments, then he proceeded thus. "That's the tavern where Barnett got directions, supposedly. Did you see him there?"

"Yes, sir, I did. I didn't take much notice of him at first. I was in the kitchen yarnin' with Jimmy Thompson. He peels the potatoes for 'em there."

"Did you see him come in?"

"No, sir. I didn't see him 'till after he'd been settled in, like. He wasn't speaking to anybody much that I could tell. Then I went outside for a bit, and when I come back, he was speaking with another fellow. They looked to have a good deal of talk, and not all of it friendly. I heard his voice raised a time or two, but there was nothing much in it, seemingly, for he calmed right down again."

"Did you see him leave?"

"No, sir. I went out the back for a bit o' refreshment with a neighbour and haven't seen the gentleman since."

A rush of wind tumbled across the fields and blew against us with a bracing chill. Old Bill turned his face to the sky with one eye closed. "We'd do better under cover before long or we'll soon get a wetting."

Proceeding on this timely advice, we followed Bill into the stables. Some of the boxes stood empty, but the oncoming weather was unsettling the few inhabitants. A long whinny sounded from the far end, and the sound of trampling hooves told of the animal's agitation. We reached the tenanted regions of the stable and beheld a tall black steed coursing round the loose box and tossing his head with spirit.

"Is this Lord Ingram's horse?" I asked.

"No, ma'am, his horses are further on. The family has none so spirited as that one. He belongs to Mr. Hardwick. I daresay no one else would venture to ride him. He's a wicked one if you ask me."

"Did Hardwick ride horseback all the way from London?" inquired Mr. Rochester.

"I believe so, sir."

"He wished to arrive betimes, before the ladies. What for I wonder? Where is Mr. Barnett's horse? The one he left behind with the ruined shoe?"

"Two stalls down, sir. A lad brought him up to the house yesterday."

"Lead us to him."

Another wind, ripe with the smell of rain, gusted through the stable. Near the door, we came to a roan with an amiable face, who fortunately showed none of the agitation of his neighbouring steeds.

"Will he stand you to have a look at his shoes? I have a particular wish to know which hoof was shod anew."

"I think he will, sir. He's a level-headed animal if there ever was one."

I reached into my pocket, pulled out my purse, and withdrew a coin, which I placed in Old Bill's gnarled fingers. He tugged his fore-lock in reply and entered the loose box.

After a careful examination of each hoof, he answered, "I can hardly tell you, sir. P'raps there was some mistake. This horse hasn't been re-shod for a year. All four shoes look as worn as t'other."

Mr. Rochester nodded, with a flash of inner intelligence passing over his face. "Your information is most interesting, Bill. Your help has been inestimable. Jane, my love, is there anything else you think our friend might help us with?"

"I *was* wondering—can you tell us what sort of man Mr. Barnett was with at the Three Brothers? Did he have the look of a gipsy or a vagrant? Did he look unkempt, or sound uncouth?"

"No, ma'am, not that I recollect. I never heard him speak, nor caught a sight of his face, but I saw he wore a kind of cloak that looked finer than any a gipsy might have. If I were put to guess, I would say it was a gentleman with him."

CHAPTER IX

"Mr. Rochester?"

"My fairy?"

We stood at the door of the stable and watched as the heavens released their heavy burden. A thick curtain of rain stretched across the stable yard, obscuring sight and blotting out all sounds but those close at hand. Old Bill and his dog had vanished into some hidden retreat of their own. Mr. Rochester put his arm round me so that his shoulder might shield me from the cool air. I was grateful for his protection, but my mind was not so comforted.

"Sir, you seem determined to suspect Mr. Barnett of wrongdoing."

"I see excellent causes for suspicion. Ought we to trust where we see reason for doubt?"

"The circumstances are suspicious, I grant you, but the reasons are yet unknown to us. There are many constructions of the event that would prove Mr. Barnett innocent."

"If I am too suspicious, your clemency will make up for it. You seem equally determined to find him blameless."

I paused and studied his visage for signs of temper. He did not look angry, not yet, but I knew how easily that sleeping giant might awake. Jealousy, wrath, and ire were so often his companions. "Are you not led astray by your emotions, sir? Are you not jealous of him, and therefore apt to find evil where there is none?"

"If my suspicions are to be attributed to the passion of jealousy, Jane, to what do I owe your steady defence of him? Why are you persuaded he has done nothing wrong?"

"I am not persuaded."

"Oh yes, you are."

I opened my mouth to speak; but closed it again. He was right. In my mind I was quite convinced that Mr. Barnett was inculpable; I saw him as a victim only. I considered this.

"You have hardly spoken to him, sir. When you do—Mr. Rochester, I have no great talent for guessing solving puzzles. It is not my way. Mr. Barnett may not be telling the truth, but I believe his motives are sincere. There is something in his manner— " I stopped, unable to give words to the conviction I felt.

"You told me once yourself if you remember. Guessing riddles is no gift of yours. You have another attribute, Jane, that is equally useful in the present case, perhaps more so. You have an insight into human nature. You are perceptive; you understand instinctively the personality of your interlocutor. I am not predisposed to love Barnett, but I trust your judgment. I shall endeavour not to doubt the man for his own sake, but where his actions lay him open to question, we cannot be blinded. His sincere manner must not stop us from seeing the truth."

The rain was slowing now. A steady rushing continued from the eaves of the roof, but the dim sky gradually brightened. "The truth can be a sharp sword at times," I remarked.

Mr. Rochester's arm tightened around my waist. "So it can— indeed it can— no one can know that better than myself. A sword may be required, to cut the bonds of deceit." My husband's strong voice dropped to little more than a whisper in my ear. "Even a good man can become sadly tangled in his own treacherous web."

I lay my head on his shoulder, sympathising for all the anguish he had endured. "You are free now, sir, no captive any longer. You are at liberty to choose a path of goodness and integrity."

"I owe that all to yourself, Janet. I have no merit in it. I claim none."

The torrent of rain was nearly done, and thick streams twisted across the gravel yard. My eyes rose to the noble house. Its yellow stone was smoking still, and the tall gaunt windows were shrouded in mist.

"I fear the truth may be unwelcome to more than one tenant of Ingram Park." I leaned in close to my husband, that I might give my words greater significance. "Mr. Rochester? Perhaps you were meant to deliver others from the false chains that encircle them. It may be you have been particularly prepared for such an office."

Mr. Rochester lifted his palm to press it against my cheek. "No, Jane. Fate has made that office over to you."

The stable yard of Ingram Park was built by able hands. The ground was firm enough to cross, in spite of the rivulets of muddy water forming a channel alongside. Lightning still flashed, but at a great distance; it was only a dim flicker on the horizon's edge. I led Mr. Rochester from the safety of the stable roof and out into the yard, but before we could gain the door to the house, we found a new channel of water that blocked our approach. Rather than wet our feet more than necessary, I directed our steps towards the front of the house.

This led us around the west wing of the building. To my right lay the gardens, aromatic with rain-drenched roses. Beyond them was the dark grove, looking gloomy under this roof of grey cloud; to my left were the tall windows of the lower rooms. I glanced up, looking for the mullioned window of the music room.

My swift halt nearly tripped my husband.

"What's the matter?" he cried.

I could not answer, for I was occupied in observing a figure in the window. I recognised the rounded music room from the outside, as it formed the lower portion of a sort of false tower. A female form stood at the window, solitary and still, with attention unmistakably given to the dark copse below. Her form was tall, her hair dark, her complexion dark also; I thought immediately of Blanche Ingram. Something drew her attention to us and her eyes caught mine. There could be no question as to her identity now. She turned from the window at once and was gone.

I half-expected Miss Ingram to appear before us as we traversed the house. I even went so far as to pass by the music room. Cherubs nodded silently to one another, but there were no recent signs of life or movement within. We repaired to Mr. Rochester's room. There was still plenty of time to dress, but as I had both myself and Mr. Rochester to prepare, I preferred to commence early. My husband underwent the business of dressing with an abstracted air.

As I was about to tie his neckcloth in place, he said, "No, it does not fit."

"Have you grown since yesterday? It fit you then."

"Eh? No, no, not that. Leave off for a minute, Jane. I want to think."

By the fireplace were two chairs. I placed Mr. Rochester in one, his collar still open, and sat down in the other.

"Are you comfortable?" he asked. "Warm enough?"

"Yes, sir."

"Well, then, what do we have? What do we know?"

"We know that Mr. Barnett was shot in the shoulder."

"In the yew grove of Ingram Park, while approaching the house by way of the Three Brothers."

" We know that Barnett wishes us to believe a vagrant attacked him. A search has been made for this gipsy vagrant, but no one has been found. We know that he met with a gentleman at the Three Brothers and later concealed the fact. We know also that a gentleman was very likely present in the grove with him."

"The same gentleman?"

"We don't know."

The clouds had melted away in the hot sun, and the scent of flowers stole softly through the open window.

"And where were the inmates of Ingram Park when the shot was fired?" I asked. "You were in the dining-room. As were Lord Ingram and Captain Fitzjames."

"Ah! Not so, Jane! They left the room. Ingram asked Fitzjames to just step out of the room a moment. They went by the window."

"Outside?"

"Yes."

"Do you know why?"

"I do not. Ingram told me they would return in a moment. Several minutes passed before the gunshot sounded. It was only after that I heard them return."

"Immediately after?"

"A few minutes lapsed. I could not be certain of how long."

"Was there anyone else in the room?"

"Yes, the servants were in and out all the time. I believe some port was spilled on the carpet and they were much concerned about it."

I meditated upon this information. With trepidation, I added another suggestion. "And Mr. Hardwick, where was he?"

"Seventy miles off, in London."

"Do we know that? And Miss Ingram? Where was she?"

"Blanche?" he asked, starting up. "What does she have to do with it?"

"I don't know. Nothing at all, most likely, but I'm curious, nonetheless. Not everyone, it seems, has been where they claim to have been. Mr. Barnett's horse was supposed to be in Millcote the same day. Was it really there I wonder?"

"That is something we have the power of finding out. We night easily visit for a day or two. We have plenty of excuses for going thither. Now that my agent has taken himself off, I have no doubt a great deal of business awaits me at home, but business can wait while our other questions are being satisfied."

"And we have the snuff-box. We have not ascertained its owner yet."

"Yes, the snuff-box that will not tell us who abandoned it there. We must find a way to discover its owner, but we cannot simply go around inquiring. That would show our hand. I'm sure there must be a way to— "

A sullen thud, as of something hitting the floor, sounded from my own chamber. The sudden noise brought me to my feet. I went to the door and opened it. Sally stood in front of the dresser where she was carefully replacing a box, some antique possession of the house that I had never touched.

"I beg your pardon, ma'am," and she curtsied in a hurried way. "I came to help you dress for dinner."

I looked at her, and then at the box she had just replaced. With a somewhat dogged expression, she said, "This is your usual time, isn't it?"

"Yes, it is."

I selected a dress myself from those that hung in the wardrobe, but before we could begin, Mr. Rochester called out to me. I returned to his apartment.

"Come here," he commanded. He was on his feet and held out his arm for me. I went to him and he drew me close, exceedingly close, his whiskers against my cheek, and his lips near to my ear. I half-expected some tender endearment, but when I saw the flash of energy in his eye, I did not know what to expect. I soon found out.

"A thought has just struck me, Janet. The maid is still in your room?"

"Yes, sir."

"And listening no doubt."

He pressed me even closer to his side and lowered his voice. I could only just hear it. "I have a scheme, and only one difficulty remained in executing it. The solution has just occurred to me. You have the snuff-box?"

"In my pocket."

"Good. Listen carefully, Jane. This is what you are going to do."

"Sally." I returned to my room, to find the servant standing by the window. She turned around to face me. "I have a service to beg of you. I apologise for its strangeness. I want you to take off your apron."

"Ma'am?"

"I need to borrow your apron, and your bonnet." I went to the closet and fetched a black stuff dress, a gown I had retained from my governess days. I had been unable to bring myself to part with a dress still serviceable, although there was no need of such an uninspired garment at Ingram Park. I carefully transferred the snuff-box to the pocket of my old dress.

"But I'm expected downstairs soon. I can't very well go to the kitchen not properly dressed."

"I won't be very long. I have a—a delivery to make. I wish to deposit a package, but I do not choose to trust it to anyone else's hands, and I do not like to be suspected of delivering it." I was already fastening the dress myself.

"Is it an intrigue?"

"It is nothing dishonest, but it is secret, nonetheless."

She frowned heavily and stared at me.

"There will not be time enough if I do not hurry."

"Well—all right," she said, with evident reluctance, and untied her apron, which I hurriedly wrapped around me. I took the bonnet from her hands as soon as she had doffed it and endeavoured to conceal my darker hair completely.

"You do look a bit like me dressed that way. From the back leastways," she added.

"And you would look far better in an evening dress than I do."

She smiled in return, a very pretty smile of even white teeth. She agreed with me, but wouldn't say so. Still, the smile made us confederates.

"I'll be quick," I said and slipped out the door.

The west wing was a simple matter. No one was staying there but Diana, who was doubtless dressing, and ourselves. Still, I saw her maid approach the stairs, and hung well back, standing behind a great chiffonier to conceal myself. In which direction might I avoid notice? The less I saw of the household, the better. Fortunately, all of the family were occupied with the business of dressing for dinner, while the servants were engaged in preparations for the meal. I crossed the great hall in solitary state. There was no one to perceive me. My occupation took me down the long hall, and past the now tentantless library. I was near the dining-room when a manservant crossed the hall. He was still some distance from me and absorbed in his own work. I fixed my eyes on the ground and he did not observe me closely.

It was necessary that I pass the dining-room door. It was open, and I hesitated before going by. Only Mrs. Harper was there, arranging hot-house flowers on the dinner table. I slid past the doorway with noiseless tread.

The drawing-room was next, my destination. The room, thankfully, was empty. I went to a small table that sometimes held cigars for the gentlemen; there I deposited the snuff-box. We would watch, then, to see if it was recognised after dinner. I turned to make my departure when the door began to open. I stepped into a side door in the room that I had never used and retreated into the darkness, closing the door behind me just as Mrs. Harper entered.

I stood in a room I did not know—it was illumined only by a dusky twilight through the drawn curtains. Once more, however, I was pursued. There were voices in the hall; I discerned the sound of movement behind the hallway door. I hastened to the nearest hiding place that I could. The curtains were both tall and heavy; I slipped between them and climbed into the window seat. Through the glass I could see that I was not much distant from the ground, but I knew the windows of the dining-room sometimes groaned on their ancient hinges. I would not risk the noise.

I turned my attention to the voices, now intelligible, that filled the room. I found I was listening to the languid tones of Lord Ingram.

"You needn't blame me, mother. I hardly think such an old friend as Rochester should be disregarded just because of his wife."

There were rustlings and creakings; through an irregularity between the curtains, I could descry a little of the movement in the room. The dowager, Lord Ingram's mother, had seated herself. A faint blur of motion suggested her son had taken a seat also.

"That woman, Theodore, is not an appropriate companion for anyone in this house. Inferior, unrefined, unprincipled— "

"Unprincipled? Surely not. Why, she ran away rather than marry the man when she ought not. You make it sound as if she were the worst of the two."

"Tedo has a point, Mama." I was surprised to hear the voice of Blanche Ingram, not only because I had not known she was in the room, but because she was speaking in my defence. "I think Mr. Rochester more to blame than his wife."

"My lily-flower, you are not reflecting. We cannot help the acquaintance with Mr. Rochester. He is one of our first families in the county, and one does not take notice of too many irregularities in such a person, but we need not recognise his ill-chosen marriage with such distinction as having them in the house. And how long is he to remain here? He seems to have permanently taken root."

"They are here at least until Mrs. Rochester is recovered from her illness. That's all that we spoke of."

"She seems recovered enough to me," the baroness said. "Running about the grounds discovering injured men in the grass. It is disgraceful that so many strangers are here when we have all this business to bother with."

"What business?" Blanche inquired.

"Your fiance's own man is injured on our property, under mysterious circumstances—it is certainly not the time for guests."

"If it wasn't for Mrs. Rochester, it might have been a mortal injury. You would hardly prefer an inquiry into a death. Let them be, Mother. They'll go away soon enough I dare say."

"Barnett is nothing to worry about," Blanche said, in an authoritative voice. "Peter will take care of that. I'm sure he is quite up to details of that kind. And I don't think Mr. Rochester is such a bad addition to our party." There was something in her voice that did not please me; it was a sort of self-satisfied tone that implied another meaning, but without the aid of face or feature, I could not tell what it was.

"Well, the woman is a disgrace. A governess! An impertinent governess! To be received at Ingram Park! It is an absurdity. I expected better judgment of you, Theodore."

"It isn't all that bad, Mother. After all, Father's first wife was only a—"

"Do not mention that woman to me!" There was a great rustling, and I perceived a hurried movement; the dowager had risen to her feet. "Your father's first wife is nothing to me. Nothing!" She moved quickly from the room; the hall door closely heavily behind her.

"That was well done, Tedo," Blanche remarked in sarcastic tones.

"I didn't mean to bring it up, but I do so hate being attacked over trifles."

"She is overburdened at present." I heard the fuss and bustle of Blanche's garments as she rose to her feet. "She will be more calm after my marriage."

"I must say, I sometimes wonder if Hardwick is really quite the thing. This shooting business, now, it's damned awkward. And there are other things."

"It can't be helped."

A moment of silence passed. I bent my head to get a better view, but they had moved from my narrow field of vision.

"It could be if you put off the marriage. I think you ought to take a little more time—look into his antecedents more. His fortune, you know— "

"I'll not have the marriage put off."

"Well, so be it. Only perhaps now, we ought to find some excuse to send the Rochesters away."

"The Rochesters will remain where they are."

"I never did understand why you pressed me so hard to invite them."

"And you needn't understand now. Come, Tedo, you will be late for dinner if you don't dress soon."

The door opened; then closed; they were gone.

I, too, hastened out the door and into the hall, now empty; but there were comings and goings around the dining-room that threatened to break in on my solitude at any moment. Was there another way back to the west wing? Yes, there was. I darted down the hall and made for the little coral room beyond. My movement was arrested, however, by a heavy step behind me.

"Sally! I need to speak to you."

It was Lord Ingram.

CHAPTER X

I stopped before the ornate sculpture placed in the centre of the room, an antique figurine of classical origin, and bowed my head. There was only a slight hope that my true identity might escape detection.

"Sally," said Lord Ingram in a subdued voice. He came near enough that I could hear him plainly, though he spoke in a barely audible tone.

"I know, this is no place to speak, but I've had no chance to see you, and now that my mother is here— "

I ducked my head even lower, bowing beneath the weight of my own fears—fear that my deceptive costume should be found out, and fear also of some awful confession on the part of Lord Ingram, some shameful truth betokened by the low and private voice he used to address a humble house-maid.

"Tell me when I can meet you."

I kept my gaze fixed on the sculpted figure, scarcely seeing what lay before me. Oh, that I had some means of escape!

"Tomorrow night I might be able to get away. Do you think you could manage it?"

There was a noise from the hall; our *téte a téte* could not be prolonged. I shook my head, hoping to convey thereby the impossibility of answering, and began to move aside. In his agitation, Lord Ingram laid one hand on my arm.

My feet halted, my breath stopped, my face turned up to his. No words were necessary. He released my arm as if bit by an adder, then he recoiled a step or two with a look, first of wonder, and then, of wide-eyed panic. I opened my mouth to speak, to beg his pardon for misleading him, but before I could do so, he spun on his heel and stumbled out of the room.

I thought no more of concealment. I cared only for finding an asylum where I might retreat to. I went out the nearest door, which led me into the wide gallery, and navigated the now familiar turnings of the west wing. I too, ran, as well as I could. I reached the music room and fled up the back stairs.

Upon entering my room, my eye went at once to Sally where she stood by the window. She stared at my hurried entrance but said nothing. If my haste aroused her curiosity, she gave no sign of it. She crossed the room and requested her apron and bonnet.

I looked at her with new eyes: I observed her pale golden hair drawn high on the back of her head, and her figure adorned in a simple black dress. Thus clad, a woman might well appear severe and plain, but Sally was no less lovely; bonnie blue eye, dewy cheek, delicate form all called forth admiration. She stared back at me with an expression that plainly evinced innocence, and perhaps no high degree of penetration. A dreadful weight of conviction seemed to cling to me.

"Ma'am? May I have my clothes?"

The repetition of her request finally made me aware of my prolonged inactive state. I took off her bonnet and apron and returned them. "Thank you for your kindness in this matter. I must beg you to mention it to no one, at least for the immediate future." She made for the door, once her garments were in place, but now I called her back. "My gown. I must change my dress."

When the business of dressing was completed, and Sally had departed for her labours below, I went to the door communicating with Mr. Rochester's room. My fingers grasped the latch, but the turmoil of my thoughts made me pause and consider the tale I was about to tell.

In truth, my spirit shrank from such revelations. I would prefer not to relate all that I had seen and heard. Both Lord Ingram and his sister Blanche had spoken things in my hearing not intended for my ears, and none of it was pleasant, nor was any of it entirely comprehensible. I did not have all the facts; I must remember that. And yet I knew enough to cast grave suspicions on the conduct of the family. I did not find it an attractive duty to pour out such a story to anyone, even my other self.

But hesitation would profit me little. Indeed, the time was growing short before the dinner bell rang. I opened the door.

My husband greeted me thus. "Janet, my love, is this you?"

I replied that it was. Mr. Rochester spoke from within a cloud of cigar smoke. This was curious enough, as he could not light a cigar by himself. Perhaps his valet had accommodated him? But no, someone else was keeping him company.

A man stood by the fireplace with his back to me, a tall figure with legs planted wide and his coat-tails over his arms. He turned to face me. It was Mr. Hardwick.

"Good evening, madam." He bowed to me. "Once I knew my old friend Rochester was in the house, I determined to come and see him as soon as duty allowed."

I bowed my head in return. "I was not aware that you were acquainted with one another."

"Oh yes. We've known each other a great many years."

"We used to meet in London on occasion," Mr. Rochester added, in a languid voice.

"And on the continent."

"Yes, so we did. I had forgotten."

"Had you?" Mr. Hardwick spoke without looking at him. He was occupied instead in a final indraught of smoke from his cigar. After he had released a mouthful of smoke into the air, he added, "I'm surprised to hear it."

"I was a different man then, Hardwick. There is little enough to value in those days for me to cherish their remembrance."

"Well, we are both rather changed, aren't we? You are well settled at last, with a deserving young wife. And I am on the very eve of matrimony. There is nothing like a change to enliven a man's spirit."

"I hope you are not marrying merely for the novelty," Mr. Rochester responded.

"I am not, as a matter of fact. Believe me or believe me not, Rochester, but I happen to be marrying for love." The bell on the wall vibrated, summoning us to our repast.

"Put this out for me, Hardwick. I don't trust myself to do it." My husband held out the burning stub to the empty air.

Hardwick took it deftly between his fingers, dropped it in the fireplace and ground it out with his heel. Turning to me, he said, "I will escort you to dinner if I may," and he offered me his arm.

"Thank you, but I always walk with my husband as his guide."

"Ah, yes. In course," he replied, and we walked out.

This had been a day of revelations, and I found it difficult to give order to each one in my mind. The strange snuff-box I had discovered in the trees might be identified before the day was done. Mr. Barnett had been proven a liar. Blanche Ingram had some unknown occupation in the west wing. There was a connection between Mr. Hardwick and my husband, although its substance eluded me. And I wondered how I was to face Lord Ingram at dinner. Here, indeed, was puzzle enough to occupy my faculties!

We paused at Diana's door to inquire if she was still within and would join us in our descent. Hitherto, she always had. This time, however, a maid came to the door and answered that she was not yet ready and would meet us below. Fortunately, there was still time to wait for Diana. We lingered in the great hall, beneath the roseate glory of the mural soaring above us.

"You needn't wait with us," I said to Mr. Hardwick, "if you wish to go ahead." It would be a relief to be alone with my husband, even for a few minutes.

"Not at all, not at all," he replied, turning swiftly from the vase he had bent to examine. "Actually, I wish to thank you for preserving Barnett for me. It would have been mighty inconvenient to me to do without him."

"I'm glad I was able to help."

"He always has been unfortunate; I can't help that. But luck turned his way for once when you put in an appearance. From what I hear, you seem to have a knack for showing up when you are least looked for. You must be akin to the angels I think."

"Hardwick," Mr. Rochester said. "You wouldn't know an angel if she knocked on your door."

"Perhaps not," Mr. Hardwick said, with a smile I did not much care for. "The divine is not really in my line, is it? But tell me, Mrs. Rochester, what did Barnett say when you found him lying there? Did he tell you anything?" I did not know what to answer. Clearly, the truth was not a possibility, as Mr. Barnett had sworn me to secrecy.

"He was in no condition for conversation, I'm afraid."

"Well, that's about what Rochester said you would say. So I suppose I must believe you. I rather thought he might have told you something. I thought perhaps— "

Before he could finish speaking, a female form appeared in the doorway to the coral room. Dressed in spotless white, with a crimson sash round her waist, she called out to Mr. Hardwick. "Peter, are you coming to dinner? Or would you prefer to have your soup brought to you in the gallery?"

Mr. Hardwick smiled. "There is my belle-flower." He went to her, put his arm around her waist, and leaned close to whisper something in her ear. She smiled, but there was little of modesty or delight in her glance. She turned towards me, a look of triumph stamped in the lineaments of her face. Although using no spoken language, her victorious brow said plainly to me, 'I have made a superior match to yours. I scorn your lot as Mr. Rochester's mate.'

Well, I am not afraid of Miss Ingram, nor jealous of her partner, nor eager for her praise. I have never been in a position to seek out her favour and did not find myself anxious for it now.

"Good evening, Blanche," said I. "I hope I see you well."

"Oh yes, very. I am always well. You have met my fiance, I see."

"We were just having a little chat, my love," said that gentleman. "She seems to be well acquainted with my agent."

"So I have heard."

"I hardly know the gentleman," I replied, bowing my head.

"And of course, you know Mr. Rochester," she replied, turning from me. "We had quite a gay season at Thornfield Hall in the old days, did we not? It is a pity, a great pity— "

"I shall value no one's pity, Miss Ingram," Mr. Rochester said, his firm voice cutting across her words, "But those who love me nonetheless for my misfortunes."

Miss Ingram looked a trifle disconcerted at this remark, but when Mr. Rochester bowed formally in her direction, she inclined her head in return. "Mama is waiting for us," she said, in a milder tone, and she left the room with Mr. Hardwick on her arm.

"Edward," I whispered in my husband's ear, once we were left alone in the great, echoing room. "Why didn't you tell me before that you knew Mr. Hardwick?"

"I hardly expected him to acknowledge me as an old friend. I thought of us as bare acquaintances."

"You met him in France?"

"In Belgium. I have a little business interest there and have stayed in Villette on occasion. He lived there for some time. One's country-men often turn up when there are visitors from home at hand."

"He was aware of your misfortunes. Perhaps he wished to con-dole with you."

"Hardwick? I doubt it. You can be sure it serves some motive of his own or he wouldn't bother with us. I have always heard him spoken of as a self-serving, grasping man."

It was at this juncture that Diana appeared on the stairs. She was dressed in a fine blue gown, but as she approached, I saw that her face was not quite composed. There was a handkerchief half-concealed in her hand and her cheek was stained with tears.

"Are you all right, Diana?" I whispered as she came alongside me. The dinner bell rang once more.

"Oh Jane, I never thought—I cannot explain it now. I will tell you later, after dinner. It will be such a relief to tell you everything."

I would have given much to attend fully to my cousin at that moment, but my husband required all my powers, and we were already late for dinner. I could do no more than show my sympathy in my expression as we walked off to the coral room.

Mr. Hardwick stood near to the dining-room with Mary Ingram on his arm. She gave me little more than a pensive glance on my entrance. Blanche had taken her place by Captain Fitzjames. The captain looked pointedly at us as we entered, but he did not smile. Lord Ingram was standing alone. I raised my face to his—and his own eyes speedily sought any object to fix on but myself. A faint flush tinted his neck, but just as quickly vanished and his features assumed a phlegmatic expression that revealed nothing.

Near to him was his noble mother, dressed in a black gown adorned with expensive lace, and a turban of dove grey. She did not scruple to look at me but appeared to take no pleasure in what she saw. She did not speak to me at all. She addressed Mr. Rochester in French, inquired as to his comfort in her house, and, reverting to English, called us all to order, that we might take our places to enter the dining-room.

The dinner began its formal sequence and a few commonplaces were exchanged, but conversation soon flagged. Lord Ingram was quite silent, as was Diana. The Captain, too, appeared preoccupied and said little. The dowager, I imagined, would not deign to start a subject that a former governess might possibly comment on. She sometimes spoke a few words to her son, seated at her right, but said nothing more.

This left only Miss Ingram, Mr. Hardwick, and Mr. Rochester to entertain the company at dinner. Seeing the onus placed upon her, Miss Ingram took up the challenge.

In an energetic voice, she addressed Mr. Rochester. "I passed through Millcote on the way back from London and had myself driven on purpose up to Thornfield Hall."

Mr. Rochester bowed his head but said nothing further.

"It is certainly a sad looking place at present. Do you mean to rebuild it?"

"I do."

"That will be quite an undertaking."

"I believe so, but your brother will recommend an able architect for me I think. I have spent so little time at home in recent years that I do not know all the local talent." Their attention reverted to Lord Ingram, but he was at that moment engaged in a low voiced discussion with his mother. "I am in no great hurry, however. I mean to do the work properly and it will doubtless take a great deal of time and labour. My most pressing need is an agent to look after the estate. My fellow left not long ago."

"His departure was unconnected with the loss of the house I hope?" Mr. Hardwick asked.

"I believe the man was a little disturbed in his mind, to tell the truth. He seemed to think something peculiar happening among the wreckage."

"Something peculiar?" Miss Ingram asked, her eyes alight with curiosity. "Of what nature is this—peculiarity?"

"Some curious fancy I suppose. You have had no such tidings in this part of the country? I suppose the wings of superstitious rumour do not fly so far as that?"

I began to tremble at the thought that someone would now make reference to Mr. Rochester's first wife, to her ghastly death, to my husband's regrettable behaviour in the past.

"Oh, we hear nothing of Thornfield here, and we have of course been in London. Tell us, what did he suspect?" Blanche asked.

"You needn't be so curious, my dear," Mr. Hardwick said, picking up his wine glass and looking through it. "Such suspicions are not worth much more than the breath used to tell them."

Blanche sat back in her chair, the eager light disappearing from her eye. I was surprised to see her so visibly chastened. Although Hardwick's voice was mild enough, he had certainly put a stop to her questions. He began to tell us a story of a famous day of fox hunting he had had in the previous season, and the conversation turned another way.

The ladies departed from the room not long after. Before I rose from my chair, I laid my hand over Mr. Rochester's, seeking to draw comfort from him. He clasped my fingers in his a moment, a firm grasp that gave me courage, and I passed through the arched doorway.

Last to enter the room, I went first to the little gilt table—yes, the snuff-box was still there. I turned then to find the three ladies of the household grouped picturesquely by the window. Mary Ingram sat demurely with her hands in her lap and her remote gaze aimed at the carpet. Miss Ingram sat by her mother and studied her rings with a proud and inhospitable visage. The dowager I found staring at me, as one would at a distasteful object that must nonetheless be borne with. I met her gaze coolly and resolved to speak as little with her as possible. There could be no pleasure in such conversation for either. I looked for the person who most interested me.

My cousin stood by the fireplace, a tall and stately figure. She was examining a collection of cameo heads on the mantelpiece. She no longer appeared distressed, but her cheek was pale; she replaced the cameo in a deliberate manner. When I approached, she turned to me with relief and gratitude in her features; she took my hand and pressed it, but before she could unburden her heart, a voice called out from the opposite side of the room.

"Mrs. Rochester, a word with you."

I looked to see Blanche Ingram, now seated at the piano, addressing me in formal tones. I gave Diana one sympathetic glance and crossed the room. Miss Ingram played the opening bars from the music placed before her, but her fingers came to a stop when I approached. I stood by the instrument and waited for her to open the business. She began by perusing my face with a look of mingled curiosity and disdain.

She commenced at last, in a low voice comprehensible only to ourselves. "I trust you and your husband are comfortable at Ingram Park?" This remark was not made in a very hospitable way, but neither was it insulting or repulsive. I could not yet gather her drift.

"Yes."

"And you, in turn, have looked after others. It was most strange that you happened to find Mr. Barnett in the woods at such an hour."

I agreed that it was.

"Well—let me tell you something that you may also find strange. It may, perhaps, surprise you. I believe you had an interview with Mr. Barnett this morning." I would not acknowledge this rather impertinent questioning about my affairs, and said nothing. "At least, Sally tells me so. She saw you come out, or go in, or something of the kind. I don't know what he said to you— "

"He only wished to thank me."

"I'm sure he did."

She had taken up a little pencil and was carefully marking a sheet of music, but now she looked up to face me, her raven curls falling back as she did so. Her voice continued even lower, even more confidentially. Her eyes flashed with what I took to be excitement. "I'm afraid I must warn you. Mr. Barnett's words are not always to be trusted." I laid my hand on the edge of the piano to steady myself. "He is not always in his right senses, you know. Mr. Hardwick still employs him, out of duty to an old friend, but you ought not to believe in everything he says."

I looked down at the clear reflection in the glossy black surface of the instrument before me. Blanche's fine features looked back at me, as if from some twilight region, and my own visage shimmered alongside hers. She was studying me closely.

I reviewed my conversation with Mr. Barnett. I might have thought otherwise if I had not seen him in the woods, quite clearly out of his senses with pain and fear. Our interview in the house had been of a different nature. His manners, voice, countenance, all spoke of a man in his right mind. He had talked to me with what I took for perfect sense. I would no more doubt his sanity than my own. I did not believe a word of what Miss Ingram said. Perhaps she read the scepticism in my face, for she said,

"I assure you, it has been coming on some time— "

"Miss Ingram," I interrupted. "Are you personally acquainted with Mr. Barnett?"

"I have spoken to him on occasion, but Mr. Hardwick says— "

"Did Mr. Hardwick commission you to tell me this?"

She opened her mouth; and closed it again. Then she said, "Forgive me if I am injuring your feelings or your judgment— "

"It is not a question of either. You make a heavy accusation, Miss Ingram."

"Oh no! I make no accusations. I only wish to put you on your guard. If he has made any confidences to you, I would only warn you not to rely too much on them. Do not regard him as an authority. He may judge wrongly, for he may perceive wrongly."

"I believe I have sagacity enough to know when a man is in his right mind."

"Have you?" she raised her eyebrows at me,

I said nothing more. I was aware of a steady tide of ire rising within me. If I allowed my feelings to gain mastery, I would surely break out into some dangerous speech, but I could hardly do such a thing; she was my hostess, an old family friend of my husband, the daughter of a lord. Besides, there was something unspeakably little in her manner of addressing me; I could not bear to be thought resentful over such a mean-spirited attack. Pride came to my aid at last. "I thank you, Miss Ingram, for this mark of confidence. I shall endeavour to be circumspect in my dealings at Ingram Park." My voice was mild, yet the last words she took as an offence. She sniffed and looked annoyed.

She picked up her pencil, gave me one last antipathetic glance, and remarked, "You needn't worry overmuch about Ingram Park. We are accustomed to see to our own needs without interference."

Are you indeed? I thought to myself. Your noble brother does not strike me as altogether master of his own concerns. Perhaps you yourself are not aware of all that is passing in your own house. Even your unused music room— I looked at her then, almost startled by the recollection. The thing seemed so simple. We were unheard by our company; I would ask her what she had been doing in the abandoned music room.

"Miss Ingram— "

At that moment, the door swung open, and Mr. Hardwick stepped into the room. Almost immediately, Miss Ingram dropped her pencil and began to play with vigour.

I retired to the opposite side of the room and waited for my husband. Mr. Rochester came last, escorted by Lord Ingram's valet, and after a brief whisper in the servant's ear, he was led to a chair near the gilt table. I moved towards him, but I could not help a last look at Diana. She stood still in solitary state near the fireplace, but when she saw me move, she approached as well. We took a seat together, on a small divan.

Mr. Hardwick assumed a place near the piano whilst Lord Ingram took up the newspaper on the table. Captain Fitzjames stood at the opposite end of the room. He addressed some remarks to her ladyship and then looked in our direction. His attention fixed on Diana, with an eager inner fire that flashed forth from his eye. He did not approach us, however. He crossed the room and gave his interest to the little gilt table and its sundry effects; tobacco, snuff, cigarette papers, cigars, matches.

I suspected him of moving in such a direction for another purpose—that of taking up a position nearer to ours, but his movement inspired the other gentlemen. Lord Ingram and Mr. Hardwick seemed equally well inclined towards the contents of the table, and before long, all three stood in its proximity. I rose to my feet, that I might have a clear view.

I watched my secretly placed snuff-box. It seemed ignored momentarily, but then—the box was seized, its clasp examined, and a voice cried, "I say, I believe this is mine!" The speaker was Captain Fitzjames.

Diana rose to her feet. Her handkerchief was already in her hand as she turned and fled from the room. The captain moved instantly towards the door, but he paused and stole one glance back at me. "Is she—is Miss Rivers quite all right?"

"A little unwell, perhaps. I will go and see. Mr. Rochester?"

"By all means, Jane. I'll wait for your return here."

Diana stood in the gallery. The air was cool here, and the shadows long. The chandelier above had not been lit, but the last gleams of sunlight had nearly gone. She kept very still, her handkerchief pressed to her face, and made not a sound. I went to her immediately; I put my arm round her waist.

"What is it, Di? What is the matter?"

I thought she might be crying, but her voice was quite calm, almost flat. "That snuff-box. That's the one you found, wasn't it?"

"Yes— "

"Then that means— "

"We don't know yet what it means."

In a near whisper, she said, "It could be him. He might have been down there with Mr. Barnett. He might have shot him."

I hesitated before speaking. "I don't know."

"Jane," this in a slower, more measured voice. "This afternoon, the captain and I, we were in the library, looking over some new books Lord Ingram had ordered."

"Yes."

"And we—he—he spoke to me. He—asked me to marry him."

"Oh, Di! And what did you say?" My hand tightened its grip on hers, grasping it rather too tightly.

"I said— " she swallowed painfully, but still her voice went on in that remorseless tone. "I said I would give him my answer tomorrow. When I had considered it."

"Diana. Do you love him?"

She looked very hard at me then, her eyes wide, but her face was cast in shadow and difficult to read. "Could you love a murderer, Jane?"

CHAPTER XI

The servants arrived to light the chandelier in the gallery. Diana and I moved with one accord, slipping from the centre of the room while a young man arranged his long pole and lighting implements. We withdrew to a recessed corner, and I felt an almost feverish sensation as I grappled with the implications of my cousin's words. Diana was pale, nearly colourless, and a clear salt drop clung to her cheek. She did not sob; it could hardly be called weeping, yet the tear remained on her cool skin and she did not wipe it away. There was always in Diana a keen spirit guided by principle, by resolve, by inward strength. Whatever fate called upon her to give or to do, she would do so unflinchingly. But what did duty demand?

I answered her question thus: "No one, as of yet, has been murdered."

"Yes. Yes, of course, you are right. My regard for the captain is—Oh Jane!" She looked at me then, and I understood her feelings. "Under other circumstances, I would not hesitate to give a positive answer, but in the present case— " She gazed at me with a strange fervency in her eyes. "There is something not right about him. I can scarcely bring myself to question his character—but there is something in his words and deeds that I cannot reconcile."

A hushed murmur of conversation in the drawing-room swelled like a distant breeze and faded away. The strain of notes on the piano vibrated the air. My cousin gripped my hand and held it fervently.

"What do you mean exactly?"

"I have been thinking it over all afternoon. When I inquired about his friendship with Lord Ingram, I found that their connection was much less than I supposed. They hardly know each other." She spoke quite low. "I believe he has pressing obligations elsewhere; his professional interests demand that he visit the Admiralty in London, but he does not go. And he answers with the most curious mix of levity and evasion. I do not think he is an old hand at deception, Jane, and yet he is playing a part. I cannot understand why. He is the most estimable of men, courageous, kind, intelligent, humble, engaging— ” She came to a stop, her lip trembling. “I am at a loss. And now this! His own snuff-box recovered in the God-forsaken glade! I can scarcely comprehend his involvement in such a deed, and yet— ” She paused, unable to continue.

The servant completed his work and the chandelier blazed forth in a glorious coruscation of light. The long gallery was now drenched in gold, but in the flickering of candles, the dim recesses turned to black and sinister shadow, encroaching from every corner, throbbing round the edge of the chamber like a palpable threat.

Before my mind’s eye there rose the image of a dark and devious being. The captain, assuming an innocent, beguiling manner, hiding a violent crime behind the cloak of civility, gathered malice in proportion to my own fears. And compounding injustice, he had practised upon the sweet and ardent affections of my cousin, whether honestly or as part of his wicked designs, he had gained her heart, only to pollute her soul with his own black deeds!

But no, this would not do. The firm hand of reason turned back these hideous phantoms and staid their dread entrance. “We cannot assume yet that he is guilty, Diana. We do not know that he committed any crime. We have suspicion, not facts.”

“I long to acquit him, to blot out all these troubling accusations, but how can I? Every attempt to justify him becomes merely the wish of a blinded heart! And then, every suspicion seems magnified, because I cannot refute it. Just think, Jane! Ever since the accident, he has kept a ceaseless vigilance over Mr. Barnett. I took it only to be disinterested kindness.”

“As did I.”

“So did we all. But is it not the best policy for keeping him silent?”

I considered this point. My own conference with Mr. Barnett had been under the full supervision of Captain Fitzjames. I remembered Mr. Barnett's hushed voice, his confidential manner; he clearly intended to hide something from the world, perhaps even from the captain. I recalled the shift he was put to, in begging a drink of water to disguise his words. Was he hiding the truth from his tormentor?

Yet he had made no reference to the captain during our interview. No subtle words, no sidelong glance suggested antagonism between them; but my train of thought led me to a conceivable solution to our dilemma.

"I perceive no other evidence of such a state of things. Diana, cousin, I am convinced there is more to this than we are privileged to see. You must not give way to idle terrors."

"But I must give him my answer. If I put him off without a reason—I believe it would be as good as dismissing him, and I—I would not lose an affection so dear— " a pause, as she stifled some pang within her. The struggle showed in her expression but as quickly passed. "And yet I cannot accept, not with so many questions left unanswered."

Diana is not the sort to break out into hysterics, to rend her garments and try her friends with an excess of emotion, but there was something so anguished in her gaze, so bewildered in her countenance, so restless in all her movements, that I could not suppress my concern. It was as if my own hand had suddenly turned paralysed and weak, or a trusted chair had given way without warning. I could not let her continue in such a state. I resolved to know what dread secret was hidden in the twilight history of that wooded grove. I would learn what had passed there, I would divine what degree of guilt was borne by this household, cost me what it may. My cousin's future peace of mind rested upon it.

"Be of good courage, Di. I will read this riddle for you, and I will do it very soon. Indeed, I know just the person to apply to."

With a great effort of will, we were enough restored to tolerable calm to rejoin the party in the drawing-room. Nothing more was said in our presence about the snuff-box—it seemed to have vanished, presumably into the captain's pocket.

Blanche Ingram had assumed her ascendancy at the piano and filled up what otherwise would have been our party's burdensome silences. Sometimes Mr. Rochester sang with her. He could not but sing well, his powerful voice filling that solemn room with rich and vibrant sound. When he was finished accompanying her, she was left to perform whatever her fancy desired. And as Mr. Hardwick leaned over the piano, with eyes only for his affianced one, she was privileged to warble ballads of love with free indulgence. I sat by Diana and said little. I was on guard, as it were, ready to defend my cousin when necessary, but as she was considered unfit for any exertion by the rest of our company, this was easy enough to do.

I could not help intercepting a look or two of anxiety from Captain Fitzjames. Indeed, I studied him long for signs of concealed guilt or worry at perhaps being caught out, but his behaviour appeared just as it always was, only less garrulous, more remote. Either he had no such fears to disguise, or he had fully regained his dissimulating manner while we were out of the room!

We stood up early in the evening to take our leave, Mr. Rochester on one side of me, and Diana on the other. The captain approached at last. Though her arm was already in mine, he directed his words at me.

"I hope Miss Rivers has taken no harm this evening. You believe her quite well?"

"Yes, only a bit overstrained I think. An unusual state for her, but none of us are quite impervious to nervous impressions."

"No," he said, a little doubtfully, glancing at last at Diana. "No, we all have our moments of debilitation, but I do hope it will pass quickly."

He looked at her with anxious, even worried, eyes. "I wish you a good night, Miss Rivers, and good health."

She smiled a little and accepted the hand he offered her. "Thank you, Captain. My dear cousin is my best medicine at present. I expect to be recovered soon."

The words were commonplace enough, but there was generous feeling in them. They melted the heavy frost of worry on his brow as the crystalline snowflake fades in an outstretched palm. Whatever faults the captain may have had, his love for her was genuine. An exceedingly quiet, "Goodnight, God bless you," escaped from his lips, and he stepped aside to let us by.

I saw Diana safely back to her room and the attendance of her maid. Then I led Mr. Rochester to his own apartment and further helped him out of his clothes and into his dressing gown. I told him as well as I could of Diana's fears and the reason for their painful import. He listened without interruption and reported the conversation that had followed the discovery of the snuff-box. Hardwick had casually suggested that Fitzjames had left it somewhere about the house by accident, and a servant had brought it there. The captain agreed that such must have been the case.

"What did Lord Ingram say about it?"

"Nothing at all."

When I was finished attending to him, I said I was going to undress and departed for my own room. Sally was there to help me out of my things, but I dismissed her soon after. I found it difficult to be in the same room with her, feeling myself in her secret, and yet doubting my authority to speak of it.

Clad in my dressing gown, I meditated on the events of the evening with little satisfaction. I must now tell Mr. Rochester of the strange words and stranger import of Lord Ingram's communication, not to me, but to whom he thought was Sally. I was loath to do so. I did not dislike Sally, for, to tell the truth, she reminded me rather starkly of myself, on my first arrival at Thornfield Hall: young, friendless, unloved, and drawn inevitably to my master. Suppose the case had been otherwise? Suppose my position had been more humble? Or my master less honourable in professing his passions? Was there not a similarity in the case? Was it not possible that they should love each other? And yet what conceivable future could be imagined between a Peer of the Realm and a humble house-maid? It seemed a most tragic and painful scenario.

I grew tired all at once of mysteries, secrets, dissimulation. I desired Ingram Park to keep its subtle whisperings and lingering equivocations from my notice. I wished the solemn grove to Jericho. I looked at the coverlet of my bed folded tightly into place. I was fatigued from the exertions of the day, and yet my couch seemed a cold and lonely resting place in my present frame of mind. I went to my husband's chamber. I stirred the small fire and crossed over to Mr. Rochester. He sat on the edge of his bed, his chin on his chest, preoccupied with deep thought.

"You have more to tell me, Jane, do you not?" I assented in a voice that belied my weariness. "Let us dismiss it for the present. I wish to turn things over in my own mind for a time before I add any more to the account."

"It will keep until morning?"

"It will keep. Come, Jane." He held out his arms to me, and I went to his embrace gratefully. "Let us put away dismal associations and distressing thoughts. Wherever we find the hollow, the venomous, the unwholesome, we will bring the flowers of precious affection, and keep green and growing the genuine fruit of paradise. To be in your arms is to plumb the depths of the pure, the passionate, the free-flowing nectar of love." His arms tightened round me, drawing me full close to him. "Come, Jane, come."

I was awake ere the sun lifted its beams above the eastward rim of the hills, yet I was not the first member of the household to be astir. I heard a knock at the door. I waited; the light tap was repeated. I began to move. Mr. Rochester forestalled me.

"The servants in this house are not being trained properly. She will wait until she is called."

I looked at Mr. Rochester. He spoke without opening his eyes. An interval of silence passed, and the knock sounded once more. I left the bed, threw my dressing-gown round me, and opened my husband's door. It was Lord Ingram.

He was dressed, but he did not look altogether as neat and exact as usual. A closer examination suggested that he had never been undressed at all. His cravat hung at a strange angle, and his waistcoat was in a deplorable state. His haggard eyes spoke eloquently of a sleepless night. I said nothing; for he held his finger to his lips and followed this by an anxious glance down the hall. His hand moved forward. A folded bit of paper was proffered to me.

"Jane, who is it?" Mr. Rochester called from within. Lord Ingram stared very hard at me then. Positioned as he was, there could be little fear of discovery: Mr. Rochester was incapable of seeing anyone; I had but to speak to reveal his lordship.

"It is only a note," I replied over my shoulder. I did not like to deceive my husband, but for the moment, I felt I had little choice.

Lord Ingram nodded. An indescribable look, almost like pain, or the shadow of it, passed over his countenance, and he went silently away down the back staircase.

"Someone brought you a note? At this hour?"

I closed the door but remained at a distance. I unfolded the letter, and read, in a gentleman's scrawl:

'I am delivered into your hands. I beg of you to tell no one of what I said to you yesterday eve. I am hemmed in by obstacles on all sides. My only hope is concealment. Keep silent, I pray you, keep silent.'

It was unsigned, but I had seen Lord Ingram's writing once before. The lines did not shake and spatter as these did, but I knew his hand. Well, I was sworn to secrecy once more, and this time even my husband could not, in good conscience, be my co-conspirator.

"Who is sending you notes at this hour?"

I would not lie. However, I wished to know more of the matter before hazarding confidences. Thinking of the task I had set myself, I thought I might change the channel of his inquiry.

"Mr. Rochester, I have an appointment to keep this morning."

"Have you? What do you mean?"

"I must speak to Mr. Barnett today."

"Ah. I see." A sudden coldness seemed to blanket the room about us.

" I must persuade him to tell me the truth, for Diana's sake."

"Very well," he said at last, with an expansive sigh, and propped himself on one elbow. "If you must, you must."

I noted the air of disapproval lingering in his expression. "I can hardly solve a mystery without interrogating the principles parties, can I?"

"Yes, yes, I give you leave, if you like, but by what certainty will you know that you have attained your goal?"

"What do you mean?"

Suppose he does not tell you the truth? Suppose he deceives you?"

"I have a lien upon him. I hold his secret, though why it must be a secret is beyond my comprehension. Still, he is my best hope of verifying facts."

Mr. Rochester lay back upon his pillow with one arm crooked behind his head. "Facts are curious things. They cannot always be made to tell an honest tale, however true they might be in themselves."

My husband's air grew abstracted; he meditated upon his own speculations. My eyes, already fixed in his direction, dwelt instead on his frame; his muscular palm open in the centre of the bed; his athletic form reclined and in repose, and his dark eye flashing in thought beneath his confident brow. I looked, and had an acute pleasure in looking.

"What is it, Jane? Why are you so silent?"

"I was only looking at you."

"Were you? And what do make of what you see?"

"It is a delightful view, Edward."

An expression flashed across his face that I had not beheld there for a long while, like that of a Turk surveying his possessions. "Is it, Jane? Do I please you?"

"Very much."

"Will you just come over here and say that again?"

I sat beside him on the bed, and he raised his hand to my mouth as I spoke; he felt with his fingers the genial smile that came naturally to my lips.

"You *do* love me then?"

"Certainly I do. Most sincerely. Does that content you, Edward?"

"No Solomon in his riches or Croesus in his wealth could have greater contentment than I possess. This is my marriage bed, Janet, with you to share it with. There is not another spot in the world that holds more charm for me than this."

I threw my arms around his neck, and to my infinite delight, he laughed.

Before the morning grew much older, I told Mr. Rochester all that had occurred on the evening before, while I was dressed in Sally's bonnet and apron. Of course, I carefully omitted my conference with

Lord Ingram but resolved to reveal all if I ever felt there was an immediate need to do so. At present, I understood the matter so little that I might easily injure Lord Ingram simply through ignorance, and I dreaded the thought of harming him. My husband said little but this:

"You say it was Blanche Ingram's idea, to have us here?"

"Yes."

"What could she mean by it? To what end?"

"Possibly to triumph over us. To feel her superiority, or else to oblige us to observe hers. Do you suppose she resents me for winning your affection?"

"That is hardly a prize she would covet. She never loved me."

"She may have valued her sense of power over you. She believed herself the object of your devotion."

Mr. Rochester proceeded to remind me of the true object of his devotion, and he would answer no questions at all. At length, I brought him back to the subject that piqued my interest.

"Do you know anything of the elder Lord Ingram's first wife?"

"Oh, she was nothing worse than a manufacturer's daughter from somewhere in the North. I've forgotten the name of the family, but they had a great deal of money. Inferior of course—her grandfather had been a barrister—but she was well-educated."

"Was she beautiful?"

"Not that I ever heard of. My father met her once, and he would have taken more notice of a great beauty in the neighbourhood. You might have a look around, Jane, if it interests you. The valet told me our chambers were used by them. However, I don't see that it will shed much light on the matter at hand." He flung the covers aside and sought his dressing gown. I helped him put it on. "What sort of day is it outside?"

I went to the window and looked up into a sky of clear and luminous blue. The sun-washed air, balmy, pure and mild, revived hope and dulled the keen edge of anxiety. I felt it to be a day of fresh possibilities; I hoped also that it would be a day of revelation. I soon had Mr. Rochester in good order and repaired to my room to dress. I took a glance around my chamber as if with new eyes, the delicate furnishings and elegant ornaments a testament to the woman who had once lived here. I had long noticed a neat trunk in the corner bearing signs of age. For the first time it fostered my curiosity, but all such speculations were cast aside by the arrival of Mrs. Harper to help me into my morning dress.

"Is Sally not feeling well again?"

"No, ma'am, she ain't, but you needn't worry your head about her." Mrs. Harper showed definite indications of irritation, but her anger did not seem aimed at me.

"Only curious," I added mildly.

To make amends for her curt tone, the housekeeper said, "Can't expect to get old wisdom into young heads, can we, ma'am? I ought to make more allowances for her." She stood behind me as I looked into the glass. "You're full young yourself, ma'am, to take on all the responsibility you do, lookin' after your husband and all. We admire you, you know, in the servants' hall. It's not every young lady would care for a husband who's so helpless."

"I suppose I am not much like other young ladies."

I straightened my collar and allowed Mrs. Harper to finish rearranging my hair. I was accustomed to doing so myself, but I wished to keep her talking. Sally had asked me not to tell of her midnight visitations to the music room, but I thought I might gain some insight without revealing her secret outright. "Perhaps Sally does not sleep well. I have sometimes known a person grow ill simply from fatigue. Do you see her into bed at night?"

With a confidential look in her eye, Mrs. Harper said, "Why, you've just hit it, ma'am. She goes to bed all right, but I don't believe she stays there."

I looked at her, somewhat startled by her words, and surprised also by the deep disapproval in her voice. "I don't think much of these foreign habits being brought here. Ours has always been a respectable house and it doesn't please me one bit to see him carrying on with his foreign ways."

I had thought myself guessing something of the truth, but now it appeared I was altogether in the dark.

"Did you say *him*, Mrs. Harper? Of whom are you speaking? I know of no foreigner staying here."

Mrs. Harper's eye glittered with the satisfaction of delivering a piece of ripe gossip. I knew I ought not to give her words much weight, as she may only be imparting false rumours, but her tone was very earnest. In a low voice, she intimated, "I mean that Mr. Barnett, ma'am."

"Mr. Barnett!"

"Aye. Born in Belgium he was. He's no Englishman. Lived most of his life there, too. Mr. Hardwick brought him here, and I wish he would take him right away again. He'll be no end of trouble for that Sally, you can be sure."

"Sally? And Mr. Barnett?"

"I saw her with my own eyes, ma'am, coming from the direction of his room after midnight. I've spoken to her about it, ma'am, and she says it was nothing, so I've only given her a warning. With our head housekeeper away, there's only so much I've got time to do, and I can't be chasing her around after dark. But every time she calls herself ill in the morning— "

"Jane!" Mr. Rochester's deep voice thrilled through me, calling me from the other side of the door.

"Well, I'd best be getting downstairs." Mrs. Harper was out of the room almost before I could move.

"Are we going to breakfast, or aren't we?" Mr. Rochester demanded.

I went into his room and took his arm. "Yes," I said, a little strangely. "Yes, we had better go."

"What's the matter, Janet? What kept you?"

"I was only talking to the housekeeper." A reply of settled calm dismissed the subject from Mr. Rochester's mind, but for my part, it was not so easily forgotten.

I led Mr. Rochester along the labyrinthine halls to the breakfast room, fully expecting an interval of calm before meeting with Mr. Barnett. My expectations were overthrown, however, by the sight of Mr. Barnett already seated at the table. He was at Mr. Hardwick's elbow. That gentleman was in close conversation with him, but when I appeared in the doorway, Mr. Barnett's lids lifted; he rose to his feet, and bowed stiffly, still careful of his injury, in my direction.

"Mrs. Rochester, good morning."

Mr. Hardwick looked at his agent in mocking amazement. "Mrs. Rochester has won your devotion, Barnett, has she? Rather unlike you, to pay court to a woman."

Mr. Barnett had resumed his seat. In a quiet voice, he replied, "She saved my life."

"Ah! A debt of gratitude is certainly a foundation for a connection. Don't you think so, Rochester?"

"It is not the first life she has preserved."

His tone was cold, and perhaps even hurtful. I regretted the turn of the conversation; it could foster no good sentiments in anyone, and hardly help the business I had in hand. I wished to soothe away any enmity my husband might feel towards Mr. Barnett, and for myself to be on a footing of unqualified friendship with that gentleman. This, I hoped, would lead to an opportunity of gaining his genuine confidence. Mr. Hardwick's badinage was no help to me.

"Has she preserved your life, also? I told you she must be an angel. A bit too good for us earthly mortals to be debating about, eh?"

"I am no angel, Mr. Hardwick," I said, having taken my seat at the table. "Any more than you might be a sort of devil in disguise. Men and women are born with the faculty of choice, to do good or evil, as the opportunity presents itself."

"No, no! I'll not allow it!" He said, laughing. "We men need our guardian angels. It is woman's peculiar office to sanctify us. If we're left to our own devices, the job will never be done, I can promise you that."

No one else joined him in his mirth, but at this moment, Miss Ingram entered the room, followed by her sister and mother. Hardwick quickly claimed Miss Ingram as his personal divine agent, and Mr. Barnett receded from the table, leaving his breakfast half-finished. He stood against the wall for a few minutes, looking over the room with a brooding face, his hands behind his back. His eye caught mine, and with a final nod, he slipped out of the door. I felt he meant to communicate something to me, but I was at a loss to know what it was.

Diana soon joined us. She still looked rather pale, but there was none of the grievous heart-rending expression of the previous evening. I was sure she had spent the intervening hours in supplicating for divine aid, to prepare herself for whatever might come. Captain Fitzjames and Lord Ingram, I learned, had gone out shooting early in the morning and had not yet returned. This reminded me of my errand to discover what arms the house possessed, but that mission would have to wait. My mind was occupied in framing the conversation I hoped to have with Mr. Barnett, and I was not attending much to what was being said at the table. My attention was claimed, however, by Miss Ingram.

"Mrs. Rochester is too weak, I suppose, for that sort of excursion."

Her haughty eyes fixed on me; she seemed to be waiting for a response. "I beg your pardon, Miss Ingram, were you speaking of me?"

"Beltenham Common is very pretty this time of year. We thought of having a picnic there today, but I'm afraid the exercise would be too much for you after your illness."

"Did you think of riding? I am no horsewoman, unfortunately."

"Are you not? You ought to learn. But then, it may be too late for lessons of that kind. A certain physical grace is required for riding. It is not every woman who can master the art."

"Going on horseback would exclude most of our party," Hardwick said. "We must take a carriage. You and I may ride, of course, my dear, but we must wait for your brother."

"No, no, he will not want a picnic after being out all morning. We shall not be delayed by him."

"Well. You'll have the barouche, Mrs. Rochester, won't you? That will leave plenty of room for you and your *entourage*." Hardwick put a curious emphasis on the final word. "And Miss Mary, of course. You would prefer the carriage, wouldn't you?"

"Oh, I will stay home with Mama. The dressmaker is coming this morning with the new fashion dolls from Paris."

"Perhaps we might have Mr. Barnett, as a fourth," was my suggestion. "This warm air could do him little harm."

There was that smile again, sarcastic and humourless, distorting Mr. Hardwick's face, "Do you really think it worth the trouble?"

"I feel a certain responsibility for him. The natural consequence, I think, of preserving him." I thought it not out of place to smile in return, although discontented at having to endure his unpleasant humour. "One hates to see the fruit of one's labours wasted."

When the time of our departure arrived, Mr. Barnett did not look particularly pleased with my plea on his behalf. He took his place in the carriage beside Diana, and across from me, with his arms across his chest and a rather blank expression on his face.

"Does the motion pain you?" I asked. He replied in the negative and did not open his lips during the twenty minutes required to take us to Beltenham common. I gave Mr. Rochester the most engaging description that I could of the scenery passing us, and Diana added in pretty details that occurred to her.

The common itself was bright with greenery. Yellow gorse and swaths of bluebells bloomed on the outskirts of a little pond that lay glittering in the palm of the hills. A pastoral ridge stretched beyond it, where a froth of white sheep bearded the brow of the hill, as foam might cling to the impending billow.

Mr. Hardwick and Miss Ingram had ridden ahead of us. They now dismounted and left their horses with the coachman. All of our party was now on foot, and we soon found seats partway up the hill, in a sheltered hollow. It would be hot before the morning was over, but the dew had only just melted away, and for the present, the sun was a blessing.

Miss Ingram and Mr. Hardwick did not retain their seats for long. They had come to be doing something and were soon on their feet and moving about. A stand of larch just below was laced with a shade-dappled path and made an inviting destination to wandering feet. Four of us remained in the hollow.

Diana pulled a trim volume from her pocket. "I've brought a book of poetry to read. If you wish it, Mr. Rochester, I shall read aloud."

"I would consider it a great favour if you would, but not just yet. Jane, did I hear you say you brought your drawing apparatus with you?"

"Yes, sir, my easel and pencils are here."

"You'd like to get back up on that ridge, wouldn't you, to see the view?"

"If an opportunity presents itself, certainly."

"Mr. Barnett, perhaps you'd be so kind." Mr. Barnett was sitting somewhat apart from us, shredding an errant leaf in his fingers. "I'd like someone to escort her, but I am as likely to be a burden as a help."

Mr. Barnett acquiesced, and Mr. Rochester said no more than, "Commence reading, Miss Rivers, whenever it suits you."

Mr. Barnett took possession of the easel and stool under his un-injured arm while we mounted the hill. At the top, I arranged my camp stool, easel, pencils, parchment; there was little wind, and my work was soon begun. I was sketching the scene before me with a re-viving pleasure; the joy of reproducing such a view animated my pen-cil.

"You draw very well," was Mr. Barnett's comment. "It does not disturb you if I watch your progress?"

"No. It is not to be a very fine work at any rate. I am out of prac-tice." I sketched on, however, stealing only occasional glances at my companion, who stood off to the side with his eyes as much on the horizon as they were on my picture. It was just as well, for while my fingers carefully traced the lines of pasture and cloud, I was busy re-volving some measure to introduce a subject so at variance with the present scene. I was helped, however, by a sound from Mr. Barnett. He sighed. A deep, chest lifting sigh that seemed to burst involuntar-ily from him. I let my pencil rest.

"There is something on your mind, Mr. Barnett?"

"Oh, I'll not bore you with my troubles."

"To tell the truth, it is your troubles that I would revert to with interest."

"What do you mean?"

"There is a mystery about you, that, if confined solely to yourself, would be no concern of mine. Deceit rarely withholds its contami-nating influence, however, and in this case, the trouble has spread to more than one of our companions. I would very much like you to clear up one or two points that perplex me."

I waited to see the effect of this speech. I had taken a very forth-right approach; I thought it best. I had a sort of authority over him, on account of his secret in my possession, his peculiar confessions in the wood, but I had no desire to extort the truth from him.

He was silent many moments, but at length ,another sigh slipped from him, and he said, "There may be a few things I can safely tell you. My position is a peculiar one, Mrs. Rochester. I have a great loathing for concealment and deceit, and yet circumstances beyond my control have forced me to commit both."

"Your conscience is uneasy."

"It is rather. But ask me what you wish to know and I will endeavour to tell you what I can."

"Have you known Captain Fitzjames for very long?"

"The captain! Only since my injury. Why do you ask about him?"

"He has been a most faithful caretaker during your recovery."

"Yes, he has."

"Did you know that he has made an offer of marriage to my cousin?"

A smile of sudden warmth flashed across his face, and his dark eyes seemed to deepen. "I did not realise he had got so far—but it does not surprise me. He has spoken of her often."

"Perhaps you see the tendency of my questions?"

"If you wish for a testimonial of his character, I can give you the highest commendation in my power."

This, I thought, did not sound like the words of one who has been assaulted by Captain Fitzjames. Either the captain had a most devious and powerful hold over Mr. Barnett—or this was a faithful representation of the man. "I must put a question to you, Mr. Barnett. I hope you will forgive its awkwardness. Just who was with you that night in the grove?"

"Who? Why, only that vagrant, as you know very well."

"There was no vagrant."

He stared at me a moment, as I had directly contradicted his words. Then: "No, there was no vagrant."

"There was a gentleman with you. Someone you knew well enough to speak with for some time."

"What makes you think so?"

"Will you tell me who he was?" He looked at the ground and assiduously dug his heel into the grass before answering.

"No. That is one thing I cannot tell you."

"Can you tell me if Captain Fitzjames was with you?"

He looked at me incredulously. "No! Why would you think that?"

"I found his snuff-box in the same place that I found you."

"Ah."

"It stands to reason that he was with you."

"It was not his snuff-box."

"But— "

"It was changed. Swapped. The one you found was nearly the same, but someone exchanged it for his."

"Why?"

"So you would not guess the true owner."

"Who is the true owner?"

He said nothing.

"Who changed them?"

Again, he made no reply.

"Do you mean to say that someone in the house committed this violent act against you, and you are determined to hide it from the world?"

"Yes, that sums it up rather well."

"This seems very strange, Mr. Barnett."

"If the *casus belli* of all this could be so summarily explained to you, it would not seem strange at all."

I looked down below and saw Mr. Hardwick and Miss Ingram ascending the slope. Our conference was nearly at an end. I rose to my feet.

"Can you assure me that Captain Fitzjames is innocent in this matter?"

"Entirely. He has nothing to do with it. His role is like yours—unconnected with its root cause, and thus far, entirely for my benefit."

"And tell me— "

"Perhaps it would be better if you did not ask anything more."

"Just one more question, Mr. Barnett. Are you still at risk?"

He had picked up my camp stool and was folding it. I was obliged to collect my drawing so that he might fold up the easel as well. We began our downhill walk.

"You have not answered. Tell me, is your life still in danger?"

"Life is a dangerous business, Mrs. Rochester. We are all of us mortal, with eternity no great step away."

"If you are in peril, we must take steps to protect you."

We could already hear Diana's silvery tones as she recited the stirring lines of *Marmion* into the still air.

"Thank you, madam, for your concern." For the first time, I could hear the lilt of a foreign accent in his voice. He took my hand a moment and pressed it most kindly. A glow kindled in his features and for once I felt that there was an animating spirit in him that was sadly oppressed. The glow faded speedily, however, and was replaced by that despairing gaze that gnawed at my heart. "But I am a man who has lost everything that was ever dear to me, and it is no great odds to me whether I live or die."

He went on ahead of me, into our little dell, and took a seat away from the others. I remained a few moments longer and occupied myself in picking the wildflowers that dwelt there. There was much in this to puzzle and perplex, but one thing, at least, was evident. Mr.

Barnett was a man in need of saving, and furthermore, a man who would do nothing to save himself.

CHAPTER XII

I strayed only a little distance from the hollow in the hill, followed by Diana's voice. Her words were rendered inarticulate by distance, but their timbre was both clear and soft. A knot of violets I had gathered occupied my fingers, but my mind wandered far off, speculating upon the strange news Mr. Barnett had given me. The snap of a twig drew my attention. Mr. Hardwick was standing on the path.

I had not seen him arrive, but his eyes were fixed on me with a darkening countenance that had nothing of its usual sarcastic humour. He said nothing, but his gaze still on me, he passed by in silence and joined the others with some bold rejoinder.

What could I have done to earn his frowns? He had called me an angel this morning, and while there was no true feeling or affection in his appellation of me, I had not expected this serious disapproval. I returned ere long to the dell for our repast. Mr. Hardwick seemed restored to cheerful spirits and laughed with Blanche in great good humour.

Mr. Barnett had remained somewhat apart, wrapt in some silent contemplation of his own. My thoughts ran continually on his strange position, his life endangered, his tongue muted, his mind confined to hapless gloom. My eyes followed my thoughts, to dwell on his sombre countenance. Mr. Hardwick once intercepted one of these looks, and that curious expression of suspicion returned.

The heat increased. A thick cover of cloud was moving in stately procession across the sky. We would wait until it had drawn its grateful screen over the sun before embarking for Ingram Park. Mr. Rochester lay back in the grass, while Blanche and Diana had agreed to walk down the hill and along the water. Mr. Barnett had wandered to the edge of the dell, to swipe at tall grass stems with a twig. It was then that Mr. Hardwick addressed me thus:

"You would fancy a walk in the shade, Mrs. Rochester, would you not? It's rather hot here for so recent an invalid, but it is almost cool in that stand of larch below. I'll take you if you like. That is, if Mr. Rochester has no objection?"

He looked at my husband, as did I. Mr. Rochester reclined with his hat over his eyes. As his face was concealed, I could make nothing of the thoughts moving in his mind, but after a moment's hesitation, he admitted that he had no objection. "You'll take great care of her, Hardwick. Or you'll hear from me."

Mr. Hardwick affirmed that he would be most careful and we walked off. My companion insisted I make use of his arm, and in truth, I found it a support in this oppressive heat. I found, too, a refreshing coolness beneath the trees. A soft breeze blew here, shivering the leaves and soothing my heated skin.

It was not, however, solely disinterested kindness that led Mr. Hardwick to attend me here. We came to a stop in a quiet glade carpeted with fallen needles. It was not secluded—we could see our companions between the boles of the trees, but we would not be overheard easily. A newly cut stump at almost the right height provided me with a solitary seat. Mr. Hardwick stood well away, his back against a tall trunk, and his eyes fastened on me with a blazing fixity, as if he might read the thoughts hidden within my brain.

"You are fond of the company of my agent, Mrs. Rochester," he pronounced.

"Yes, I like him."

"*Like* him? Oh come, you need have no reservations with *me*. Tell me now, you are tired of the old man, aren't you? Tired of playing nursemaid to a withered old thing?"

"Mr. Hardwick, how can you— " I was not allowed to finish. He hurried on.

"Barnett's handsome enough, young and vigorous, in spite of his injury. Now that you've gained your fortune, you are free to please yourself. Is that not the case?"

"You know nothing about me, Mr. Hardwick, if you think— "

"I remember the first day I met you, you spoke up rather quick in Barnett's defence. And now, you see, I find you holding hands with him behind your husband's back— "

"You are wrong, sir!" I cried, stung into defending myself. "You have imagined what is not there."

He remained leaning against the tree, but his eye bore full force upon me. "You may know less about Barnett than you suppose. I ought to warn you, he is not always reliable."

"Do you say he tells lies?"

"Lies? Not *lies* exactly. One may not mean to deceive and yet still do so, but I thought it best to put you on your guard. Don't you think that's humane in me?"

I declined to be baited into conversation on such a topic and therefore said nothing.

"Come, you *do* take an uncommon interest in him, do you not?"

Still, I held my tongue.

"I suppose he has not told you about his wife?"

"His wife?" The words flew from my mouth. A gleam of triumph showed in my interlocutor's eye. "Where is his wife?"

"She, poor thing, is no longer for this world. What abode she has been taken to I don't pretend to know. I hope she is singing with the angels, I'm sure. I never knew much of her, but the grief of losing her has driven Barnett hard."

My inner eye revealed to me all that this imported: the heart-rending plea when I found him in the grove, his addressing me as if I were his loved one, who had come to take him with me from this earth; it was all plain.

Mr. Hardwick continued staring hard, and as soon as this moment of inward comprehension passed over me, he left his post by the tree and crossed the glade. Three strides brought him directly to me. I stood up in a hurry but could do no more. "He *has* told you something, hasn't he?"

"I am bound—I promised him not to speak of it."

"Ah! Well. His father knows nothing of the business. You know about his father?"

I shook my head.

"It would do him harm if the connection were known, even with the poor girl dying off like that. His father's ambitious and meant him to marry above his station. He'd never forgive Barnett if he knew his son had married a girl of that kind. But you see I'm already acquainted with the details. You need not conceal anything from me."

On the contrary, I said to myself, I trust you the least in his business.

Mr. Hardwick turned from me and took a few paces across the glade, his hands behind his back. When he faced me once more, he held my eye with his: it was a hard eye, cold and searching. I wished he would turn it somewhere else, but could not look away myself.

"I know you take an interest in him. I have seen it in your face more than once. I guessed either that you loved him, or that he told you about— " he hesitated.

"I love my husband."

He waved away my words. "What did he tell you?"

"I cannot say. And your manner in addressing me in no way tempts me to do so. You cannot be any true friend of his."

"You are altogether out, madam. I am the very best friend he has. He relies a great deal on me." His posture changed: he seemed less fiery, less like a bird of prey seeking to devour. When he spoke his voice was cool, yet putting out a certain electricity. "As I said, his grief has wrought heavy on him. He is not himself—your conviction that

I am his enemy springs from a disordered mind. His words cannot be relied on."

"You doubt his sanity?"

"At times, he can be very rational, very plausible; at others, wholly unreliable. Whatever he has accused me of, be sure it is his mental confusion that gives him such a perspective."

Now it was my turn to watch, and to contemplate the visage of my opponent.

"Well, Mrs. Rochester?" said he, with a familiar turn of his lip. "Does my face interest you so much? Do you make physiognomy your study?"

"I am more inclined to wonder at your words. Mr. Barnett has accused you of nothing. What is it, pray, that you imagine him to be accusing you of?" His cheek blanched; he bit his lip. "What have you done, that you are afraid of him telling me?"

In an instant, he turned on his heel and strode away from me. Not another word did he speak. I did not follow him. My limbs took to trembling, in spite of the heat, and I sat down once more on my stump to listen to my palpitating heart. I heard Mr. Hardwick's voice calling out with artificial cheerfulness to Diana and Blanche, where they stood by the water.

"Are you all right, madam?" I looked up to see Mr. Barnett before me. "Your husband thought you had been gone long enough. He asked me to look out for you."

"Thank you, I am quite well." Mr. Barnett's look showed that he did not quite believe this, but he said no more and offered me his arm. We left the wood in silence.

The journey back to Ingram Park was uneventful. On our return to the house, we were welcomed by Lord Ingram and Captain Fitzjames, and we were invited to repair to the drawing-room for tea. Mr. Rochester I could see preferred to go, but there was scarcely a member of our party that did not disrupt my feelings in some way. I

asked Diana to accompany me to the library and she went gratefully.
I gave her an account of my conversation with Mr. Barnett, not without some residual fears that his words were as confused as Mr. Hardwick suggested. I said nothing on that head to my cousin. While neither man could be entirely credible, I still considered Mr. Barnett the
most trustworthy of the two. I had hardly finished my tale when the
door opened, and our solitude was interrupted by the captain himself.

"I beg your pardon," he said diffidently, "if I am intruding."

"No, not at all," I answered, but he did not seem to attend much
to my words. He looked at Diana.

"You are very welcome, Captain." Her voice was rather soft and
subdued, but there was a look of charity in her eye that spoke more
eloquently than words. He was wearing his coat, the deep blue of the
royal navy, and carried a valise under his arm. He crossed the room
and laid it on the table, and in doing so, came to a stop directly in
front of Diana.

"Miss Rivers—I will call you Diana if you will permit me?" She
nodded.

"Shall I go?" I asked quietly.

"No. Mrs. Rochester, do stay. You must hear my plea for forgiveness."

"Forgiveness?" asked Diana. "What could you need to be forgiv-
en for?"

"For speaking too soon. Yesterday, I—I am afraid I was caught up
in my own feelings. Feelings very ardent, very real—I assure you, my
feelings have not changed. They are as strong as ever. Nothing would
give me greater pleasure in life than to receive your hand in marriage.
I have never met another woman who—but there I go. I always find
it easiest to get direct to the point. However, I must lay my heart
aside, though it pains me— " In a lower tone he went on. "Please
believe that I would have you know as much of the truth as I am

vouchsafed to give. You have inquired once or twice as to my reason for coming here, and for staying on so long, though my acquaintance with the family was so negligible. The truth of the matter is—and this is to go no farther than this room—his lordship asked me to give him advice. As an outside party, you understand, he thought I could help. However, it seems my opinions are not so much use to him as he hoped—they are, any rate, to be disregarded."

A dark scarlet flush passed over his face, but he speedily quelled his anger, a most vital, mastering emotion judging from the visible effort required to abstract himself from it. "I have resolved to leave—immediately. My things are packed and the horse is already preparing to bring me to the mail coach."

"What! So soon?"

"Yes, my dear. I regret it extremely. I will not ask you for an answer to my ill-timed proposal. My affairs are so unsettled—I must not presume—but you have my heart. There can be no doubt of that. You can be assured of my affection and all my intentions, but I will bind you to no promise, not until—Lord willing, I will find you here, or follow you to Moor House. I would follow you to the ends of the earth— "

"William— "

"I hope you will understand my feelings, even if I cannot explain my motions. You are not angry with me? Or disappointed?"

"No. Only I wish you were not going away."

"Dearest Diana."

He took her hand in his and drew near her. I stepped aside to the window, but I could not help observing them. A long minute they stood, her glossy curls drooping, a glowing blush covering her cheek, while the captain's head bent down to hers. He brought her fingers very near to his lips, and trembling, pressed them tenderly together. With a rapid farewell and an air of resolution, he took up his valise and hurried out the door.

I drew Diana's arm into my own. She said nothing, but she looked her agitation, a potent blend of pleasure and regret. I led her to the window, facing the road leading away from Ingram Park. We watched his erect figure ride away, while a groom followed on a second horse.

"Jane," Diana murmured. "What on earth are we to do now?"

The only thing to do immediately was to repair to our rooms. It was time to dress for dinner. In my quiet chamber once more, I went to my window. I viewed grove, garden, and lake unseeing, my mind revolving in fruitless circles upon the knowledge I had received. The only possibility I could see was to lay aside caution and begin asking questions directly, which would doubtless draw unwanted attention, even unwanted vehemence, down on myself. Or else I could do no more, simply wait and abide by time to reveal the secrets of the case. Only suppose Mr. Barnett was injured, even killed, before that happened? Suppose this was to drag on for years to come, and the captain and Diana were alienated by some force at present indiscernible?

On the other hand, the malignant person pursuing Mr. Barnett may decide to target myself instead. Sobering thought! I was young and newly married; I did not feel any great partiality for death. And my husband depended on me entirely. Had I any right to risk myself in the cause of another?

At this rather wearying juncture, I heard a knock on the door. The valet serving Mr. Rochester was there.

"A letter arrived for you, ma'am. I brought it along. And Mr. Rochester is asking for you."

I returned to my post by the window as I wanted the light to examine the envelope. Mrs. Edward Rochester was written in bold letters across the envelope, in careful but unpractised script. Just who *was* Mrs. Rochester? Had she any business meddling in the affairs of Ingram Park?

I went to my husband's room, and once there I unfolded the letter. It was from Adèle Varens, Mr. Rochester's ward; my former pupil at Thornfield. She was at school now in a nearby county.

"What is it, Jane? Who is the letter from?"

"It is from Adèle."

"Little Adèle! Is she well?"

"Oh yes, she writes cheerfully. She misses me, and you too. She has her complaints, but she is well enough for the present."

"Then why is it that you are crying?"

"Oh, I am not crying."

"I know the source of that tremble in your voice. I am blind, Jane, but I am not deaf. Come here."

I went to him with the tears still wet on my cheek. He caught me close in an embrace while I wept into his collar, a cold steady rain that would not abate for some minutes. When at last I grew calm, he took my face tenderly in his hand and inquired what was distressing me.

"It was only the letter. It brought everything back to me, when we were at Thornfield, and I first knew the genial bliss of your affection. I had Adèle, and Mrs. Fairfax, and— "

"And then I destroyed your peace and marred your happiness."

"Yes, of course you did. I'm not talking about that. Do you remember, Edward? Under the chestnut tree?"

He bestowed a kiss on me then. "I'm not likely to forget, my darling."

"And all this— " I waved my hand vaguely in front of me. "All these dreadful lies. I had imagined a smooth path ahead, if only we could be united, and yet now that we are, we seem surrounded by trouble."

"And is that all?"

"I depended on you in those days. It was my chief joy to do as you bid, to be your helper, to be led by you."

"It is up to you now to do the leading," he spoke a little ruefully, but he did not sound unhappy. "I have long acknowledged it."

"But to where? I feel myself a ship lost at sea, with no beacon to guide me."

"You have reserves of strength in you, Janet, that you yourself are not aware of. I have never known another being so keenly possessed of the steel to do what is right in adverse circumstances. I do not believe you have learned to exert even a tenth part of your powers on behalf of those you love."

"How can you know?"

He smoothed my hair with his hand. "I know you. I have studied your nature as no one else has. I have seen into your heart's core—you have revealed it to me hourly. Your courage, compassion, faithfulness, your determination to do what is right: they will not fail you."

I thought of Lady Ingram's cold eye upon me. "I shall not make a very great lady if I undertake interrogating my acquaintance."

"I am not over fond of great ladies, Jane. Do what you know is right, and you will have the full approbation of both your Maker and your husband. Is there any other worth caring for?"

No, I thought, no there was not. My plans were formed in that instant. Tomorrow, I would act.

CHAPTER XIII

The Three Brothers stands on the bank of a trout stream, the same that wends its way below Ingram Park, through Mr. Barnett's ill-fated grove, and down into the valley, wherein lies a little village. While the morning was still young, we used the same path that Mr. Barnett had ascended the previous Tuesday.

Mr. Rochester went beside me, my arm wrapped about his waist and his own locked round my shoulders. Travelling thus, we made good time, and arrived at the tavern just as the barman was taking the shutters down from the windows.

"Good morning, ma'am. Good morning, master. The room's open if you're wanting some refreshment. It'll be a hot day before long." The tavern keeper led the way inside, but I stopped before entering.

"Well, Jane?"

"I only want to have a look around." I left Mr. Rochester near the door a moment and took a brief tour of the region in which the tavern stood. The stable yard was empty and bright, and the stream running faithfully behind boasted a pair of boys engaged in fishing. A sunk lane beyond it led away from the tavern and thence to the little hamlet beyond.

We went indoors. When rewarded with small mugs of coffee, I asked the tavern keeper to remain while I put a question or two. A stout woman in a gingham apron, presumably his wife, was at work in the kitchen, but otherwise, there was no one else present.

"I wish to inquire about a particular gentleman who did business here last Tuesday evening." I took from my pocket a rough sketch of Mr. Barnett, drawn from memory, which I had prepared for the purpose early that morning. The tavern keeper held it at arm's length to examine it, then he studied me with a keen, wary eye.

"I saw him, yes."

"You know who he is?"

"He was the gentleman set upon that very night, in yonder grove." A nod of his head in the direction of Ingram Park indicated his knowledge of the sad event.

"I understand he spent a considerable time here that evening."

"That's so, ma'am. He was here an hour or two."

"He had a companion at one time, a visitor, while he was here."

The man looked at Mr. Rochester a moment, as if expecting that gentleman to rein in his too inquisitive partner, but my husband was mute. His sightless gaze was directed elsewhere, but he was, I knew, listening with interest.

The barman shifted in his seat. "You seem to know quite a bit about what went on, ma'am. Why d'you ask me about it?"

"It is always best, I find, to be certain on all points, however trivial."

Mr. Rochester nodded in confirmation of my words.

"Very well," the barman said. "As you say, there was a man with him for a time. How do you come to know about it, if I may ask?"

"My informant is most likely familiar to you. Bill, who works in the stables at Ingram Park."

"Old Bill! Was he here then?"

"He says he was in the kitchen."

"Aye, just so." The barman meditated on this information.

"He's here often, is he not?"

"Oh yes, as often as he can. And always of a Tuesday."

"Do you find him an accurate observer?"

"Well, that depends." Another uneasy glance at Mr. Rochester. "I don't know if this is exactly fitting for a lady—but since you ask—if he hasn't had anything much to drink, he's reliable, but he's apt to stray when he's had too many pints. I've heard him tell some wild tales."

Mr. Rochester spoke for the first time. "Go on, what about?"

"He's worked at the park for about as long as he's been alive, and he sometimes tells strange stories. Fairies carrying away babies at birth, strange spirits abroad at night, that sort of thing. It's a curious thing what'll stick in a man's mind when he's had too much."

"That's nothing to do with us," I said. "He was sober enough when we spoke to him. He says Mr. Barnett had a heated conversation with someone."

"Yes, that's so."

"Do you know who he was?"

"Oh, a regular nob, with a spirited animal tearing up my yard while he drank up his sherry."

I produced a second picture, a pencil sketch of Mr. Hardwick. "Is this the same man?" The barman took the picture, and I noticed a curious tremor in his fingers.

"I don't believe I've ever seen him before."

"Why, Joe! How can you say such a thing!"

All three of us raised our heads in surprise, startled by this sudden address. The stout woman at work in the kitchen had appeared behind her husband's chair. So engrossed were we in our conversation that none of us had noticed her approach.

"You know perfectly well that was the very same man. We talked about him, Joe, don't you remember? He paid you extra on account of that horse."

I looked at the tavern keeper, his countenance blushing pink up to his ears.

"He paid you extra?" I asked. "Because of the horse? Because of the damage it caused?"

"Yes, ma'am."

"Is that all he paid you for?"

His red cheek quickly blanched. "He told me it was on account of his future mother-in-law. He thought she might not think it respectable for him to be here. I didn't see no harm in it."

"He paid you to conceal his presence here?"

"Well, yes, ma'am, when you put it that way."

"I never thought I'd see you take a bribe, Joe!" cried his wife.

"You know how that old lady is. For all her money and her title, she acts as if she's been a-sucking on lemons all day long. If I had all her gold an' jools I think I'd find something better to do than frown on everybody. She's not one to forgive even a little step out of the way, like havin' a quiet drink with a friend. She ain't understanding like you, Maggie."

"Well, that's so," Maggie conceded.

"We will bear no tales to Lady Ingram's ear," Mr. Rochester interposed. "It is this gentleman then, who was conversing with Mr. Barnett?"

"Oh yes, sir."

"And what did they talk about?"

"Honest, sir, I hardly heard a word of what they had to say. I was outside stowing the new barrels after a bit, and he was just leaving when I came back in."

"Did it raise no suspicions in your mind that he sealed your lips about his presence shortly before his companion was attacked?"

"Well, now, it did rather. But not too much, if you see what I mean, for I had his reason for it."

We all pondered this in silence for a few moments. I stood and went to the window and looked out on the stable yard behind the building. Then I turned back. "You spoke to Mr. Hardwick before he left, about the horse?"

"Yes, ma'am."

"And did you see him leave?"

"I did."

"On horseback?"

"No ma'am, he went away on foot."

"By himself?"

"He went with Mr. Barnett, ma'am."

"Did he?"

"At least I thought so. They walked off together."

"On their way to Ingram Park?"

"As far as I know."

I remained at the window a moment to contemplate the implications of what I had just heard. It was as I had thought: Mr. Hardwick had gone into the grove with Mr. Barnett. Were only the two of them present? And did Mr. Hardwick fire the fateful shot? And where had he gone to afterwards?

I sat down once more beside my husband. "Tell me, what became of the horses? Did Mr. Hardwick ride away after?"

"No, ma'am. Both gentlemen left their horses behind, but Mr. Hardwick paid for them to be taken away the day after."

"Where were they taken?"

"I don't know, ma'am. No one ever told me."

"Not to Ingram Park," Mr. Rochester said. "Had he no groom with him?"

"No, sir, he asked me for a reliable lad to lead them off."

"That wild horse of his? That made such a disturbance?"

"Oh, our lads are used to that sort of thing. Little Pete's been bred and born around horses. He knows just what to do with 'em."

"And can little Pete tell us where he brought the horses to?"

"I'll fetch him," Joe's wife announced, and she bustled out the back door. Little Pete was soon produced, his skinny frame and freckled face nearly obscured by the outsize cap that engulfed his ears. He was one of the twain who had been occupied by the trout stream and he still bore his fishing net in his hand. He spoke, however, with a knowing authority, particularly when promised a new sovereign.

"I took 'em quite a ways, sir, but it was a tidy bit he paid me, sir. The next day I had to go all the way to Millcote."

"Millcote! To the blacksmith's?"

"Blacksmith? No sir. I went right on beyond Millcote, right past Hay even."

"And just where did you leave the horses?"

"I brought 'em to Mr. Hardwick himself. He was there to meet me."

"But where?" I asked, with a dreadful foreboding in my heart.

"Well, I forget the name of the place, but everybody knows about it. It's that big gentleman's house that burned to the ground last year. And a creepy old place it is, ma'am. I wouldn't like to hang about it myself, but Mr. Hardwick was there all right."

"Do you mean Thornfield Hall?"

"That's the name of it, ma'am. The very same. You know about it, ma'am?"

"Yes," I said, in a voice scarcely to be heard. My face must have changed, for the woman of the house looked at me with concern. A great weight seemed to settle on my shoulders. "Yes, I know all about it."

We left the tavern behind and made our way along the smooth grass plat that would bring us back to Ingram Park. The sun shone merrily and a thrush warbled a melodious sound from the treetops, but I was heartened by neither. Thornfield Hall! Why should Mr. Hardwick be there? What business could he have among its burned posts and ravaged beams? A cloud of doubt darkened the way before me. My husband's hand crushed my own, and I felt that he, too, was consumed in the same worrisome fears that troubled me.

"Janet!" he cried, "that was remarkable."

"Remarkable indeed, sir. Who could have imagined such a thing? Mr. Hardwick at Thornfield! It is a dreadful thing to think of."

Mr. Rochester brought us both to a sudden halt. "Thornfield! It's you that's remarkable. Why, you wormed that fellow's secret right out of him! You did splendidly, Jane."

I smiled. "Do you really think so?" He kissed me and affirmed he was convinced of it. "But why would Mr. Hardwick want to be at Thornfield?"

"Oh there's no great difficulty about that, is there? Surely you no longer fear that house for all its sombre associations? A mere pile of brick dust and timber; it can do you no harm."

We resumed our walk into the woods. "But why should he be there at all?"

"Can you think of no solution? The place is uninhabited. The neighbours frightened off by tales of supernatural malevolence. He requires an easy spot for a stranger to locate, with clear roads to travel on. It was a mere stopping post, Janet. A place to meet and depart from where he might do so undetected. He wished to return to London unseen."

I considered this suggestion and felt it had merit. Still, the whole conference with the innkeeper was disconcerting. "If Hardwick left the tavern in company with Barnett, then the two of them would have been together in the grove."

"Yes, yes, of course. Rally your intellect, Jane. What conclusion do you draw from all this?"

"The snuff-box, the one I found was Hardwick's. When he found it was missing, he went to my room to make the switch while I was not there. Hardly anyone would be about in the west wing to see him do so."

"What then?"

"Then Mr. Hardwick may have shot Mr. Barnett. Indeed, he seems extremely curious about what passed between Mr. Barnett and myself. Perhaps he imagines Mr. Barnett's first words betrayed his employer. He is afraid I know that he is responsible, but why injure him in the first place?"

"Why indeed? There are myriads of possibilities. There may be some long-standing feud between them that we know nothing about. Or some secret that Mr. Barnett has threatened to expose. Or perhaps Barnett drew his weapon first, and Hardwick was only defending himself."

"But what for?" I tried to imagine the listless Mr. Barnett, disinclined even to protect his own life, drawing a weapon on anybody, but without much success. "And now they simply continue on, doing business with one another as if nothing happened? It seems absurd."

"Well then?"

"Well, suppose Mr. Hardwick left him. It seems he intended to do so in any case, having left his horse behind with instructions that it be taken away. Where did he go, or mean to go, do you suppose?"

"We don't know."

I shook my head. "I can make nothing of Mr. Hardwick. Captain Fitzjames was outside of the house at the time, but as we know suspicion was intentionally cast on him, it is unlikely he is actually at fault."

"We have only Barnett's word on that."

"True, but the captain knew very little of either party, so there cannot be much reason for him injuring Mr. Barnett. Unless it was an accident. Suppose the captain took a turn in the grove, and Mr. Barnett came upon him in the dark and accidentally frightened him—but no, he's hardly the sort to run away from an injured man and return to the house to play the flute in the drawing-room. We must leave the captain beyond suspicion for now." We were, by this time, coming near to that same grove that had raised so much speculation. "Of our party, that leaves Lord Ingram."

"What possible reason could he have for shooting Barnett?"

Here I was forced into silence. I knew a powerful motive for why Lord Ingram might wish to attack Mr. Barnett. I knew there was a peculiar intimacy between him and Sally. And based on Mrs. Harper's information, there was also an intimacy between Sally and Mr. Barnett. Jealous passion was an ugly motive to attribute to anybody, but if the past was a reliable guide, it would not be the first instance of jealousy inciting violence. Of this, I could say nothing to Mr. Rochester, for I had been asked to remain secret about Lord Ingram's connection with Sally.

I left the question unanswered, and he pursued his own conclusions. "We have three gentlemen, all presumably in the area and unaccounted for at the time, yet without reason for firing at him."

We were standing now under the shadow of the yew trees. I remembered the thrashing noise in the branches the last time we had come to investigate this spot. Could it have been Hardwick himself? Lurking about the scene of his crime to see who had found him out? Was it Lord Ingram, returned to the house in secret, hiding behind the trees to find out if he was betrayed?

"We have too many questions, Janet. We have a need for information, and it is you who must get it. Have you any ideas?"

I had, in fact, one or two ideas of my own to pursue, and I promised to act on them as soon as opportunity allowed. My husband safely bestowed in the care of his valet in the parlour, I went first to the region of the house frequented by the domestic staff. A bevy of servants were at work in and around the kitchen. I was glad to find Mrs. Harper on hand, counting the silver. I asked if I might have a private word with her. She looked surprised, but she stepped aside into a commodious storeroom, stone-flagged and chilly even in the summer heat. Except for casks of flour and barrels of apples, the room was empty.

"Mrs. Harper, be so kind as to cast your mind back to last Tuesday, the night that Mr. Barnett was found injured on the grounds."

"Yes, ma'am, I remember."

"Did you hear the gunshot that was fired?"

"I did indeed."

"After dinner that evening, Lord Ingram and Captain Fitzjames stepped outside for several minutes Do you know where they went to?"

"No, ma'am. You might ask Mr. Nichols, the butler you know. He might be able to tell you."

"Thank you."

She looked at me curiously but said nothing more. We were both moving towards the kitchen door when a new thought struck me.

"Do you remember what you suggested to me about Mr. Barnett and Sally?" She nodded but added nothing more. "Do you think their peculiar relationship is known to others in the house? Is anyone else aware of it?"

"I did tell Mr. Nichols—I mentioned it to him, ma'am. I was a bit upset, like, when I had to talk to her about it. I asked for his advice, seeing as how the head housekeeper was away. I wanted to be sure I was doing the right thing."

"Do you suppose he told Lord Ingram about it?"

"I don't see why he would, but then, I didn't ask him to promise secrecy or anything like that. He might have I suppose. What do you want to know for, ma'am?"

"Just something I was thinking about. And it may not matter at all."

I went away from this interview with little encouragement. After all, Lord Ingram probably had other ways of gaining information than through his butler. It seemed clear, however, that my next object was to find Mr. Nichols, but he was occupied in the service of the gentlemen in the billiard room. I thought next of approaching Lord Ingram himself. I could send a message through a servant perhaps, and that way secretly bring him to a private conference, but I shrank from the thought of accusations without anything more solid than a vague suspicion to justify my interference.

I could also ask Sally. If she were actually concerned in the business, she could surely tell me, but then, suppose the conflict had been kept from her? If I were to tell her my suspicions, she might pass them on to some other party, thereby ruining my chance of catching him out. Well then, what about Mr. Barnett? Maybe his disinclination for revealing the facts was due to a wish to protect Sally's reputation. Perhaps if he knew I was already in the secret, he would tell me all.

I went to his room; he was not there. I asked a passing servant and learned that he was on the east terrace. A few minutes more found me standing on the same, looking out over the decorous hedge to the lake below. Mr. Barnett was indeed there, a book in his hand and a cup of coffee on the little table before him. He took no benefit from the beverage however—the cup was full, but steaming no longer. The book was half-open and unexamined. He did not even seem aware of my presence. I accosted him in a low voice.

He looked up with a mild start. "Forgive me," he said, with a hesitant voice. "I was only reading."

"You are fond of poetry?" I asked, perceiving the name of the author on the spine.

"I don't know. I have never read this before. It was left out, in the library. I only thought— " he never completed the sentence, but closed the book and laid it on the table.

I took up the volume. "Scott is a favourite of mine," I said. "I believe I left it out myself. My own copy is packed away in a trunk at Ferndean Manor. I have outpaced my belongings." I smoothed the cover with my hand. "A good book is a grateful relief to an agitated mind, but not always so efficacious as a listening ear."

I looked from the cover to Mr. Barnett's face. He was staring at me with that curious expression I had noticed before.

"What is it?"

"I beg your pardon, Mrs. Rochester. The turn of your head, and the way you speak—they have a most uncanny resemblance to— "

"To whom?"

The sound of distant laughter rippled upon the sunlit air. The rest of our party had gone into the drawing-room, a little way along the front of the house. Its windows were open, and silvery refined voices mingled with the scent of jasmine and thyme. Yet a most pregnant silence reigned upon the east terrace.

At last he said, "No, I am wrong. You do not look so very much like her. Only I think of her so often—Mrs. Rochester, will you sit down a moment?" He got to his feet and brought a chair, his good arm bearing the weight of it.

I drew near and took a seat by him.

"You had a rather long walk with Mr. Hardwick yesterday, did you not?"

I agreed that I had. "I believe he suspects me of knowing something to his disadvantage, but I am bound by my promise to you. I told him nothing."

He nodded. "I have, maybe, put you to unnecessary trouble in asking you to keep a secret on my behalf." He gave me another long, searching glance. "It may even be unjustified, unwarranted—I will explain what I can—you always seem to appear when I am most in need of your assistance. I feel ashamed of taking advantage of your kindness, but if you are willing, you might do me a most essential service, in listening for a little while."

"I would gladly hear more of what occupies your thoughts."

"The fact is, Mrs. Rochester, that I have long kept certain facts of my past concealed. I have a father, you see, who has very strong opinions. He was born the son of a doctor, but through a combination of good business sense and a great deal of perseverance, he has risen in the world, and now owns a sizeable property in the North. I am expected to continue this happy sequence of prosperity. My father asserts that he has done all this for my sake, but he would most certainly cut me off from all chance of inheritance if he finds me unworthy of the responsibility."

He looked down at his feet and shook the change in his pockets while he gathered his thoughts. Then he commenced: "You have never been on the continent, Mrs. Rochester?"

"I have not."

"My father has built up considerable business connections in Belgium, most particularly in Villette. He sent me there when I was twenty years old to learn how to manage the business. I was a different creature then from what you see before you now. I was raised in an atmosphere in which commerce and wealth were the two almighty gods of our existence. My religious instruction was formal but uninspired. What I found in Villette—I burned, Mrs. Rochester, with a desire for a greater life—for something fervent, passionate, elevated—something transcendent—I suppose this does not make much sense to you?" He looked at me sceptically.

"I understand you very well, Mr. Barnett. Thoroughly, I assure you."

I had a sudden vision of myself in Mr. Barnett's eyes. I must appear a conventional, prosaic figure to him. A former governess, a schoolmarmish sort of creature, who has taken on the job of nursing a crippled husband in exchange for worldly gain. How little we know of our fellow beings!

He still looked unsure of what kind of mind he was communicating with, but he went on. "There was a community of people at that time, devoted to a teaching that was not quite orthodox—but they seemed to me to possess all the spiritual, generous, heart-whole devotion that was lacking in my youth. It was a fellowship ripe with hidden wisdom, promising a better path than that trod by our fathers. And after I met Celeste—that was not a very church-of-England marriage, but in our hearts, it was nonetheless sincere." He fixed his eyes on some distant unseen object. "I should have been brave, Mrs. Rochester. I should have married her, formally, at once. But it's easy to defer a hard task; easy to keep hoping a solution will turn up to extricate you from your difficulties; besides, it seemed unimportant at the time. I thought I had found a better way, but it seems that there are few ways to break rules with impunity.

"Celeste—she was rather like you. And yet different, too—I will not attempt to describe her, but our happiness in one another was complete, perfect, pure." he sighed. "It was business, of course, vile business, that called me back to England. My father knew nothing of how I had occupied myself in Belgium and lost no time in directing me to marry for money. I, in turn, considered myself bound already, and returned to Villette as often as I could. My income, both present and future, depended on my father's goodwill, and once our little girl was born—I could not risk disclosure, solely for the sake of providing for the ones I loved."

He went on in a dreary voice. "In the meantime, the fellowship in Villette that I loved had begun to dissolve. Our leader proved unworthy of his responsibility and his followers departed in a hurry. My dear ones were left without support, for Celeste had no family. A little over a year ago, I was laying plans to bring them both to England." His face darkened with the shadow of despair. The cheerful laughter of the drawing-room seemed a cheat to the words he formed so painfully. "At that time, I was negotiating some matters for my father in London. I was sharing rooms with Hardwick—he and I had actually met in Villette, although he never shared what he called my 'religious enthusiasm'. I remember, the day the letter reached me— " he said nothing for a long moment, and with a voice even more dismal, he said, "she was gone. Celeste, my wife, my wife to me, was gone. A fever had taken her."

"And what about the little girl?" I asked when he fell silent.

"I can't find her." The restrained sob in his voice cut my heart. "When I arrived, her lodgings were empty. The neighbours had left. All our friends were scattered to every corner of Europe; no one could help me. No one knew what had become of her. I looked as long as I could and stayed until every penny was spent—until my father cut off my income and promised to disinherit me completely if I did not return. I have complied, feeling I owed it to him out of filial duty, and to preserve some inheritance, if—if Claudette is ever found. But I could no longer engage in business. My father has given me leave for a time, and Hardwick offered me a position as a sort of agent of his. I have sometimes helped him in such matters before."

"Can nothing more be done? To recover your daughter?"

"Hardwick has many connections there. We are making what inquiries we can, but there is hardly anyone left that we have not already inquired of. I am very much afraid, afraid she is—I can say more."

He covered his face in his hands. I would have liked to take his hand, to comfort him in his misery, but it would not be quite right. I was Mrs. Rochester, not solitary Jane Eyre, free to comfort whom I would. Mr. Barnett must bear his pain alone. In time he stood up and paced the terrace, his head bowed, his hands folded behind his back.

"What was her name, Mr. Barnett? Her full name?"

"Claudette Marie d'Anville. Maria was my mother's name."

"And how old is she?"

"She would be nine in September."

In that instant, a plan made its first stirrings in my mind, but it required consideration, and I would say nothing to Mr. Barnett about it yet. It would be unfair, I thought, to give misplaced hope. My mind, however, was taken quickly from the hopeful prospects of the future to the more perplexing events of the present.

"You asked me to keep secret, then, for fear that your father might someday hear of your wife?"

"Yes. He is very strict himself. Such a connection would surely condemn me in his eyes."

"Mr. Hardwick evidently believes you confessed something else to me. What did he think you said?"

"Do not ask, Mrs. Rochester, I beg you. I can say nothing about that."

"But— "

"I have no one else to turn to—no one else who knows Villette is left to me. He is my last hope." Mr. Barnett looked at me then. His pacing had brought him under the shadow of the porch, and his black eyes gleamed beneath their dark lashes. "I need Hardwick, no matter what he has done. I cannot offend him; I cannot part from him. Can you understand?"

I bowed my head; I understood very little. After pacing a few more minutes, he seemed to recover some of his former placidity. He resumed his seat.

"Mr. Barnett, perhaps you can tell me this. Have you ever been to Thornfield Hall?"

He rose from his chair in a hurry. "Let secrets lie, Mrs. Rochester. There is nothing to be achieved by prying into the hidden things of this world. I have tried, and you see what I have gained by it." He turned on his heel and departed.

CHAPTER XIV

I rose from my seat on the east terrace, where I had been meditating in solitude on my interview with Mr. Barnett. Did I think now that he was a man not to be trusted? A man whose sanity was doubtful? I did not. I now understood, at least, some of what had made our previous conversations so perplexing.

The words that dwelt longest in my mind, however, were these: 'Whatever Hardwick has done.'

If Mr. Hardwick had fired a shot at him, here was a powerful motive to keep silent, to invent a story of a passing vagrant and behave as if he and Mr. Hardwick were still on good terms. But why would Mr. Hardwick fire on him? Mr. Hardwick had a firm hold on Mr. Barnett, did he not? He could be assured that Mr. Barnett would keep his secrets, at least so long as he continued his search for his child.

But suppose the child was found? What then? Could it be that Mr. Barnett's death would be most expedient to his employer? An icy foreboding crept into my veins; it nearly chilled my heart, in defiance of the heat. I resolved at once to do what could be done to find this unhappy girl: Claudette Marie d'Anville. Mr. Hardwick could not be trusted with the mission of finding her; his motives were compromised; I must find news of her. I would apply to Mr. Rochester. He had already told me that he had connections in Villette; perhaps he knew someone who moved in circles that Mr. Hardwick had no access to. If she was alive, I hoped she was not destined to become an orphan.

The voices in the drawing-room had withdrawn and a lark sang blithely somewhere in the park below. I turned from the sunlit scene and went through the door into the house. As I went in quest of Mr. Rochester, I remembered Adèle, an orphan herself, who had lived some time in France with neither father nor mother to care for her.

How had Mr. Rochester found her out? Surely he would know how a child was to be discovered.

The drawing-room was now empty, but for a servant clearing the glasses. She directed me to the front door. Our hosts and their guests had gone for a ramble in the gardens, with Mr. Rochester on the arm of the valet. I pursued them as far as the hall. They had only just passed down the steps, and the butler retained his place by the door as I crossed the long hallway. He made to open it once more as I approached.

"Thank you, but I am not going outside at present. I would like to speak to you, if I may."

He bowed. "Certainly, madam. I hope there is nothing amiss in our service to you?" Mr. Nichols stood politely in front of me. For the first time I noticed grey blended with his dark hair, most especially at his temples. His face was quick and intelligent but carefully veiled by correctness.

"No, not at all. I have no complaints. I only wish to ask you about last Tuesday. You heard the gunshot?"

"I believe so, madam."

"You aren't sure?"

"I was in the office, madam. I had received a letter from her ladyship about a matter regarding one of her tenants. An overdue mortgage I believe. I was retrieving the papers to put in the mail the following day. The office is in the middle of the house—the door was closed and there are no windows. I thought I heard something like a door slamming, but I was not certain."

"I see. And Lord Ingram? Do you know of his whereabouts at the time?"

His eyes narrowed. "His lordship? He was in the dining-room, was he not?"

"I understand he stepped out for a time, with Captain Fitzjames. He was out of the house when the shot was heard."

"Ah." He looked at me sceptically. "Mrs. Rochester, I have been employed in this house since his lordship was a boy, and I can assure you, he would be as likely to put a bullet hole in a man as he would be to grow wings and fly. Nothing is less probable."

"I should only be too happy to believe it."

He tipped his head to one side and studied my face. "Forgive me for saying so, but I don't think you do."

"I am not sure yet what to believe. I only know that friends whose welfare concerns me are now bound up in this unresolved matter. I am not persuaded that all parties are telling the truth, and it is the truth that I intend to find out."

An uneasy expression flitted across his features but he said no more.

"Mr. Nichols, I understand from Mrs. Harper that you are aware of a peculiar circumstance concerning one of your staff. Sally, I suspect, was seen coming from Mr. Barnett's room in the night?"

In a slow voice, he answered. "Sally? Have you got as far as that?"

"I'm afraid so."

He drew a deep breath, let it out as a long sigh, and his formal demeanour wore away, leaving behind an almost parental anxiety. "Yes, Mrs. Harper told me about that. I encouraged her to speak to Sally about it. I thought it might be a help, to know that she could not keep secrets forever."

"Tell me, does Lord Ingram know that she was visiting Mr. Barnett in the night?"

"I have certainly not informed him of it. Nor would I. I have been a long observer of events in this house, and few have distressed me more than his lordship's behaviour towards her. I confess, the situation has troubled me. To be fair, I know very little. I hope, I *hope*, I am wrong."

"So do I." A tinge of relief showed on his cheek. "Have you perceived anything peculiar, between his lordship and Mr. Barnett?"

"There is little to observe. He hardly speaks to the gentleman, although he directed us to give him every attention that might further his recovery."

Well, thought I, that does not tend one way or another, does it? No great culpability there, and yet a man privately racked by guilt for assaulting another may well make efforts to speed his recovery.

"Thank you, Mr. Nichols. I promise you, public accusation and scandal are the farthest from my aim at present. I desire it as little as you could wish. I only want to find out the truth."

"I hope the matter may be settled amicably on all sides."

I agreed with him and departed, but how, I wondered, are matters to be settled amicably when someone is willing to sacrifice a man's life? Previously, I would have been inclined to agree with the butler; Lord Ingram did not strike me as a bold, passionate, vindictive man. He was unlikely to resort to violence against his fellow man, but there was, I thought, a kind of weakness exhibited in the event. Why inflict a wound that does not kill, and then run away? There was a cowardice about it that I thought Lord Ingram capable of. I did not regard him as a bad man, but in a moment of panic, his reasoning powers distorted by jealous passion—at any rate, it seemed more likely than the captain, who was by habit and temperament accustomed to responsibility for the lives of others.

And as for Mr. Hardwick, he was in nowise lacking in boldness or vindictiveness, and perhaps had a motive for relieving himself of his agent. He seemed unlikely, however, to do an incomplete job of the business. Could he have been stopped by someone? Perhaps Ingram or Fitzjames had interrupted him and he fled?

This was all conjecture. I had no way of verifying anything. I could, however, seek out some servant acquainted with the events of last Tuesday. I betook myself to the kitchen. Neither Mrs. Harper nor Sally were there. The cook reigned supreme here and did not look inclined for conversation. Fortunately, I found a kitchen-maid sweeping the back steps. I addressed her.

"What is it, ma'am? Did you need something?" She was a frail, young thing, with wisps of mouse-brown hair escaping from her cap.

"Only a question, if you would be so kind."

She stopped sweeping but seemed at a loss for what to do with the broom. Her face blushed pink, and she took her lip in her teeth.

I smiled reassuringly. "You need not worry. You are in no trouble." I spoke in my most cheerful, engaging tone and her features composed themselves. "Were you working in the kitchen last Tuesday?"

"Yes, ma'am. You mean the day poor Mr. Barnett was shot? Oh yes, ma'am, I was working in the kitchen that day."

"Did you go into the dining-room after dinner?"

"I'm not sure I remember exactly."

"There was spilled wine that needed cleaning."

"Oh! Yes, ma'am, you're right. I was scrubbing the wine out of the carpet."

"Mr. Rochester was there, yes?"

"Yes, ma'am. He was very quiet like, just sitting with his hand on his glass."

"And Lord Ingram, was he in the room the whole time?"

"No, he went out for a bit. He and the captain. They went to talk to Thompson."

"Thompson? Who is that?"

"He's the gamekeeper, ma'am."

"Did you hear what they said to one another?"

"I think Thompson come to tell him about a fox they were chasing the day before. Or maybe it was a gun."

"A fox and a gun do not sound very much alike."

"Well, Thompson always calls a gun, 'her'. I can't think why, but I heard him say, 'I've found her at last, yer lordship,' and then he gave it to the master."

"Gave him what?"

"The gun."

"The gamekeeper gave him a gun?"

"Yes, ma'am. A long pistol."

"But what could he want it for? Why should Lord Ingram desire a gun after dinner?"

"I'm sure I don't know, ma'am. Oh! You don't suppose— " her voice turned quickly to a hoarse whisper. "You don't think it was him who did the shooting, do you? The master? I never thought of it, but he had the gun, just then!"

"I don't think anything yet. Let us consider this for a moment. You did not think anything about it at the time. There was nothing unusual in Thompson having a gun?"

"Thompson's usually got summat of the kind on him. He's fond of 'em."

"It did not strike you as strange at the time, that Lord Ingram should take it from him?"

"Oh no, he might've just been takin' a sight, like, or Thompson mighta' been repairing it."

"Did he give the weapon back?"

"I don't know. I had to go to the kitchen to help Cook with the petit fours and I didn't come back in until later, when everyone was gone."

I thanked my informant liberally and left her with a sovereign in her pocket and specific instructions not to speak of our conversation. It would be a great evil if my questions were to set all the staff gossiping about their employer. I also made a mental note to replenish my stock of change—my purse was pitifully small and there seemed to be a surprising need for sovereigns in this sort of inquiry.

I thought of going immediately to the gamekeeper, but surely, if he knew anything, he would either have spoken up already or was purposely concealing the truth. I knew also that I had been absent long enough. I had already heard the bell, summoning me to luncheon.

I met my husband in the coral room. "There you are, Janet. My fairy girl must be flesh and blood after all. She disappears on gossamer wings and returns to earth for good bread and beer." He drew me to him and touched my cheek with his lips. "Have you had a successful morning?"

"Perhaps. Only time will tell if it is to be of any use."

As soon as our repast was over and I could be alone with Mr. Rochester, I endeavoured to enlist him in this search for Mr. Barnett's little girl. He was less sanguine than myself about our chances of finding her.

"We will write, Jane. In fact, I believe I already know the person we should apply to. There is a gentleman who knows Belgium well and is always piqued by the opportunity to right other people's wrongs. Furthermore, he is acquainted with a professor there who may know where we should inquire. She may have been left at some institution or other, or else taken in by some private family that was unacquainted with the father's whereabouts. Don't mention the business to Barnett, however, for it's only a slim chance. The little girl may well have perished with her mother. It seems most likely, I'm afraid."

"But we will write?"

"This instant, if it pleases you. Take pen and ink, Janet, and address it to Mr. Hunsden."

"How long will it be before we hear from him?"

"It depends on the occasions of our informant. If he is not otherwise occupied, he will turn to the business with a will, but there's no telling what he has in hand at the moment."

The letter was written, and my hopes ran high as I gave it to the servant to be placed in the outgoing mail. I felt emboldened by my ability to act for some good in this matter, tangled and fettered as all other chances seemed to be.

Hope is a deceptive emotion, however. At times it gives us the strength to strive and endure against all odds; at others, it is but a weak support that melts away the moment one wishes for a prop to rely on. I received a swift reply to my letter. Mr. Hunsden was already departing for the continent and bore my note with him. As the days passed, however, I suspected the futility of my efforts. A matter of great import to me could not be of much concern to a stranger engaged on his own business matters. I dared not confide my plans to Mr. Barnett, for he grew more morose and dispirited every time I encountered him. Not long after this, he departed from Ingram Park for a week or so on some commission of Mr. Hardwick's.

I had at first imagined this to be my chance for making inquiries, but I had no further opportunities to question the staff of Ingram Park, for I soon found that the baroness had forbidden the servants to talk to me about any but every-day matters. That noble lady refused to speak to me at all.

Blanche Ingram returned to the indulgence of her dislike of me. What little passed between us by way of conversation was formal and sharp. Her sister Mary looked as if she would like to converse, but her courage failed and no audible remark passed between us. As for Lord Ingram, he could not but look at me with pain. I felt sure he avoided me.

Doubt stirred my mind, suggesting that I had done wrong to busy myself in the affairs of others. I had only produced hostility in our hosts and antipathy in Mr. Barnett. What use was all of my questioning? I began to think it best if I packed my trunk and persuaded Mr. Rochester to seek some other bourne of safety.

Dwelling much on thoughts of this nature one afternoon, I sought the garden as a solitary refuge. The sky was overcast, but a still and oppressive heat bore down upon me. I felt, at least, that I would be alone, which is what I desired. I reviewed all that Mr. Barnett had said to me. My mind went in pursuit of some addition to the puzzle, as my feet carried me deeper into the garden.

I pursued a gravel path that disclosed neatly arranged vistas at every turn, and I soon arrived at a view that encompassed the lake. A new thought struck me. If there was a weapon to dispose of, would not that prove a convenient depository? After the shot was fired, Mr. Barnett's interlocutor had perhaps run to the water, tossing away the reminder of his guilt. Any footmarks would doubtless be lost by now, but might not the weapon be found there?

Unless the gun was still in someone's possession, or merely hidden in the house. Perhaps it was, at this moment, secreted away among the family pistols installed at Ingram Park. A fresh wave of discouragement sent me walking once more, but I did not go far, for I soon heard a noise I had not expected. The snap of a branch sounded somewhere behind me. I paused, listened, and walked; then I stopped all it once and heard footfalls that seemed to cease only a step or two behind my own.

"Who is there?" I cried. There was no answer. I took a few tentative steps behind me, then, summoning my courage, stepped around the corner to look past a hedge. There was no one on the path. I felt foolish, imagining anyone near me. I continued on, wondering if my own perceptions were trustworthy. Suspicion, I knew, could breed itself, preying greedily on a mind already given over to speculation and fear.

And yet I found my pace increasing, my feet driven by a panic that my reasoning faculties failed to persuade away. I reached the house in record time. I gained the gallery and found, to my delight, that the butler was there with a tray, bearing a solitary letter.

"Mrs. Rochester! I was told you were out of the house. You were asking for a letter not long ago."

It was true. In my anxiety, I had asked Nichols to keep one eye on the mail, for fear that I might miss any news sent to me. It was, however, only a note from my cousin Mary. I was hot from my walk and seated myself in the cool gallery. I perused the letter but found nothing of great consequence within. I was about to rise when I discerned the sound of hurried footsteps upon the marble. I rose to my feet that I might see who it was.

"Mr. Barnett!" I cried. "I did not know you had returned."

"Good afternoon, Mrs. Rochester." He stopped and bowed. I perceived he was still dressed for riding. "I have only returned this moment."

"I am pleased to see you well."

He bowed again but said no more. He appeared agitated.

"Is anything the matter?"

"I did not sleep well. The previous evening, I— " He opened his mouth to speak, then hesitated. Some deep well of emotion had been touched before ever he entered the house, for he closed his lips, and to my surprise, a tear fled the corner of his eye and coursed down his cheek. "Forgive me." He wiped it away.

"You have had a hot ride, sir, and are tired. You must rest." I desired with all my heart to tell him I was waiting for news of his daughter; to buoy him with some unlooked-for hope. And yet, supposing the news ill? If he were already agitated, a false hope might strike a fateful blow to a grieving father's heart. I said nothing of my letter.

"Thank you, madam, I will." He continued his stride out of the gallery and disappeared. The grandfather clock boomed its hollow chime; the solemn tones echoed from all corners of the enormous room. I had walked longer than I thought and would be late for dinner. The envelope still in my hand, I hurried to my room to change my dress.

I expected Sally to be there to help with me; she did not appear, however. I found Mr. Rochester waiting for me in his own chamber. In my absence, the valet had helped him to dress for the evening. I hurried into my gown, doing the hooks myself with some additional difficulty, for I was dusty and damp with my walk, and departed with my husband. Diana met us on the stairs and repaired my dishevelled shawl for me.

"You look quite abandoned, Jane."

"I was walking overlong in the garden. And then I had no maid to help me dress."

"No maid? Where has Sally got to?"

"I don't know."

Dinner might have been a solemn and silent affair that evening, were it not for Mr. Hardwick. His spirits were high, and he kept up a garrulous stream of talk about horse racing and famous card parties in London. The raffish conversation did not suit the baroness, but she only pursed her lips and frowned. I wondered if he had taken too much wine earlier—or had he received some report from Mr. Barnett? Had his affairs altered? Had some news come for him?

The ladies retired to the drawing-room, but with energy for little more than waving a fan. Mr. Barnett did not appear at all, and I did not like to ask Mr. Hardwick about his return, for I dreaded laying myself open to any more scandal or false accusation. The heat had moved into the house and lay all about us. There was no singing that night. A grey pall, foreboding rain, stretched across the sky, whilst a ragged and watery sunset closed the day. The inmates of Ingram Park retired early.

I dressed for bed in a dismal mood and approached the window. All was dark and sombre under the close canopy of a starless night. My heart was oppressed by a gloomy sense of waiting, and my eye wandered over my chamber as if to seek the answer to my many questions. I noted once more the trunk standing in the corner. I held my candle aloft to examine it once more. There was a glimmer of light reflected from the hinges as the flame moved. I knelt beside it and reached for the clasp. I could see now that it had been recently oiled, and I was not surprised to find that the lid moved easily under my hand.

Inside was a great nest of linen. This, I supposed, was some part of the wedding trousseau belonging to the first wife of Lord Ingram's father. The cloth was yellowed with age and scented with camphor, but very fine nonetheless. There did not seem to be any item of significant value, mostly monogrammed handkerchiefs and tea towels. Well, a fitting reward to idle curiosity, I thought. What else might I expect to find?

But for caution's sake, I pressed my hand down to the bottom—and came in contact with something hard, knobby and cool. With greater eagerness, I pushed aside the folds of fabric and withdrew it, the sole object, it seemed, possessed of hard and distinctive lines.

I brought it forth—and felt as if I had pulled a viper from a basket! I suppressed an impulse to toss it away from me, as one might rid oneself of a serpent in one's palm. I held in my hand the barrel of a pistol. I knew little of firearms, but I perceived that the barrel seemed quite long, and the metal shone from recent polishing. It glimmered in the candlelight. I hastily wrapped it in one of the squares of linen and went to Mr. Rochester's room.

"There you are, Jane. I was wondering what happened to you."

"Oh, Edward." I explained the discovery I had made.

He ran his fingers carefully over the weapon, searching out each groove and line. "A curiously long barrel."

A strange and wary certainty come upon me. If this was the same weapon Lord Ingram had possessed at the time of the shooting—was it not hid in a safe and clever place? Surely it would be taken for some old and forgotten piece, forsaken years ago, just as the trunk had been ignored, but it would take a member of the household to know of this trunk. Or, dread thought—I had seen Blanche Ingram in the west wing before, when I was verifiably out of it. She would know about the trunk. She might well have disposed of the guilty person's weapon. Would she do so for her brother? Or for her Intended? Why not? And why not? Were they all in league together?

My mind went round and round in a futile whirl. I sat down heavily in the chair by the fire and leaned back, momentarily defeated by the conclusion taking shape before me. Mr. Hardwick had purposely led his agent up the path. Lord Ingram and the captain had met with the gamekeeper, almost as if by appointment, and taken a pistol from him. Mr. Hardwick slipped away, to disappear in the night, while Lord Ingram sought his jealous revenge, and the captain, wittingly or no, kept watch while he made his attempt. Or perhaps it was the captain who prevented the fatal shot, thus preserving Barnett's life until I discovered him. And the weapon? Miss Blanche Ingram, arriving from London, conveniently hid the weapon. Could it be possible? Could they all be involved in the crime? Could Lord Ingram truly possess the passionate impulse that would drive a man to such an act?

Mr. Rochester's hand seized mine. "You are trembling, Jane. What is the matter?"

"Mr. Rochester, do you remember, not long ago, I asked if you had always found Lord Ingram to be a truthful man?"

A frown crossed his forehead. "Well, Jane, what of it?"

"Will you answer that question now?"

Mr. Rochester sighed. "I've known Ingram all his life. He is not, and never has been, a man of profound intelligence, or penetration, but he has always had a generosity that I valued in him. Consequently, I have never told this story to anyone.

"Shortly before the passing of his father, he spent a season alone in London, and there fell into the clutches of a set of card sharps. I was on my way to the continent, to drown my unhappy spirit in whatever panacea the world could offer me, but a friend informed me that Ingram might be in some trouble. I went round to see him and taxed him with my concerns. He flatly denied his difficulties. I came a second time and he denied it once more. Only on the third repetition did he at last confess himself deep in debt and unable to extricate himself.

"I had a word with the discreditable vultures preying upon him and lent him enough capital to put them off until repayment could be arranged. As his father died shortly after and he inherited his full income, he was able to rid himself of his debts and the scoundrels he had taken up with. And, I think, he became a little wiser. As you can see, he has not always been as honest as he might, but of course he was younger then, and rather embarrassed by the whole business. Why do you ask?"

"I believe Lord Ingram may be in a far greater difficulty now. I am sure, Mr. Rochester, you will keep this secret safe as well."

I poured out the story of Lord Ingram's accidental confession regarding his meetings with Sally, his possible motive of a jealous rival in Mr. Barnett, and finally, the conceivable history I had constructed of the long-barrelled pistol. Mr. Rochester looked extremely grave.

"It is not a pretty tale, is it, Jane?"

"No, sir."

"Still, it is not proven. Many another speculation might suit the same circumstances. I should particularly like to know more about Mr. Hardwick. There are too many unknowns about what he has been doing. The hour is late now and your fingers," he said, taking my hand in his and kissing it. "are growing cold. We will see what we can do on the morrow. Come to my bed, Jane. I want you by my side."

Before retiring, I took the pistol and returned it to the trunk. I looked out my window once more, at a night deepening into an inky darkness. Then I went to my pillow to be wrapped close in my husband's embrace, but little rest did I find there. I slept fitfully, sometimes woken by a blast of wind that made the windows tremble, and again by strange dreams of hurried flights and dreadful panic.

I dreamt at last of Thornfield. It was not the fine mansion I had once known, but the tumbled wreck, scorched and dilapidated, of recent memory, where I now walked. The same uneasy pall of cloud obscured the sun, and the rookery at the edge of the field swarmed like a hive. Birds cried out and spun round in the wind.

I was looking for someone, always looking, and at last I found him—Mr. Barnett, huddled against the remaining wall, standing with his head bent and his hands clenched—the very image of mute and struggling misery. I took his hand and we tried to depart, but the ruinous house had grown; at every turn lay yet another tumbled pile of blasted brick or beam. We could find no way out.

The sound of gunfire pierced my ears, a resounding crack that echoed above my head. I gripped his arm and we ran, our feet flying over the rabbit-shorn grass, but there was nowhere to hide. Again and again, we were forced back against that high and windowless wall, and the fearful sound of bullets smashing into stone clutched at my heart.

Then all at once we broke free of the walls and fled the house into the overgrown garden. Down the path we raced, only to find the lightning struck chestnut tree, and the moment we arrived there, another crack shook the air, and the tree burst into flame—

I sat up in bed. A sudden flash of lightning, followed by a long-enduring rumble, low and distant, told me whence these dream bullets came from. The clock struck the hour. It was not yet midnight, and my nightgown was damp with sweat. I rose from my couch—Mr. Rochester turned and some half-formed word dropped from his lips, but his good eye remained sealed. I sought a drink of water from the pitcher. I fain would have opened the window, but I knew I would wake him if I did so. The wind shook the window panes, but the storm was far distant. The Moon's light gleamed through her shading veil of cloud. I turned away from the window. I thought perhaps to pace the opposite side of the room and find relief in movement, ere I returned to bed.

As I did so, I caught a passing glow of light beneath the bedroom door. Someone was crossing the hall. Sally! It must be she, come again to contemplate in solitude, but what business could she have there on such a night?

"Jane." Mr. Rochester's voice was barely audible. I dropped to his side at the edge of the bed.

"Someone is in the hall," I whispered in a low voice. "I am going to see who it is."

He seized my hand for a moment, although he said nothing more. I left him then, with a disquieting sensation, as if I was leaving him far behind.

Once in the hall, a grim darkness covered my vision; it was an almost tangible blackness. Thunder pealed long and low in the distance. I ran my hand along the wall to help me on my way, and soon found the spiral stairs. The music room was just below, and a line of light under the door suggested the portal I sought. I crossed the hall, gripped the handle and stepped inside.

It was not Sally.

CHAPTER XV

A woman stood by the window with her back to me. Tall, and crowned with raven hair wound into a simple braid, she wore a sober black dress. Her ghostly visage looked at me from the windowpane, as from a mirror.

"Blanche!"

She turned with a start when she saw me. "Why are *you* here?"

"I saw a light pass my door. I came to see what it was."

Her lip now curled into a sneer. "I have heard much of your curiosity, Mrs. Rochester. You have been prying into a great many things since your arrival here. As it happens, I have been charged to inform you that my mother does not take a favourable view of you questioning our servants."

"It is not my intention to trouble your household."

"Then your intentions are at variance with your behaviour. You have no business here tonight. You had best return to bed."

"Miss Ingram— " I paused. She is taller than I; her face and posture easily assume the habit of superiority. I would not be put off by her, however. "My movements are not yours to command. I shall not leave until I have asked you some questions and obtained satisfactory answers."

She tossed her head with affected scorn, but I would give her no further opportunity to snub me. I walked into the room and stood well within the circle of candlelight.

"You were here, in this room, when I was out of the house."

She hesitated to speak. The window behind her flashed; her outline showed black for one luminous lightning strike—then we returned to dim candlelight.

"You know that I saw you. Why were you here?"

"I was meeting my brother. He wished to speak to me in private."

"Did you see him?"

"Yes."

"And what course of action did you agree on?"

She said nothing.

"I am certain your brother is in difficulties. In this I did not pry—it is pure accident that I know about Lord Ingram and Sally."

"Sally!" Blanche took a step towards me. The candle in her hand wavered, shaking the shadows around us. "It is not Sally!" she spat out the words with vehemence. "She is only the messenger. It is your precious Mr. Barnett. If only we could be rid of him!"

"But what has he done?"

"He is blackmailing Theodore."

"On account of what? His relationship with Sally?"

"Sally is nothing I tell you. Sally is only his tool. It's Barnett who— "

"But what else could your brother have to hide? What must be concealed at such a cost?"

Blanche shook her head and muttered something I did not catch.

"What is it? What has he done?"

"Tedo?" And then, most peculiarly, she laughed. "Tedo has done nothing. Nothing but try to protect—I'll not tell you. It's no business of yours."

"Very well. Barnett and Sally are old acquaintances, are they not? But blackmail—and Sally! She seems so innocent. I can hardly imagine her scheming against anyone."

"Innocent enough to be the tool of the insidious Barnett— "

"How do you know that Barnett is the source of this?"

"Sally told Theodore so."

"Miss Ingram— "

"What is it? Why have you gone so pale? You know something."

"Were you here to meet your brother now?"

"Yes. And he is late. You must— "

"He's supposed to meet you here?"

"Yes!"

"We must find him. We must go immediately."

"But what—?"

"He wants Barnett stopped, does he not? I suspect Captain Fitzjames tried to restrain him before—but there is no captain now, and he has made sure you are out of the way before he strikes. We must find him at once."

Her dark eyes flashed with instant comprehension. As if we were one, we fled the room and mounted the stairs. I wished to stop at Mr. Rochester's door, but the fear that gripped my heart spurred on my rushing feet. I could think of nothing but whatever portion of the house Lord Ingram inhabited. The dark halls of Ingram Park wavered fitfully in the candlelight. With swift but silent tread, I followed Blanche, her stately form gliding before me like a dark sail let loose among the shadows. We did not speak until we descended the stairs to the gallery and our steps sounded on the marble tiles.

She halted suddenly, and when she turned around I saw that her skin showed ghastly pale against her dark coiffure. "I thought we would meet him in the passage. I cannot believe— " She looked at me full in the face, and for the first time in all my acquaintance with her, I saw there something new, something different from her bold, haughty nature. Terror was steadily mounting in her eyes. I feared she might lose her resolve, and with it all sense of purpose or plan; but our mission was too grave for hesitancy.

"We must look for Mr. Barnett first. If Lord Ingram is plotting his revenge, that is the first place to go. He is in the east wing. Captain Fitzjames took me there once."

"No, we cannot go alone," was Blanche's plea. "What good will it be? How could we stop him, if he is—if he is plotting some dreadful deed? We must get help."

"Ring the bell then. Rouse the servants."

"No! There must be no talk, no scandal. I will go to Mr. Hard-wick. He will know what to do. Wait here."

"Leave me a light!" I cried, feeling an answering rush of panic as she fled the room. She stopped near the door and hurriedly lit a can-dle held by a decorative candelabra on the table. I was now alone in the gallery.

I crossed the room and wrested the candle from its holder. When I held it aloft, enormous shadows leapt away from me as I turned to look about me. Yes, I was quite alone, and I dare not seek aid; there was no time. With hurried step, I turned towards that region of the house inhabited by Mr. Barnett. I climbed the stairs, crossed the hall, and approached the door. I knocked but received no reply. I quelled a momentary dread within and opened the door.

The darkness at least did not reign in this quiet chamber. A lantern burned steadily from the tall chest of drawers. I looked at the bed; it was empty, still neatly made. No one had sought repose there this night. I entered with slow and cautious movements. The room appeared empty, but I was not the only visitor, I thought. The draw-ers stood open, and stockings, shirts, and other articles dangled hap-lessly from them. The cupboard door swung open freely also and pa-pers were strewn about the floor. I paused where a letter lay at my feet, torn from its envelope with obvious haste.

I felt a presence behind me, a split second of awareness, and then a gloved hand passed over my mouth and took a firm grip. My heart, beating rapidly but a moment before, came to a sudden halt in my chest, like a bird attempting to rise from the woodland floor, its flight suddenly arrested by the bullet in its breast. I gasped but could make no sound.

A voice spoke in my ear. "Do not cry out, I beg you. It is only me." The painful grip of his hand released my arm. I backed away and turned to face my interlocutor. He appeared unnaturally tall in the dim light, his shirt collar open and his cheeks grey. It was Lord Ingram. "Do not cry out," he said again, extending empty hands in my direction.

"Where is Mr. Barnett?" My voice was ragged but audible.

"He is not here. I do not know where he is. I came to find him—I wished to speak to him—but he is not here."

"You have done him no harm?"

"I have not! I swear it. Do you think I would harm him? That I would injure him? Never! I would risk exposure first."

I remembered the fears that had driven me to this chamber in such haste; they evaporated under the pale expression on Lord Ingram's face. Awkward, diffident, and yet dignified; he bore the look I imagined a martyr might have worn, before facing his inquisition.

"Do you believe me?"

I answered cautiously. "Yes, I think so. I couldn't be sure. We do not always know even ourselves when we are driven by strange and unknown impulses."

"Well said, Mrs. Rochester. You see what I have been at." He could scarcely have missed my eye upon the ravaged cupboard as I spoke. "I had not thought I was capable of even so base a business as this: digging through another man's belongings. But I could not resist the opportunity so freely given me. You will not understand all this. I do not ask you to understand, or even to alter your judgment of me— "

"I understand, at least in part, I think. I am come just now from your sister. I found her in the music room."

"Ah! Where is she now? Still there?"

"No. She has gone to find Mr. Hardwick. We were frightened that you might be plotting something deliberate. If you are really being blackmailed by Barnett— " I did not finish. His lordship sighed.

"You know the truth then."

He took the chair from beside the wall and placed it in the middle of the room. "Sit down, Mrs. Rochester, and I will tell you the tale. It does not make a long story, but likely it will explain a number of things that seem strange to you."

I sat down as I was bid; Lord Ingram took my candle and fitted it into an empty holder on the table, but he did not commence speaking. He gathered up the papers so carelessly tossed around the room and began to stack them neatly to replace them in the cupboard. Then he leaned against the tall bedpost, folded his arms, and set his face in a most resolute expression.

"It is as well, perhaps, that you should know. Shortly after Hardwick and Blanche announced their engagement, Hardwick came to my mother and said that he knew of a lady's maid in need of a place—some acquaintance or other had recommended her—and he thought she might be suitable for Blanche. He requested that she be placed here until his own establishment required her. The marriage, you see, needed to be put off for several months, due to some business concerns of Hardwick." Another sigh. "I thought little of this at the time. A few months ago, however, Blanche and my mother resolved to spend the season in London, as Hardwick was there also. I remained here on account of a note, an anonymous note, requesting I stay behind, and intimating some knowledge about Hardwick that I did not possess. I did so, and was told to be in the grove on a particular night. I was confronted by Sally. It seems she had long been acquainted with both Hardwick and Barnett. The latter have been long-time associates it seems."

"I am aware of it."

"Ah. Well, she confronted me with a disconcerting tale of Mr. Hardwick's life on the continent. While living in Belgium, he had pursued a pattern of life both corrupt and shaming. Loose living, and poor repayment of debts I could understand, but it seemed he had become an accomplished blackmailer while there and had incurred the wrath of a great many wealthy personages with secrets to keep. I attempted to verify this through other sources and uncovered enough to convince me that there was a real danger to be avoided.

"Hardwick, it appeared, had meant to leave this life behind, but Sally and Barnett did not. I knew my sister was pretty well in love with Hardwick, and I thought that if he were resolved on leaving such habits behind, it was best to keep all secret. Barnett's demands became much more outrageous than I expected, however. And Sally, as his collector, became a dreaded figure to me.

"I first sought the help of Captain Fitzjames. I had known him at school, and also by reputation. I knew his ship had been paid off and I felt he would be just the principled outsider I needed to advise me."

"But you did not like his advice."

"He said I should risk exposure and go to the authorities. I could not bear to do this to my sister, or to my mother. Barnett continued to demand payment—I was forced to go on meeting Sally in the grove. You met me once, returning from a meeting with her."

"Yes. And did you meet Sally in the music room as well?"

"No. That was a private place to Blanche and I when we were young. No one else has used it in ages."

Would that it were so! I thought. Others have used it for their own purposes.

"It is why I invited you and Rochester to come. I had another motive you see," he smiled rather diffidently, "to my concern for your well-being. I thought if there were more witnesses about the house they would withdraw and relent for a time; but no, it has only made things worse. Barnett's demands grow with each new application. I had to know where I stood; hence the busy searching you find me engaged in. If he had committed anything to paper, my situation would indeed be desperate."

"And have you found anything?"

A pause. "No, I have not."

I rose from my seat and took up my candle. I drew near to Lord Ingram and caught his eye. He turned to move away, but I arrested his motion by laying a hand upon his arm. The dilation of his eye was visible in the glare of my candle.

"Mr. Barnett is in Hardwick's power." I forced myself to speak in a slow and measured voice. "He would do nothing to harm his employer. He is relying upon Hardwick's aid in a deeply personal matter. It would be wholly irrational for him to be the author of this blackmailing scheme. Tell me, has he ever spoken to you of this directly? Has Mr. Barnett told you of this business himself?"

A barely perceptible shake of his head told me that my guess was right. Mr. Barnett's name was only a blind, a feint, to confuse his lordship. My mind's eye presented me with a clear vision, accurate in every detail, of Sally alone in the music room and suddenly surprised by my arrival. Caught unawares, that one glimpse had proved the right one. Wary, angry, guarded, vindictive: these were her true qualities.

"It is Sally then. It is she who has been taking your money and threatening exposure."

"I have sometimes wondered— "

"Where is Mr. Barnett now?"

"I don't know."

I remembered the housekeeper's insinuation that Barnett and Sally were secretly meeting, but surely it was for some other purpose than she imagined. Bereft of his dearly loved wife, it appeared highly unlikely to me that he would carry on such an affair with the housemaid. But might he not, instead, give her a word of warning? If he knew all of her history, he might know of this too. And if so, he could well be the only one who could expose her for what she was.

"Someone wishes harm to him, someone in this house. If it is not you, and it is not likely to be Hardwick, then—it is Sally that we need to find."

Lord Ingram put his head in his hands and groaned. All his limbs conveyed antipathy, sorrow, defeat. "My soul is worn to a shadow. I have not the strength to do any more tonight. I have already polluted my honour to such a degree— "

"You have done your best to protect your family, but you must do more. I tell you, Mr. Barnett is in danger. If we do not act now, there may be far worse to regret."

With a weary look and another shake of his head, Lord Ingram rose. I feared he would refuse me. I tried to conjure up fresh arguments, but I could but compare him to Mr. Rochester, all will, power, decision; how I wished it was he by my side! But I had to make use of what tools I could. I was determined to locate Mr. Barnett as soon as possible, and every passing minute only increased my fear of some fresh harm befalling him. I watched with relief as Lord Ingram took the lantern in his hand. The light illumined a face both determined and grim. Before the night was older, we departed.

In a moment. Lord Ingram had rung the bell and summoned forth every inhabitant of Ingram Park. There were soon servants scattered along the halls to peer into darkened chambers and call out to empty passageways for the elusive Mr. Barnett. For my part, I knew what I must do. Searching parlours and pantries must be done, but not by me. I did not know the house as its rightful tenants did. I had my own mission to pursue.

Fortunately, I had retained my candle; it aided me in my haste as I approached the gallery. Here I found a glittering constellation of lights, a dozen candles and lanterns tracing their orbits in and out of passageways. A chorus of voices called out Mr. Barnett's name by turns, their echoes strangely exaggerated in the darkness. I perceived the voice of the dowager demanding of her butler that he find Miss Ingram—that Blanche be brought to her once.

"I thought we were to look for Mr. Barnett, your ladyship?"

"I don't give a fiddlestick for Barnett. I want my daughter."

"But Mrs. Rochester said— "

"And who, pray tell, is mistress of Ingram Park tonight?" She declaimed, with most impressive authority. "Is it I, or is it not? I will not have such outrages perpetrated in my own house. If you find that Mrs. Rochester, I insist she be kept under lock and key— "

I would not give her the opportunity. I slipped away towards the west wing, unmarked as I passed, no doubt taken once more for a servant passing. I wondered myself who retained mastery of this house in the dead and drear night? At length, I arrived at the door that led onto the gravelly path among the shrubbery and wended its solitary way down to the solemn stream, the grim and crowded yew trees, the moss-lined path. I had met with Mr. Barnett there before; it could not be overlooked now.

I opened the door and was greeted by a wind that darted up the hillside. It bore on its wings the heady scent of rain. The dismal cloud-wrack had completed its circuit and was sending its marshals back upon us. A flash of lightning dazzled my eyes; an ominous growl of thunder made the air tremble with foreboding.

My candle was immediately snuffed out, but above me, a great rent was torn in the clouds, and a yellowish, mournful half-moon cast its light upon me. It was enough. I leapt like a deer upon the path, as heedless as prudence allowed, and followed its winding course. I thanked providence that my feet were sure and carried me without incident to the dense shadow under the trees.

Here the stream murmured swift and mirthless in its bed. I called out Mr. Barnett's name—my voice fell blank and empty beneath the crowded branches. I was soon at the well-remembered spot where our first meeting had been, but there was no light, no voice, no sign of visitation; not even a ghost of memory seemed to abide here. The trees groaned and writhed in the strength of the wind, their stiff unyielding branches shuddering around me.

The wind died; I stopped; I listened. A twig broke in the gloom. I spun around, but another flash of lightning obscured my night vision. I called out but heard no answer.

"Who is there?" My voice quavered as I spoke. "Show yourself!"

No voice replied to my own. Beyond a dense thicket that had grown up round the bole of a massive yew, I thought I saw a movement, a shadow that could be no branch or leaf. I willed my feet forward, but they would not obey me. I realized, with startling dismay, that I had told no one where I was going; that I had brought no means of defence. I had thought of nothing but finding Mr. Barnett, but who, in all this ominous darkness, had found me?

A spear of lightning sprang from the clouds, surrounding us in vivid brightness, and revealing the outline of a being whose form I could not identify. I tried to discern its face, but in the sudden glare, it dodged and ducked its head, as if it had thought itself unseen until the blinding shaft illumined us. I half-expected Mr. Barnett, but this, I knew, was not he. This was not his shape, nor his height; I feared it was Sally, bent on some premeditated evil; but this was no woman's figure. I did not recognise it, and yet there was something familiar about that outline, something that summoned a fear I had kept confined; prompted it to spring, to rise, to seize control of my limbs and will. I turned and ran, my feet fleeing eagerly between root and stone. A hair's breadth behind me came my pursuer, his boots pounding the earth.

"Wait, Mrs. Rochester, wait!" His hand took hold of my arm; his voice, too, I knew at once, and I realised why terror had been wrought to its highest pitch.

"Captain!" I cried and came to a stop. Of all people to find in this desolate spot, Captain Fitzjames was the last I expected to meet with. There was something so fundamentally wrong in the sight of him at such an hour and in such a place. I recoiled as if in pain from his hand. "What are you doing here?"

"That is just what I was going to ask of you. What is happening in the house? Why are there so many lights?"

"But you—you— " I gasped, my breath forsaking me.

"Yes, I said that I left Ingram Park, but I could not bring myself to leave completely. You remember how uneasy I was on the day that I left. I knew something was not right in that house. But I could do no more good there. I have been staying at the Three Brothers."

"What! In secret? No one knew you were there?"

"I made every effort at concealment, but I could not remain aloof for long. I was in the garden this afternoon; I believe you heard me at one time and I nearly spoke to you, but my dread in revealing too many sordid details held me back. Tell me now, what is happening? I was nearly turning mad with guessing. If you had not come, I might have forced an entry. What is happening inside?"

"We cannot find Mr. Barnett. Or Sally. They are not in their rooms. They are not anywhere."

"Good God! It has come at last. And Lord Ingram?"

"He is searching too."

"You don't know what fears have wracked me, with nothing to do but wait and watch as much as I could. So they are searching the house? What brought you out here?"

"I found him here, once before."

"Yes. I understand, but he is not here. I've occupied this spot all evening. Come, we will search the grounds together. You ought not to be alone. We will inspect the gardens, or the stables." He turned his head and waved his arm towards the distant stable, but as he did so, his expression altered. His eyes opened wide and I heard the sharp intake of his breath.

At this distance from the house, it was possible to see just beyond it, to where the stables lay, cloaked in night. And there, where there ought not to be, was a light. It was not a dim lantern winking; no pale ghostly glow; it was the hostile burning of firelight.

"We must run," he said. And we did.

The fear of an unknown is of a certain quality; it compels unreasoning fancies to life. As my feet ran over the stony path, across the manicured lawn, and to the garden gate, pursuing me with furious haste was a new fear: the terror of what was known. My midnight search was ended; I was no longer troubled by uncertainty, attempting to second guess what weapon would be drawn; my course was set. This did not frighten me, or if it did, it was the fear that strengthens one for the fight, that drives one to a desperate courage. I ran with purpose and without hesitation. But a creeping dread, that murmured in my ear even as my breathing echoed in my brain, certified that this was all inevitable. The fiery walls, the hopeless entreaty, the horrible end of all searchings and wanderings; from the moment I perceived the light of the flames, I knew that this was like my dream.

Captain Fitzjames vaulted over the gate in one enormous spring; a feat that I could in no way imitate. My hand searched hastily for the latch, flung it open and pushed the door from me. The path, I knew, would lead me in the right direction, if I turned at the centre. I heard the captain's boots beating hard upon the ground. I could no longer perceive his form. I ran on.

I reached the edge of the stable yard in time to see the captain dashing through the back door. While smoke poured upward from its frame, the portal was brightly lit from within, although the fire must have been some way further along the building. A great cloud of smoke rose above, lit from underneath by a wretched orange light. The desperate scream of a horse in fear, an utterly terrifying sound, echoed in the night. I turned my steps to the house in time to see Lord Ingram stumbling from the kitchen door. He was calling out, and the household servants poured into the yard behind him. Buckets were fetched, a line was formed, and above all, a great clatter of thunder sounded, while the first drops of rain hit the anguished earth.

Someone, Old Bill, I thought, was pulling on the lead of a horse, dragging the panicking creature forward. A dog barked unceasingly. I watched as a tall form stumbled from the stable, familiar to me now as a dim outline. I rushed forward.

"Captain! Did you find them? Did you find Mr. Barnett?"

He coughed hard and said, "No, no one. But the back stall is locked. Axes!" He cried and lunged forward. "We need axes!"

I looked up at the building. The rain had begun but without any great earnestness. The downpour was not yet commenced, only a cruel wind that howled uphill and beat the flames into greater fury. 'No time,' a voice cried within me. There was no time for axes.

A quick search revealed what I hoped to find: a trough of water outside the building. I still had my shawl around me. I plunged it in the water and threw it around my neck, then over my mouth. Alone and unnoticed, I ran through the door by which the captain had entered.

A wall of heat halted my steps; the very air wavered and shook. It was like my dream, uncannily like. And as if in the grip of a dream, I went forward into the unendurable heat. The blaze had been lit in one of the stalls, I thought, on the far side of the building. I remembered the key hanging from the nearest wall. It hung there still, a decrepit object that had doubtless been long ignored: a spare key that was never needed. I seized the ring and ran to the door of the stall. By the time I had forced the key into place, the metal latch was growing hot to the touch, but when I applied enough force, it turned.

At first glance the stall was empty. There was no flame here, and no one within that I could see. It was lit only by the glare cast behind me. Was this just a fool's errand? I called out and hurried forward into the gloom, only to trip over a long, soft form. It responded with a convulsion and a muffled cry. It was lying on its side, its head wrapped in a sack and its frame clad in black. It was a woman. I tugged hard at the sack—to my surprise it came away easily—and was astonished to find myself staring into the terrified eyes of Blanche Ingram.

A heavy handkerchief was tied tightly over her mouth. I grappled with the knots until I was able to loosen it enough to remove. She coughed, shuddered, moaned, and turned over.

"Someone is going to pay heaven and hell for what has been done to— " her words were halted by a renewed fit of coughing. Smoke was pouring greedily into the darkened room. She went on anathematizing whoever had done this to her, but I spared no more time for her epithets. I turned to her feet, but these were bound also with strong cords. I had begun to cough myself; I pulled my shawl more firmly over my mouth. My efforts to untie her were of no use, however. She had struggled hard against her bonds and the knots were wrung tight.

"There is a knife," cried Blanche, finally coming to grips with her predicament.

"Where?"

"I don't know. It was tossed somewhere. Over there?"

She threw her chin up in an effort to point. I searched the ground on hands and knees, shoving aside the dirty straw; my hand gripped the blade at last. The sharp point nicked my skin, but I paid no heed.

"Be still, or I shall cut you." I severed the cords with alacrity.

Her hands were still tied, but I pulled with what strength I had and brought her to her feet. Now a dreadful roar assailed my ears.

"It has caught the hayloft."

"We shall die!"

A threatening red glow tinted the outer room. I threw my arm round my companion's waist, and half-helped and half-compelled her toward the door. A stumbling rush brought us swiftly down the passage and into the outer darkness, where we collapsed on the ground in a wretched tangle. Raindrops fell lightly against my cheek, and an enormous sound, like the indraught of a giant, bellowed in my ears. A crash, a rush, a tremendous crackling and crumbling filled the air.

I got to my feet as well as I could. Blanche lay in the mud, her expression of horrified spite flickering in the scarlet light. The roof had fallen into the blaze, and the naked beams of the stable burned like a portent against the midnight sky. I wanted to call out, for my night blinded eyes could just discern a crowd standing in the stable yard, backing away from the disastrous, flaming wreck. My voice, however, was no longer at my command. Neither did I feel altogether safe where we were. Great scraps of burning matter were lifting and spinning in the waves of heat. Like enormous sparks, they were falling around us. The wind had changed and soon my vision was obscured by clouds of grey smoke.

"Get up," I cried, in a choked voice, and endeavoured to drag my companion to her feet. Without her arms to balance her, she leaned heavily against me, and we made our clumsy way in the direction I thought the house lay. I was disoriented, however, by the smoke and the heat and the exertions of the evening. The hard dirt of the yard beneath my feet gave way to tall grass, and the twigs of trees brushed my face. I stopped and looked around in an attempt to find a clear route, but we were enveloped in a dense cloud that stung my eyes. It was easy to perceive the inferno we had escaped from; it glowed redly behind us; but all other paths remained obscure. I tried once more to cry out, but my voice was lost in the universal roar. Blanche collapsed, dragging me half down. I could not leave her; where, indeed, would I go to?

"Help," I cried but in feeble tones. My lungs laboured to take in breath.

I, too, felt my knees give way.

Another rending crash; the stable was beyond hope now; the building had collapsed upon itself. I struggled to rise, but no answering strength in my limbs came forth to meet my will. We were trapped here, I thought. To what end, I knew not. I implored my Maker for aid—I could do no more than wait and hope.

I did not wait long, however, for a flaw in the wind tore a gap in the screen of smoke. A familiar form appeared over me. I regarded it not with fear, as before, but with a kind of awe that he had found us out.

My voice was hoarse and my throat raw; fortunately there was no need of words. The captain lifted Blanche bodily from the ground and held her in his arms. I pulled myself to my feet and leaned on his arm, and together, we made our way back to Ingram Park. A curious procession we must have looked if any could have seen it.

Mr. Rochester met us in the yard. The captain called out to him and the moment he reached me, his arms were round me; he held me fast—a brief moment sacrificed to the unutterable joy of reunion, and he then demanded, "Are you hurt, Jane?"

From the first moment we were visible, a cluster of servants flocked to us. Lord Ingram himself took possession of his sister and carried her in his arms, but I would not part from Mr. Rochester. The firm support of his arm was the only conveyance I would have to carry me to safety.

It was not so long after that the rain descended, a steady downpour that dampened but did not quench the flames entirely. I had no wish to watch the angry fire subside. We entered the house and came to rest at last in the servants' dining-room, close at hand.

A pitcher of water was provided to clean our faces and assuage our thirst, and soon the labours of the night no longer lay so heavy on me. My desire for news was greater than my desire for rest. Diana appeared, in her nightgown, shawl, and incongruously, a bonnet. The captain came also, looking weary. And yet I deduced he was holding my cousin's hand beneath the table. There was no occasion for mirth, however, in our present company.

"Where is Mr. Barnett? And Sally?" I asked.

Lord Ingram answered my inquiry. "They departed from the house before we were even aware of the fire—perhaps they were scared off by our search for Mr. Barnett. Three horses are missing. Old Bill spotted them as they left."

"When?"

"Not long before the fire was seen."

"Three horses? Was one of them riderless?"

"Alas, no!" Mr. Rochester said. "Mr. Hardwick has gone with them."

"We must summon the magistrate at once," said Lord Ingram. "Eshton must be told as soon as possible, but I hardly know who to send. I dare not expose any of them without knowing more of the matter, yet questions are bound to arise."

"Let me go," Captain Fitzjames said. "It would give me the utmost satisfaction to be at work at the present moment, and I will endeavour to explain the situation in the best possible light. I have had more than enough of watching and waiting."

Lord Ingram thanked him in strong terms, and with a final glance at Diana, he departed.

"I would not be idle either. Tell me what I can do," Diana said, looking from myself to Lord Ingram.

"I must return to my mother's room. She is extremely distraught. But it is Blanche that most troubles me. I am afraid she breathed in a great deal of smoke—she is far from well."

"I will stay with her, and help relieve the servants with their task. I am accustomed to nursing."

"That would put my mind at rest, Miss Rivers."

Diana departed on her mission of mercy, while our host rose to his feet. "If only we knew where they were going," he said, and nearly shrugged his shoulders to dismiss the thought.

To that question, however, I already knew the answer. "I have no doubt they are on their way to Thornfield."

"Thornfield! They are beyond our reach then," Lord Ingram said, and sank back in his chair with relief. "There is nothing more we can do."

"It is not so very far. They have anticipated us by an hour, but there may still be time to reach them."

Lord Ingram stared at me as if stunned. "You cannot be serious. It is the middle of the night—and after all you have been through! No, it is absurd. You must go to bed at once."

I said that I would go, the moment I found a conveyance to carry me thither.

"Rochester," his lordship said, "You must not let her go. You ought to order her to bed."

I looked at my husband. Would he exercise his authority to command my movements? Could I disobey his word, loving him as I did, valuing our union above all earthly things? A struggle ensued in my breast, agitating me almost to pain. I bowed my head and waited for him to speak.

"Order her to bed? *Order* her?" Mr. Rochester declared. "Like a naughty child who has broken her curfew? When she conceives it her duty to leave at once? I'd sooner command the wind to stay in your pocket. Where Jane feels herself right, there is no use in my interference. But whither Jane goest, there I shall go also."

My hand strayed from my side and seized his arm in a grateful grip. How I valued my husband at that moment! How I cherished his impulsive, independent nature, for by it he could comprehend my own.

"But this is madness!" Lord Ingram declared. "Neither one of you is fit to confront them. How the devil will you get there? Who will drive you?"

"I will, sir, beggin' your pardon."

We all turned at once to see a servant in the doorway, bent and grizzled, smoke-stained and clenching his cap in his hand. It was Old Bill, our friend from the stable. "I've already got the coach in the yard, lent by the Three Brothers. If they didn't go, I'd a-gone myself, just the same. Why, all my horses might've been killed! There ain't no punishment too hard for the likes a' them."

CHAPTER XVI

The carriage ran over hill and bridge, the horses panting in their traces, in such haste that we might have been driven on by a final stormy blast. The equipage was a sturdy one, well oiled and ready for its run, but no haste could be too great for me. Swift as our pace was, I felt the miles pass too slowly. I dreaded lest Sally, or Hardwick, or Barnett himself, might succumb to the temptation of violence.

Mr. Rochester covered my hand with his. "Jane, who do you suppose left Blanche Ingram bound up in that burning barn?"

"It could only be Sally. I'm sure Mr. Barnett did not. If he had not the energy to denounce his attacker, he would hardly wreak havoc on Miss Ingram."

"What do you say to Hardwick then? Might he not be in league with Sally?"

"You think they are running away together?" I asked.

"I consider it very likely."

"Setting the barn on fire seems a remarkably vindictive way to run off, and unnecessary too. Miss Ingram could hardly stop them."

"She may have offered to betray some other crime she was aware of."

"Perhaps— "

"What is it, Jane? What are you thinking of?"

"Forgive me the thought, Edward, but I was thinking of something I heard once—about Thornfield Hall."

"Yes?"

"I was told that the fire broke out first in my former bedroom."

"That's so, Jane. Jealousy is a powerful motive, and a dangerous one. Let us grant, then, that some close intimacy existed, not between Sally and Barnett, but between Sally and Hardwick. The case becomes rather more clear, does it not?"

"Sally was meeting a man in the music room at night. I heard a laugh; a low voice that must have been a man, but afterward, she never accounted for it. I thought later that it was Lord Ingram, but it must have been Hardwick."

"And Barnett would not give the identity of his attacker in the grove, because it would reveal Sally and Hardwick's infamous conduct— "

"And risk offending Hardwick, his present hope of finding his daughter."

Was this, then, the dangerous piece of knowledge Barnett possessed? That Hardwick and Sally were conducting an illicit affair at Ingram Park? It was no great wonder, then, that Sally was terribly jealous of Blanche. She would have felt her own influence over Hardwick slipping away—

"But then why shoot Barnett in the first place?" I asked.

"Perhaps Barnett threatened to tell all. Hardwick obviously prizes his engagement with Blanche. It is a step up for him, you know, and he seems to have conceived a sort of affection for her."

"Then why go on meeting with Sally? Why run such a risk?"

"When one becomes habituated to vice, Janet, it calls for an uncommon character to break from it at once, to cut out, root and branch, the deceitful desire one has submitted to so often in the past. They have snared themselves in a trap of their own making. They suffer the fate of all conspirators; treachery has undone them."

"And yet they must be saved if they can be. All three of them, if it can be done."

"Assuredly, Jane, but do not hope too much. You cannot save a man who would not save himself."

Our conveyance crested a rise in the land and Millcote spread out below us, its silent chimneys now invisible in the darkness. I considered my husband's words, wise and practicable as they appeared. I could not accept them.

"But I mean to try and do that very thing. Mr. Barnett is operating under a delusion. He believes his search for his daughter is futile. I intend to persuade him otherwise. It is the only way to deliver him from the folly of his companions."

The carriage slowed its harried pace as we entered the environs of the sleeping town. One could not dash headlong at this late hour over the cobbles, but our journey's end was approaching.

"Jane— " Mr. Rochester chafed my hand with his. "I shouldn't let you do this. We ought to have called on the authorities. Or at least waited until the captain could come."

"No—no, I do not think so."

"Why, what unassailable argument do you possess? What good will you do amongst them?"

"I am not certain. I only know that I must make the attempt."

"You are ever a faithful soul, Jane. God bless you, my love, for your sympathetic spirit—it has ever drawn me irrevocably to you. I cannot deny it now, though it sunders my heart—hold me now, Jane, before you go."

The rain vanished, blown far into the west, to be replaced by a dank, cool air that settled over the landscape. As we descended Hay Lane, I saw a haze brewing over the streams that coursed alongside it. A night mist was rising; it enveloped the approach to Thornfield as if in a thick blanket.

"You shall go with that fellow on the box. I shall be of no use here, but Janet," and Mr. Rochester gripped me once more. "You will take great care of yourself? Every earthly hope I have goes with you. How can I spare you, my darling, even in such a cause as this?" His grasp grew painfully tight.

"I shall be very careful, Edward."

"I will not remind you of where your great care has led you thus far." His grip relaxed, but only a little. "The truth is, I trust your sagacity and wit, even in such a dark and dismal place as this. I believe you are equal to it, but God knows I do not part with you willingly!"

I soothed him as well as I could, for I knew in my own breast the tremulous fear of all that might befall my beloved husband if I were torn from him. On our instructions, Old Bill slowed as he near the wreckage of the house. It was difficult to discern, for we could see almost nothing. Fog lay over Thornfield, dim and colourless, obscuring even the gaunt outlines of the ruined house.

I gave a final hand clasp to Mr. Rochester and descended from the carriage. The coachman tied the horses and followed me. There was no sound; our own footsteps on the pavement were scarcely to be heard. When we left it behind, there was nothing. No light was visible, no sound of movement or life assailed our ears. All was blank and silent. Had I led us on a useless errand? Was there anyone in this everlasting murk? This hazardous ruin?

But no, at last my straining ear perceived a noise. It was the low sound of a horse, snorting in the mist. I altered my direction to pursue it. When I held aloft my lantern, it illumined no more than the pale walls of fog that surrounded us. The grass was tall; our progress slow; my feet were already dripping and my dress increasingly damp and heavy.

Old Bill followed at my elbow. "Mrs. Rochester," he whispered. I turned to face him. He had evinced sure confidence when driving his horses, but now I saw that matters were changed. His eyes shifted from one direction to another in anxious inquiry. "You ever hear tell of—of ghosts, about this place?" I shook my head at him. "I heard stories, ma'am, that'd make your blood run cold."

"There are dangers enough," said I, "without our imagining more."

"I ain't imagining, ma'am. I've had it on good authority. Why, that boy at the Three Brothers, he saw— "

"Never mind what he saw," I whispered urgently. "I must listen. Be quiet!"

I heard at last what I took to be the stamp of a hoof upon the turf. Somewhere near here was a long avenue of beeches. That must be where the horses, at least, had come to. I toiled over the dimly lit ground. Old Bill remained behind me, but his steps lagged, and I amended my pace so as not to lose him altogether.

The sight of a horse's long face loomed into view, causing both I and my companion to fall back. A careful search discovered all three animals tethered to a low hanging tree branch, but the riders who had brought them were nowhere to be seen.

"Ma'am!" gasped my companion. His face paled and his eyes widened in a glassy stare. One gnarled finger pointed over my shoulder. I turned and faced the shrouded avenue. I could see nothing more than the shifting curtain of earth-bound clouds; but now a flash of white, the hem of a garment moved in the mist, a stark line amongst all these amorphous forms. A scream split the night and Old Bill fled the scene, his heavy footfalls clumping through the dank grass. An expostulation died on my lips, for a sudden blow smote the back of my head. I was engulfed in darkness, swift, silent and complete.

Mr. Rochester heard the scream, a high-pitched cry that cleaved the solemn night. He bolted from the carriage on an impulse, his hands finding the door and his feet the step on the command of unconscious memory. He stopped, however, when he reached the ground, one hand still holding fast to the carriage, the last sure and solid object in the blank void around him.

The scene of the fire had not been so bad as this. There he had been able to see somewhat in the strong light. Forms and outlines were perceptible, and that harsh orange glow had at least told him where not to tread. He could make out nothing in this darkness, but there were other senses that might aid him. He already knew without being told that he was in a dense fog, for the dank and clammy air on his skin told him as much. Well, they must all be blind then.

That scream had not belonged to Jane; of that he was certain, but the note of terror had been unmistakable. Someone was plainly in trouble, but from what? To remain in idleness while such a scream as that rent the night—no! It was unendurable. He called her name, twice, thrice—he listened but heard nothing. He called again but there was only the desperation in his own voice to answer him. He groped his way to the front of the carriage and felt on the seat for the whip he guessed was lying there. It was a sort of crop, a thin rod with a cord at the end that swung freely. After he wrapped the loose cord around his wrist, he held tight to the shaft and let the handle drop. He found it long enough to feel the ground before him and prevent his feet from encountering any truly disastrous obstacles.

At all costs, he must avoid the broken remains of the hall. He believed the fallen house to be unsafe—he disliked all he had heard of it—the lofty wall, alone and unsupported, the leaning, blackened rafters. He thought of it often; indeed, it haunted his dreams. He remembered well his final departure from this house. Thornfield had possessed an almost preternatural power, a malevolent force that had seemed to draw him back within its grasp—

As he walked, he tapped the ground before him with the horsewhip, in case of some lump of stone or entangling pit that would cause him to fall. He pushed through a fence of overgrown hedge, fearful that he was simply wandering into empty fields, but his boot kicked up a spray of gravel. He had found the garden path. He thought he had heard that cry from somewhere in this direction.

With his bad arm, he kept up an occasional contact with the hedge, and in this way pressed deeper into the garden.

The cold dew lathed his brow; the fog was increasing. The hedge gave way to the trunks of cherry trees. He stopped to listen; he waited long. At last he heard voices, speaking low, the words indistinguishable. He followed his ears now and successfully cut through the overgrown flower beds.

All at once they seemed on top of him. The fog played odd tricks with sound, for he could hear them speaking plainly, yet no one cried out at the sight of him. He guessed himself unseen. He could not hear Jane's voice but knew not what he had stumbled upon.

"It's no good." This was Barnett's voice he was sure. "I told you from the start it would be so."

"Oh buck up, Barnett, you know you never can see the good in anything." Hardwick, he thought. "The debts are nearly paid, anyway."

"You ought to be marrying a woman of fortune. Someone in a cleft stick like yours can't afford to be romantic."

"Romantic! I thought you wrote the book on that subject. Come now, Barnett, what is life but a gamble? You can't win if you never play. Besides, it's her own family's money. It ought to be mine if she's marrying me, not her doleful brother's."

"I suppose blackmail is one way to get a dowry. A pity the family couldn't pay a more worthy man to marry their daughter."

"Oh! I'm quite good enough for her. I'll be a model husband, you know, once I have some capital in my pocket." A pause; a peculiar sound; if he didn't know any better, he was tempted to say it was the sound of coins clinking against one another. "What's got into you, tonight?" Hardwick asked. "Why all this moralizing?"

"I'm only telling you what I've always believed. I thought I ought to say something to provoke your conscience, if indeed you have one."

"That's rather harsh. You know I'm capable of a little good feeling. I'm not absolute bereft of the organ. I've looked after you, haven't I?"

"You needn't look after me anymore." There was a new note in Barnett's voice that made Mr. Rochester hold his breath so that he might not miss a word.

"And what is that supposed to mean?" Hardwick asked, and the curious clinking noise stopped.

"It's over, Hardwick. I'm through."

"What are you talking about, man? You aren't—Good God, where did you get that?"

"Goodbye, Hardwick. My life is not worth the bullet, but I cannot bear to live any longer."

Mr. Hardwick cried out, "Take that gun away from your head—this minute."

Somewhere in this wasteland was his wife, alone, and possibly in the grips of something or someone truly terrifying. And here, the man his wife had risked herself to save was nearly brought to his end not by any criminal hand, but by his own despair. God help me, Mr. Rochester cried within, what choice was right? What choice!

"You won't talk me over anymore. I'm through listening to you."

"Just give it here, Barnett—"

"This is a night of ill-tidings. Can not you see it in the air? Feel it in the atmosphere? It is a good night to die."

"Curse it, the man is going mad! You are not yourself."

"I tell you I am!" he cried, and his voice cracked. "I have done your dirty work for nothing! Claudette is dead and I must go to her!"

"You do not know that," Mr. Rochester said, his voice emphatic and clear.

"Who is there?"

"Your daughter may still be alive."

"What? Who are you?"

"Rochester. Who else? It is my property after all, and I believe you are trespassing."

"Rochester? Where are you?"

"I can hardly come to you. You will have to find me."

Footfalls ensued, and the two men approached. Hardwick found him first and muttered a curse under his breath. "What the devil are you doing here? Of all places?"

"It's my wife's doing. She guessed where you would be."

"But why—?"

"Yes, why?" demanded Mr. Rochester. "Why are *you* here?"

"I knew it would end like this," Mr. Barnett moaned. "I knew it. It's all up, Hardwick."

"Oh, do stop being such a shrew. You're worse than a wife."

"Don't be a fool! You can't lie your way out of this one."

"I could give it a good try if you would just hold your tongue!"

"Oh, I can't face it! The whole pathetic story's got to come out now. Damn it all!" Then the swift click of the hammer coming into place sounded on the dead and empty air.

"Barnett, don't— " Hardwick began.

"She'll know what a weak creature I am; she'll hate me."

"Who? Your daughter?"

"My daughter; I dreamt of her last night, all laid out, with her hair in braids, and flowers wilting at her feet." Judging from the stumbling thump, he fell to his knees. "My daughter is dead, and Mrs. Rochester will never respect me again. Rochester, I know you were jealous of me, and I never meant it to be so. It is just that your wife is the only person alive who cares if I live or die. I can't face it now, that she should know what I am."

"She wanted to save you."

"And she has wrought my destruction instead. My cup is full I tell you! My suffering is greater than I can bear. I will not have another drop added. I cannot bear it!"

"We wrote to a friend on the continent. He may have news of your daughter— "

"No! No! I saw her! She is dead! I will stand no more false hopes, no more last chances."

"You must not give way. You must not give up hope."

"You bid me to hope? To *hope*? You! You, with your wife to love! Your happiness is only condemnation to me. You cannot understand what I suffer!"

"Cannot understand?" Mr. Rochester cried, his swift ire rising at last. "Cannot understand? You know the story of my misfortunes, Barnett, I have no doubt. A dozen wagging tongues have repeated it to you, have they not?"

"Yes, I know of it."

"You think I cannot understand losing the only happiness I ever possessed? The only woman that I ever cared a farthing for? She was cut off from me in an instant; I was condemned to perpetual worry, and waiting, and weariness of spirit. My God, man, you think I didn't pass every day thinking of the brace of pistols in my room? I walked this very path, hour after hour, in agonies of remorse and pain. Blindness is nothing in comparison. Are you listening to me, Barnett?"

A long moment, and at last, a hushed, "Yes."

"I have known despair. Her harsh and steely gaze was my companion for nearly a year—like a suppurating wound, incapable of healing. I drank the bitter cup to its dregs and finally believed as you do—that she was dead."

"At least," Barnett choked out the words. He was certainly weeping now. "You didn't know it to be your fault."

"Even that dagger pierced my soul. It was not only my fault; it was my *falsehood*. I had lied to her, in the most grievous way. It drove her away—" His voice was in danger of breaking down—he must pull himself together. "It was my own folly, my own falsity, that drove her from my very door. I could rely on myself no more. Trust in God, Barnett. Let providence be your guide. Your own light is but a shadow—you cannot see the path marked out before you. Despair if you must, but stay the hand that would steal the sun before it dawns."

A series of loud sobs racked the sullen air. A sudden movement followed, a struggle, and then Hardwick's relieved voice said, "Oh, thank God. I've got the gun."

Barnett was weeping openly, the sound muffled somewhat—Rochester guessed that his hands covered his face.

Hardwick was quite near now. "We must get him away from here. He must be put to bed. Take this blasted thing— " He pressed the revolver into Mr. Rochester's hand. "I will try to get him back to the horses. How did you come here?"

"The coachman brought us."

"Brought who?"

"Jane and myself."

"Mrs. Rochester is here?" Barnett said, in a voice mingled with both pain and alarm.

"She went looking for you, and now I can't find her."

"But Sally is here. Mrs. Rochester is in terrible danger." Barnett was on his feet now. "Hardwick, come on, we must find them."

"But you're— "

"You know how that woman hates her! You know what she is capable of!"

"That was an accident, Barnett. She didn't mean to shoot you."

"The deuce she didn't."

"She's done worse than that," Rochester said. "Sally met with Blanche Ingram after you departed. She left her tied up and locked in the stable."

"What?" Hardwick cried.

"And set the stable on fire."

Both men cried out at this. "And is she—?" Hardwick stopped, unable to finish the phrase.

"Blanche has been saved, Hardwick, through no work of yours. If you don't believe me, come and smell my coat. It still reeks of smoke. Keep your secrets if you like; I don't care about them. Only help me find my wife!"

CHAPTER XVII

It was Adèle I heard calling to me. Her childish tones rang out over the sunlit grass. The air was balmy and mild; a curious languor had stolen over me. We would go to the orchard this afternoon, I thought, and see if the cherry trees had begun to bloom. I was fortunate to be at Thornfield Hall.

"Miss Eyre, wake up. They will give us nothing to eat if you do not hurry."

"Yes, you told me in your letter," I replied sleepily, without getting up. "You went hungry all day once when your teacher made you stay late."

Was this Thornfield?

"Come, Miss Eyre, come. Why are you still lying there in the sun? You are like a—what do you call him? A lily-eater."

"A lotus-eater," I corrected, and sat up. My body felt surprisingly well, light and free. Adèle was capering over the grass, dancing in perfect time with the music that poured from a vivid blue sky.

"Do come, Miss Eyre, come and dance with me." A voice in the back of my mind assured me that I ought to check this impetuous behaviour in my pupil. But the music was so moving that as soon as I rose to my feet, I began to dance with her, our bodies swinging round, and birds in great clusters swirling round us. I have hardly danced a step in my life, yet this buoyant movement came naturally to me, and we both of us laughed with delight.

"Now we must fly!" Adèle exclaimed: she clapped her hands, darted into the air and flew away. I cried out to her to wait, but she was already gone.

The music altered; the tune was strange and curiously sad. I wondered that I had been laughing a moment before, for now I felt near to tears. I heard a voice I knew, but couldn't place. I must answer, I thought, though no words came to my lips, nor did I know what I ought to say. I felt only a dull urgency. I must answer—

I sat up, or tried to. Something was restraining me. I thought I had opened my eyes, but it was of little use, for I could see nothing at all. Perhaps I had not really opened them and must try again. My head still hurt—a deep and abiding ache. I tried to move, to find a little relief, but this only brought on a fresh pang that shot through my brain. The grassy fields were gone; the birds were no more. There was a dim greyness about me that brought to mind something primitive and remote. The words came unbidden to my mind.

'The spirit of the Lord hovered over the face of the deep.'

In what deep waters had I been cast? I was like a log tossed into a pool of water, rising slowly and reluctantly to the surface. My limbs were sensitive enough, for I felt keenly the damp air chilling my skin and the tight cords tied around my wrists, but my mind was still sluggish and dull. I called out, but my voice was weakened by the pain in my head. My effort was not ineffectual however, for a light approached, a steady tread was nearing, and its source bore a lantern, a brilliant beam among these shifting shades.

"Are you awake, Mrs. Rochester?"

"Sally?"

She smiled. It was not the sort of smile one wishes to see when awaking in a strange place with an unfortunate injury.

"Oh, yes, Sally is here to help you, ain't she? Always ready to come when she's called." A spiteful laugh followed as she hooked the lantern on a neighbouring tree branch. She was dressed in a pale grey riding habit, with her hair in a long braid that coiled down her shoulder. I recognised the ghostly white form I had glimpsed earlier in the mist. She stood over me with her gloved hands planted on her hips. I had thought the fog as thick as ever, but in the light of the lantern, dim edges of cloud could be seen, drifting gently above us.

Then I remembered.

"Blanche Ingram!" I cried and tried to sit up, but my hands were tightly bound behind my back. Nor could I move much, even if I had wanted to. My vision swam before me with every sudden movement. I groaned and lay still.

"Tell me about Miss Ingram. Do you know where she is?"

"She is not dead. Your plot did not succeed."

Sally grimaced, and a veil of hardness descended over her eyes. The soft, reluctant tones of the naive servant had dropped away. She spoke in a fast, hard voice. "That's a pity, but it's no matter. I've got you now, don't I? I shall have to be content with that.

"I believe you preached contentment to me once. Thought you'd do me some good, didn't you? Give me a bit of your philosophy? Well, I've a philosophy of my own. I take what is mine, and God help the poor fool who stands in the way. I've played many roles, Mrs. Rochester," she drew out my name with angry, bitter venom. "I dazzled the London stage not so long ago. And perhaps I will again. Who knows? But never again will I play a lady's maid. Such a servile, miserable job! Yes, ma'am! No, ma'am! Right away, ma'am! I have had quite enough of it. I suppose you did too—I doubt a governess gets much better—and got out as best you could. I can't say that I think marrying a blind cripple is really a good way to go about gaining independence—seems like a poor showing if you ask me— "

"I was independent before I was married."

"Well, isn't that lucky for you! The rest of us must make shift for ourselves. You might have stuck to your task instead of busying yourself in my affairs. Stirring up Barnett, and Ingram, and the rest. I had it all well in hand."

"And Mr. Hardwick, did you have him in hand too?"

She struck me across the mouth, a fierce blow that stung long after she had planted it. "He was safe enough before you came."

"And after his marriage to Blanche?"

At this she laughed, a sound I had not expected. "Marriage? Marriage? He was never going to marry her! It was all a part of the plan. He would drink them dry of money to cover his debts, and then we were off. There was Paris, you see, and Italy. Only we needed the money."

"That's not what he told me." I spoke in a quiet voice. I could hardly do otherwise in my weakened state, but my words had their effect.

"What did he tell you?"

"He said he was marrying for love."

She hit me again. She cursed Blanche Ingram in a fluent spate of foul language. "He never loved her! He loved me—he has always loved me!"

"If you have not been wise before, you must learn to be wise now. A gentleman will marry for many reasons, but love may not be the first."

"You're one to talk, aren't you?"

"I'm sure he did love you or profess to, but he might also have deceived you, or, it may be, you have deceived yourself."

"You'll pay for that." She pulled a revolver from her cloak, the spit of the weapon I had found in the trunk. The metal felt cold against my temple.

I did not tremble; I hardly felt any fear; I was too dizzy, I think, my mind still labouring at a remove. "Is this why you shot Barnett? Did he try to tell you the truth? To prepare you for what would come?"

"Barnett and his foolish scruples! He tried to persuade Hardwick to tell them everything—to give me up! I had no choice but to silence him."

"You were in the tree, the night that he was in the grove. Just as you were when I went to look at that same spot the following day."

"You think yourself clever, don't you? Not that it's likely to do you much good now."

I heard the cock of the revolver near my ear, and felt a cold and heavy weight descend on me.

"Do not kill me. Please."

"It is your own fault, for minding my business instead of your own."

Struggled to rally my faculties. "Murder would make your escape from England more difficult. I have saved your victims twice now—I have spared you the trouble of a murder trial. I think you owe me thanks instead."

"Oh! We're going to play the fine lady, are we? All high and mighty now? No doubt you mind your book and bell and candle, don't you? Mind what the priest says now." She brought her face close to mine, her hand boring down on my shoulder, and hissed in my ear. "The mighty shall be brought low." She pressed the gun hard to my head. Her hand was shaking, and the weapon with it.

"Sally!" Hardwick's voice cut through the fog. My attacker sprang to her feet, her face flushed, her eyes glittering wildly in the lantern light. The gun vanished from my sight.

"Have you finished already?" She demanded.

"What's going on? What are you doing?"

"A stroke of luck, Peter. Mrs. Rochester turned up! Our difficulties are over, aren't they? No one else will trouble themselves with our business anymore."

I saw Mr. Hardwick glance down at me in my prone position, but I found his expression inscrutable. "What were you telling her just now?"

"Oh, it was only a little encouragement. I was quoting scripture as a matter of fact. I know a great deal of it."

"Yes, I know you do. Sally—I don't think tying up Mrs. Rochester will exactly suit the case. We ought to be more discreet."

"It isn't my fault she's blundering about Thornfield in the dead of night. I think she's out of her senses. It's for her own good."

"Well—she's not alone you know. Her husband's here."

She laughed scornfully. "*He* isn't likely to see much, is he?"

"No—but we'll have to be done for tonight. We must get back."

"We aren't going back. We've got plenty of money now. Enough to begin with anyway. And it's too dangerous to keep on with it. You said so yourself."

"Yes, well— "

"You must tell her," I said to him. My words were spoken mildly enough, but for a moment, his eyes locked with mine. A look of distress that he could not disguise marked his brow.

Sally went to his side. "You will never have to fawn over those noble fools again— " She put her arm around him; he slipped from her grasp.

"What did you do, Sal, at Ingram Park? What did you do to Blanche?"

"I didn't do a thing to her. No one saw me do a thing."

"No one *saw* you? But what *did* you do?"

"I—Peter—nothing, love, only I knew we weren't going back."

"Did you hurt her?"

"Mrs. Rochester says she's all right. It's all right now."

"Did you start this fire? She was nearly killed. The whole household could have been destroyed."

"It—it was an accident."

"Just like Barnett was an accident?"

In a steely voice, she answered, "It was time we ended things."

Hardwick passed his hand over his eyes. "You must face the truth, my dear. The money was for you."

"You always said so; that we might be together."

"That was a long time ago!" His voice had risen to a shout. He drew a deep breath before he went on in a measured strain. "I meant to establish you somewhere—without me."

I turned my head, cringing with pain as I did so, that I might see Sally's face. The colour disappeared from her visage; her features turned to marble; all but her lips, that shone like coral against her pale cheek.

Hardwick held up his hands. "I am engaged to be married."

"No!" The word broke from her as if it was the cry of a small animal cornered by its pursuer. The gun flashed from the folds of her dress. She pointed it at his chest with an anguished shout, but Hardwick dived for the barrel and a wretched struggle ensued. A spark of flame, a cloud of smoke, and they sank to the ground as one.

I swooned once more but came round at the sound of Mr. Barnett's voice.

"Mrs. Rochester! Are you all right?" He knelt at my side. "Thank God, she breathes. Hardwick— "

But Mr. Hardwick did not answer. He only went on murmuring in a low voice. With an effort, I succeeded in turning my head and encompassing Mr. Hardwick in my field of vision. He was sitting on the ground, while his tears ran unchecked. He held Sally's body cradled in his arms and her lifeless eye stared blankly at the dim and starless night.

"Poor Sal, Sally, my dear—Oh God, I never meant for this to happen— "

The remainder of that night was a confused recollection of dreaming and waking. At times, I was chasing Adèle through the fields; at others I was being carried on a stretcher. Doctor Carter was present I think, for I recall him saying that Ingram Park had not supplied the healthy atmosphere he had expected for me, but this might all have been yet another dream.

The first solid impression I retain is a quiet bedroom at The Rochester Arms. Mr. Rochester was seated by my side, his good hand settled on his knee, the other tucked away in his coat. His eyes were closed, as if in slumber.

"Mr. Rochester?"

I soon found that he was awake. My hand was seized in a familiar grasp. He slid from his chair and onto his knees, pressed my fingers to his lips, and held my palm to his cheek.

"You are awake, Jane? You are my living darling still?"

His raw, visible distress wrought upon my heart. "Dearest Edward, I am here. You need have no fear for me." The slightest motion caused a paroxysm of suffering at the back of my head, but I said nothing about that.

"You are absolutely certain? You have been prone in this bed a night and a day. I could neither see you nor hear your voice."

"Do not be so sorrowful. I am all right."

He rose to his feet, laid down on the bed beside me and twined me in his arms. I closed my eyes, for the light oppressed them, and touched gingerly the bandage covering much of my head. By feel alone, I passed my fingers over his shuttered eyes; I laid my hand in his. It was the best I could do. At length, Mr. Rochester spoke.

"It appears, Janet my love, that I am to loose my heart from the confines of my breast, and keep it on a long lead. I am not to have my treasure kept safe at home in cotton wool."

"Shall I promise you never to commit so outrageous an act again?"

"I would be too frightened of the result. A wild creature, once liberated, ought not to be confined to its cage. I shall exact no promises from you, but this one. That you will act with that strong sense of principle that has always directed you. And that you will always come back to me."

I passed a quiet day, held close in my husband's embrace. He could scarcely bring himself to leave me when the doctor or the servant attended to my needs. I have never forgotten those long hours, reader, encircled by his arms, as if he feared that I would never more be contained within them. I had long trusted in the enduring power of Mr. Rochester's love, but never had it been so thoroughly impressed upon me.

The following night I slept in a deep slough of unconsciousness. I believe I hardly moved. My rest was restorative, and my curiosity woke with my limbs and brain. I inquired of Mr. Rochester the extent of my injuries.

"Carter said you had quite a concussion, but he expected no difficulties in your recovery. Tell me if the pain grows worse. Do not pretend you are well if you are not. I do not wish to be spared any suffering on your account. I would rather have your confidence."

"You will have it. But I have so many questions."

"I am sure you do. What would you like to know first?"

"Sally—she is—she is gone, isn't she?"

"She is. Mr. Hardwick has gone to see her people. She came from a family in Kent. She was a clergyman's daughter who lost her family to an epidemic many years ago, all except a pair of poor, penniless aunts. She ran away to join the stage in London when she was young. That is where she met Hardwick."

"And Miss Ingram?"

"She is nearly recovered. Lord Ingram has already come and gone. I have told him the truth, but the ladies of the family have only a vague notion of what has occurred."

"And Mr. Barnett? Where is he?"

"He is sitting outside the door. He has not left us for an hour, and will hardly stir from the inn in case he can be of any service to you or me. Shall I call him in? Can you see him?"

"Yes, I think I would like that. You do not mind?"

"I do not."

"I have worried you terribly, poor Edward."

"We do not seem to be fated for a quiet hearth and home, Jane."

Mr. Barnett approached the bed. I could just remember the last time I beheld his face, bending over me in the fog. I had never seen a man look so wild. It was a startling contrast to the clean, brushed, and above all, controlled man who came to my bedside.

I spoke at once. "I have news for you, Mr. Barnett. I have written to a friend, about your daughter— "

"I know it. Rochester told me." A smile appeared in his eyes, though it barely lifted his mouth. "I am in your debt once more, Mrs. Rochester. That was a dark night under the fallen eaves of Thornfield. But I will not give up," and here he looked, with a swift glance of gratitude, at Mr. Rochester, "not while there yet remains a new day."

"That is right. And what of your plans?"

"I am acting now as Mr. Rochester's agent. And as yours as well. I shall work for you, so long as you will have me. It is the least I can do, although I can hardly hope to repay the debt I owe you."

"Except for our first meeting, I don't see that I was ever of much benefit to you."

"It was enough, Mrs. Rochester. More than enough."

I was forced to keep my bed for a time, but at last Doctor Carter allowed me to get up and resume a little activity. Diana came to see me almost as soon as I was fit for visitors, and Captain Fitzjames came with her. Their plans, I learned, were rapidly developing. They sat side by side and hand in hand throughout our interview. Diana would be leaving soon for Moor House, to begin putting her affairs in order, and the captain would depart to his father's estate, to make what arrangements he could.

"You must take your time and get well, Jane," Diana said, and she took my hand in both of hers. "It will be a little time still. There is no great hurry."

"But neither is their need for delay," I said. Diana laughed, a sound I rejoiced to hear.

"We are in your debt," the captain added. "I hate to think how events might have unfolded without your help. We all owe you a great deal, but I am afraid you have suffered more than your fair share in this matter."

"It will all be forgotten. Diana has long been regarded by me as a sister, and I shall take great pleasure in calling you brother."

CHAPTER XVIII

When I was well enough to walk a little, and no longer in need of a bandage over my head, I obtained permission to leave the inn. The doctor had shaved away a part of my hair to treat the wound, but such faults were easily concealed by a bonnet. As Mr. Rochester did not feel he was a strong enough companion for me in my feeble state, Mr. Barnett walked with me. We made our way along the quiet lanes at the edge of Hay, that I might gather a few late summer roses.

"Tell me, what are Mr. Hardwick's plans now?"

"Hardwick is a will-of-a-wisp. There is no telling where he might end up. Judging from his letters, however, I think he is rather chastened by circumstances. I do not think he will venture on any—what shall we say?—adventurous undertakings in the near future."

"It would be a blunted creature that would do so."

We neared a rise in the lane, and in the distance, I could discern the road that ran to what was once Thornfield Hall. He found a dry seat for me on a low stone wall, meditated a moment on the ground at his feet, and then commenced his narrative.

"I can't say that I can justify his conduct towards Sally. She was his mistress, and he did make some rather fatuous promises to her at one time. She was fond of repeating them to me. And of course, she helped him in these blackmailing schemes in Belgium. So did I for that matter, for I sometimes carried his earnings to his bank in England.

"It was not entirely Hardwick's fault, however. She was so pretty, you see, and gentlemen had always admired her. She had determined that her beauty was enough—that she would raise herself in the world on that alone. She had no real conception of the gulf between herself and a true lady. She valued only looks as an indication of value, and never understood the inferiority of her own mind. I believe she took Hardwick's words and changed their meaning—she twisted them into something he never meant. Against all her careful planning, you see, she fell in love with him, but he could not afford to keep her as the sort of woman she wanted to be.

"Hardwick had tried to dismiss her in the past—I think he was rather tired of her—but she always managed to re-establish herself in his life. The lady's maid bit was her idea. She wished to be near him, but he thought he was only giving her a new start in life. Then she dreamed up the blackmail scheme involving Lord Ingram."

"It was dreadfully dishonest. Poor Lord Ingram was tortured over the whole business."

"Oh, it got quite out of hand. But you see what happened to me when I told Hardwick I would confess it all to his lordship. I think she was already going a bit mad."

"I thought she was only jealous."

"She certainly was, passionately so. Both of you and Miss Ingram."

"Of me! Why would she be jealous of me?"

"You had been raised up in life by your marriage. She always felt she was your superior—it infuriated her to see you so elevated when she thought of you as beneath her. She could not understand that a man would value anything more than beauty." He paused. "Forgive me, I seem to be implying that you are— "

"That I am not beautiful. I know I am not and do not pretend to be. No, I see the case more plainly now. She already disliked me, and then to have me perpetually upsetting her schemes— But do you know how the second of her pair of revolvers came to be in my room?"

"Ah. She put it there herself; she hoped it would implicate you. If you made any accusations, she could accuse you in return of harbouring the weapon. I thought it unlikely to convince anyone and did nothing about it. I was in such a muddle of my own—I'm afraid

I was not thinking very clearly. I tried more than once to warn her, even at the risk of my reputation— "

"When she was seen at your door late at night."

"Yes. And I tried to warn you too, but somehow nothing I did seemed to make a difference."

"I am glad it's sorted out now, but I have sometimes wondered what happened to the coachman. I assumed he made it home, but I always forgot to ask."

"Old Bill?" Mr. Barnett laughed. "He was found the next day cowering in a ditch with his hands over his head, waiting for the world to end. He was sent home ashamed and I hope his neighbours never let him forget it!"

Upon our return to the inn, I could see plainly that a carriage had arrived in the yard. The arms of the Ingram household were emblazoned on its door. Who among the Ingram family deigned to visit us in our humble establishment here? I inquired if Mr. Barnett knew anything of this, but he only replied with a shake of his head. I mounted the steps and went inside.

Standing in the empty parlour, in a queenly dress of sky blue silk, was Miss Blanche Ingram, waiting for my return. I dismissed Mr. Barnett and gave her a slight bow. Her eye on me was, as usual, cold and uninviting. Yet there was a look of anxiety on her brow that strengthened as I entered the room.

"Mrs. Rochester, will you sit down?"

I did not answer immediately, for the innkeeper's wife appeared just then. I begged her for a vase of water to house the roses I had gathered. When this task was completed, we took seats opposite from one another. The parlour was an old-fashioned one, and Miss Ingram appeared a little incongruous seated in its shabby venerability.

I inquired after her family. She answered in brief replies. When she did not speak, I added, "I hope you are fully recovered from the night of the fire."

Her haughty chill thawed at once. "I shall never forgive that woman." Her words were laden with venom and disgust. "You cannot imagine the horror I endured at her hands. If I could have faced her myself, I would have— "

"Miss Ingram," I interrupted. "Do not desire revenge on her. She wronged you terribly, yet she herself was a poor and wounded creature. She was tortured by her own self-deceit."

"Do you defend her to me?" Blanche cried. "After what she did to me?"

"She tried to kill me too," I added, in a quiet tone. "And nearly succeeded."

"Surely, you have not forgiven her? What a—what a soft-hearted, indulgent creature you must be. I can hardly understand you."

"We are called upon to forgive as we ourselves hope to be forgiven, Miss Ingram."

She stared long at me. Then she inquired somewhat abruptly how Mr. Rochester was? He had seen Lord Ingram?

"Yes. I understood that to be the case. I did not see him. We owe much to his lordship's hospitality and kindness— " I stopped, and a question I had pondered but had not yet considered how to ask swiftly fell from my lips. "Miss Ingram, was it by your desire, that my husband and I were invited to Ingram Park?"

She gave me another long look, haughty, assessing and cool. "Yes," she replied at last. "Yes, it was."

"Not out of liking for us, I'm sure."

I thought my rudeness might sting her, but somewhat to my surprise, she laughed. "No, I confess, I do not delight much in the sight of either one of you, but Peter insisted I encourage Tedo to invite you. My brother fell in with my plans, for he has always had a high opinion of Rochester. I can't think why."

She did not know then, I thought, of my husband's aid to her brother years before. "But why would Mr. Hardwick want us at Ingram Park?"

"You are so good at guessing other people's secrets. Surely you have guessed that much. It was to keep you away from Thornfield! As long as only Mr. Rochester was at Ferndean, he was not likely to meddle in the estate, but after your arrival, Peter grew afraid that you would find out."

"Well. And do *you* know what he was doing at Thornfield?"

"That horrible woman! She made him hide the money there."

"But where? Under a broken wall? Or a burnt beam?"

"There is an old horse-chestnut tree, at the bottom of the garden. The one with the little seat around it that was struck by lightning. Perhaps you remember it?"

I certainly did, and said so.

"All the inside has rotted away. It is perfectly hollow. They hid the gold there." I considered this a peculiar circumstance, but Miss Ingram's thoughts were clearly on her transgressor. "It was all *her* doing—he never meant to get involved. He intended to put a stop to it, but he was only waiting for the right opportunity."

The opportunity that would most profit himself? I wondered, but I did not fully comprehend Mr. Hardwick's motives. I would be generous to him if I could. "He wished to protect Sally?"

"Of course."

"But what will become of the money?"

"He has offered to return it to my brother."

"Has he really?"

"You needn't sound so surprised. He is an honourable man, Mrs. Rochester, even if he does not suit some people's ideas. Tedo will not take it, however. My brother has asked him to pay off his debts with it."

"That's very kind of Lord Ingram."

"He feels culpable for what has happened. If he had not been so weak as to submit to the blackmailing scheme, all this could have been avoided. I told my brother as much at the time, but he didn't listen. He ought to have prosecuted her instead of paying her."

"Sally has paid a high enough price for her deeds now."

"In any case, I did not come here to discuss that woman. I beg you not to mention her name. I came here with an express purpose." She tugged fretfully at her gloves before she continued. "I came here to thank you. For saving my life."

I bowed my head. "You are very welcome. A just return for your hospitality, whatever its motive."

"You *have* got a sharp tongue, haven't you? I don't suppose you speak to your husband like that."

I smiled a little at this reflection, but I only replied, "He doesn't seem to mind my way of speaking very much, but I apologise, if I sound ungrateful. It was not my intention."

"Oh, I am not bothered by a little plain speaking. I prefer it, rather." She rose to her feet, and I did the same. "I wish you a swift recovery. You will not return to Ingram Park just now?"

"No, I don't think we shall."

"Tedo wished me to tell you that you are welcome to return, but I doubted you would. I think it likely you have had enough of Ingram Park for a time."

Of this statement, we were in perfect agreement. I saw her to the door, watched her stately carriage as it rattled away, and carried my roses upstairs. On the way to my chamber, a servant met me with an imposing stack of envelopes. The mail had arrived. Upon entering the room, I saw Mr. Rochester sitting with his unseeing eyes to the window.

"Mr. Rochester, I am back."

"Are you there, my fairy? Are you weary from your walk?"

I placed the roses on a table, folded the mail into my lap and then seated myself on his knee. "Only a little. A quiet resting place is all I am in need of."

He drew me close to him. "My wandering bird has flown home to me once more. Well, Jane! We have not been married so very long after all, have we? And how do you find your married life? Not tired of your old and surly spouse?"

"I have barely had time to enjoy him yet. I feel as if the fruit is hardly tasted."

"No doubt the bitter is yet to come."

"If there is any bitter, sir, it is merely a pungent flavour and gives zest to the sweetness of the whole. My happiness in our union grows with each passing day." I parted his locks and laid a kiss on his brow. His good eye, bleared as it was, yet seemed to look into mine, to divine the spirit within that kindled with joy in his presence.

"*Mon ange*," he whispered. He held me in a close embrace; his lips pressed my ear; I knew well what would follow, but I never liked to defer any task that lay at hand.

"Mr. Rochester, I have a matter of business to discuss with you."

"Have you, Jane?"

I drew his hand to the stack of letters in my lap. "The mail has come."

"What, all of that? You don't mean to look at it now, do you? Just put it over there on the table."

"Certainly, sir, when I am finished looking through it."

"Provoking elf! Leave the letters, if you please. I have no mind for business just now."

His arms clasped me closer than ever, but I only answered with, "This one is from your lawyer, and this, from your banker."

"And I suppose there is one from my candlestick maker. Put them by for Mr. Barnett. You know as much about London banking as this cufflink of mine."

"Here is one from Mrs. Fairfax. I shall enjoy that one later."

"Yes, later!"

"And this— " I tore open the envelope in haste.

"What is it? Is anything the matter?"

"No, no, it is only from Adèle."

"And are you in such a hurry to receive her school girl missives?"

"She has been strongly in my mind of late, that is all. I have often wondered— "

"You always were partial to half-phrases. What is it you have wondered?"

"I'm sorry—I was reading. She still uses too many exclamation points. Her present teacher is not doing her duty."

"Oh, never mind the mail! You may correct every lapse of punctuation you like, but you must wait until tomorrow. We may not have had much of a honeymoon yet, Janet, but I do not intend to give it up altogether."

We read no more letters that day. On the morrow, however, I informed Mr. Rochester that I wished to take a journey. "I shall only be gone a day I think."

"I believe I can guess where you are going."

"To see Adèle."

"I thought so. Are you sure you are well enough?"

"Yes, I think I am. I know you and Mr. Barnett have a considerable amount of business to occupy you, and I have put off the visit far too long."

"Well, take great care, Jane, and hurry back."

The school was a long, brick affair, set down on the outskirts of a busy industrial town. As I was now the wife of a landed gentleman, I was no longer suffered to travel about alone and must have a maid to accompany me. The Rochester Arms had provided a sober matronly servant in need of a holiday. It suited us both to make the journey in relative quiet, and on reaching the school, she departed for a row of shops in search of some muslin for her sister, and I, for my former pupil.

The schoolgirls, I found, were occupied in their lessons. I asked the directress not to interrupt; I would observe the class, I explained, being well qualified to judge whether the lesson was up to standard. The girls presented an orderly appearance, neat in their braids and dark dresses, and seated in several long rows. The lesson was in literature, and the students looked on with dull and placid faces, although one or two showed a certain animation that suggested their faculties were more awake. There was one in particular, a slender, dark-haired girl, who looked rather small to be seated near the back, yet she observed the lesson with a keenness I admired, her fine eyes shining. I moved silently round the room that I might catch sight of the paper before her. She was at the end of her row; I sought a glimpse of her desk, and the sheet she was so carefully marking with her pencil.

"Dearest Papa," it ran, in fluent French. "the teacher is such a sleepy creature. I wish she would read as you used to do, and wake us all up. Do you remember when you read to us from the play that Shakespeare wrote, and you did all the voices? How Maman and I laughed! Oh! I do miss her— "

A loud clanging pealed across the room. The bell had rung for the midday meal. The girls quickly rose and packed away their slates. I no longer observed the class however, for a familiar voice cried out my name.

"Oh, Miss Eyre, I knew you would come!"

Adèle threaded the crowded room and threw her arms around me. I returned the embrace with an almost equal enthusiasm; I had not realised how much I had missed her. I was soon trying to keep up with a hurried tumult of words.

"Are you quite all right, Adèle?"

"Oh, I am just so happy to see you, Miss Eyre!"

"It is Mrs. Rochester now."

"Oh yes! I had forgotten! Is Monsieur Rochester well?"

"He is, but I must not keep you from your meal. You must be hungry."

"I am always hungry, but I am used to skipping meals. How long do you stay?"

"I must leave in an hour. I promised to be back this evening. Perhaps the kitchen can provide us with a little bread and cheese, and you can show me your room."

To her room, accordingly, we went. Adèle consumed her food before we passed the stairs. "Do you always eat so quick?"

"Oh yes. I can't seem to help it. This way, Mrs. Rochester. It is not so very pretty, is it?"

It was not. I had not expected more, but I wanted an opportunity to look around me before I passed judgment. I was acquainted with the signs of both a cheerful, well-conducted school, and with those of a severe, unhappy one. The drawn, pale faces and cheerless movements I had seen round me suggested that I was beholding the latter.

"Are you happy here, Adèle?"

"Oh, no, Miss. That is—Mrs. Rochester. Not a bit."

"You miss Mr. Rochester, perhaps? And Thornfield?"

"Yes, but it is not that. I am not lonely. Only the teachers are so very mean. And I understand nothing. They do not teach me like you used to do. They only make me feel stupid."

"Should you like to come back with me? Today?"

"Oh yes! I would love to! Oh! But I cannot leave my friend."

"Your friend? who is she?"

"I am the only one who understands her, and she is my very best friend."

"Does she speak French?"

"Almost only French. She has not been here long, but I love her so. She is an orphan and has no one else."

"Oh, an orphan?" Fancy had painted a most appealing picture, but of course it could not be.

"She has no mother or father. At least, her mother is gone, and her father has disappeared."

A keen hope cut through me. I could not help asking. "Has he? And what is her name?"

"Here she is! I knew she would come up—I have told her all about you." Adèle turned and hurried down the dormitory, skipping past the long row of beds to greet her friend. I noted with interest the same young girl I had observed in the schoolroom. She was very thin and pale, but her dark eyes shone with a brilliance that was fully recognisable. Still, it would never do to be mistaken on such a point. I approached her. She curtsied prettily, and in halting English, attempted to say, "How do you do?"

I addressed her in French. I asked her about her home, her time at the school, her long lost Papa. I learned she had been placed here by a benefactor in Belgium who knew she had relations in England, but could not locate them.

"Have you ever tried to find your Papa? Or to write to him?"

"I write to him always," she replied. "But where am I to send the letters?"

"Perhaps I can help you. Will you tell me your name?"

"They call me Mary here. They say now I am in England, I must have an English name."

"But I wish to know your given name. The name your Maman and Papa gave to you."

It was soon offered, and my hopes were confirmed. I informed the directress of my plans, and within the hour, their trunks were packed, my maid was collected, and we were speeding towards the Rochester Arms with a full carriage. I reflected on the mysteries of providence. I reviewed all that seemed miraculous and strange in the course of my existence, and wondered at the Divine hand that measures our days and plans our steps.

I reflected, too, on the great blessing of wealth, that at so little comparative cost to myself, I could lift two poor souls out of the misery of an unfortunate school, and unite them with the ones they love. It was rather a grand thing; I quite delighted in my own power, and delighted still more to stop at an inn and indulge in a plentiful supper that was speedily consumed by my young charges.

When at last we reached the environs of Hay, the girls were sound asleep and rocking gently with the motion of the coach. It was past eleven, and I had already arranged with the maid to find beds for Adèle and her friend until further plans could be made. The gentlemen might have already retired, I thought. I would not disturb them with any new revelations tonight.

All my plans were overthrown, however, at our arrival. The girls woke up and instantly began chattering like magpies. I entered the inn first and found Mr. Barnett and Mr. Rochester seated in the parlour, waiting for my return by the fireside. I greeted them cheerfully, and my husband had hardly begun to express his satisfaction on my return when an eager cry met our ears.

"Mr. Rochester!"

Adèle bounded across the room and embraced him with enthusiasm. Mr. Rochester withstood the shock of impact and held her with an amazed expression. "Was this your errand then, Jane? To bring Adèle back with you?"

"You are happy to see me?" she cried.

Mr. Rochester laughed. "*Très content, ma petite-fille*, but you are little no more, I find. You have grown an inch at least! So you are delivered from bondage, are you? Your guardian angel has found you out?"

"She watches over more than one lost soul, I see." Mr. Barnett had risen to his feet on our arrival, but only now did his eye stray to the door. A small, timid, upright figure lingered there, as if half afraid to join in this scene of happy reunion. Her face was concealed by the shadow of the doorway.

"Come in, my dear," I entreated. She stepped forward. Mr. Barnett opened his mouth to speak, but no words came.

"Mr. Rochester," I said, "allow me to present a friend of Adèle's, whom I took the liberty of bringing with me. Her name is Claudette Marie d'Anville— "

A great sob burst forth from Mr. Barnett. A look of utter astonishment, and of complete and unspeakable joy, flushed his countenance. He held out his arms for her embrace.

"Papa!"

Thank you for reading The Hour of Fatality. I hope you enjoyed the story. I have a website and a mailing list where you can sign up to stay up-to-date on future books. Feedback from readers is important to me, so if you would like to read future mysteries for Jane and Mr. Rochester to solve, let me know!
Leannemckinley.com

ACKNOWLEDGEMENTS

Many thanks to the faithful fan fiction readers who cheered me on while I labored over the first draft of this story, to Entrada publishing and to Bev Dow, for the helpful feedback, to my family, for their patience, and especially to my husband, for suggesting the snuff box.

Made in the USA
Columbia, SC
21 March 2022

57974849R00162